Magnolias and Mayhem

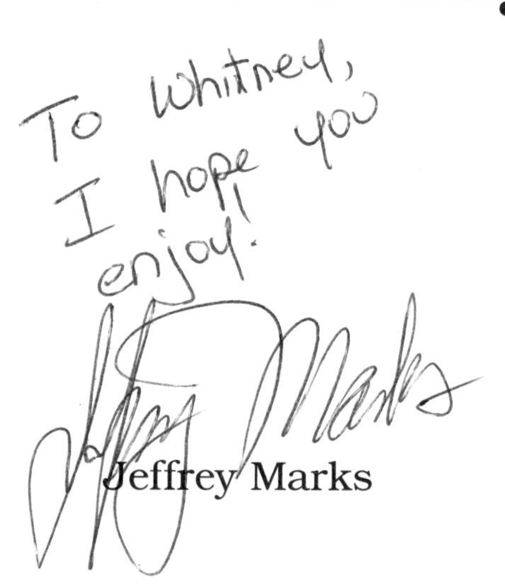

Jeffrey Marks

This book is a work of fiction. All names, characters, places, and events are the product of the author's imagination. Any resemblance to actual events or persons, living or dead, is entirely coincidental and beyond the intent of either the author or the publisher.

"With This Ring" was originally published in February 1995 in *Crimes of the Heart*, Berkeley Prime Crime edition.

"Her Good Name," copyright 1991, Carolyn G. Hart. Reprinted by arrangement with Gelfman Schneider Literary Agents, Inc.

"Waiting for Snow" previously appeared in *Brier County*, University of Missouri Press, April 2000.

Hardcover ISBN 1-57072-112-2
Trade Paper ISBN 1-57072-128-9

Printed in the United States of America

1 2 3 4 5 6 7 8 9 0

To Don Maass, my agent, mentor, and friend . . .

TABLE OF CONTENTS

INTRODUCTION

The logical successor to the proper British mystery, Southern crime novels—known for their impeccable manners and ladylike belles—have formed an American scion of this subgenre. The manor house has been replaced by the family homestead, the butler and staff by family friends. But the core of a more gentle place and time where crimes are expected to be solved with a minimum of bloodshed and fuss have replaced the earlier generation of English novels.

Southern authors have long been known for their ability to weave stories for their readers. Readers can easily imagine those warm summer nights filled with the chirping of crickets and a Southern grandmother feeding stories of the past to enrapt children. In today's market, Southern authors have taken the place of oral storytellers, but their works are still filled with stories of the past. Just as the Civil War is never quite completed south of the Mason-Dixon line, the tales of the past are never finished.

Even with this reputation, it wasn't until the start of the second Golden Age of mystery fiction that the Southern writer came into being. The major thrust of the first half of this century was the big-city crime caper. Few novels took place outside the realms of the metropolis, New York, Chicago, Los Angeles, and San Francisco. Only with the advent of the 1980s did the crime novel go to a more regional approach; and when it did, the South rose again.

Simultaneously, the writings of the varied, but all Southern novelists such as Margaret Maron, Joan Hess, Carolyn Hart, and Sharyn McCrumb sprang to life. No clearer indication can be seen of their acceptance than Maron's sweep of mystery awards for the first book in her Deborah Knott series, set in rural North Carolina. As one of the nearly dozen children of a bootlegger, Judge Knott has to solve a crime with roots in the past, a common theme for Southern mysteries.

I think you'll find the stories included here have that strong voice expected from Southern authors, along with some incredible storytelling. We've tried to collect stories from all parts of the south—Florida, Georgia, the Carolinas, Tennessee, Texas, and Kentucky. Indeed, the South has risen again—in a way that no one expected.

Chatty Patty

by Taylor McCafferty

As a resident of Kentucky, Barbara Taylor McCafferty has so many noms de mystere that she has no idea who she really is. As Taylor McCafferty, she is the author of the Haskell Blevins series, set in small town Kentucky; as Tierney McClellan, she writes the Schuyler Ridgway novels. With her twin sister (whom you will meet later in this book), she has created a series featuring identical twin sisters.

The doll was the first thing I saw when I walked into the room. It was lying on its back across the living room on the floor, its yellow yarn head resting against the wall on my left, its pink cloth arms and legs askew. Lying there, smiling at the ceiling, the doll looked as if it might've been dropped there just minutes earlier. Perhaps by a little girl too busy playing to bother putting away her toys.

I stared at the doll, knowing even as I stared, that I was just putting off having to look at the stain on the carpet in front of the door. Not two inches from my right foot, the stain was large and dark and made an ugly, reddish-brown circle in the beige wool carpet.

The stain was just inside a tape outlining a small figure.

For a second my eyes began to sting, and I couldn't seem to swallow. But then, Grieber was right behind me. Even when he's in plain clothes, there's no mistaking that Grieber's a cop. He's got that look. Like he's seen it all, and most of it he didn't like. Going through that front door, I could feel Grieber's eyes on my face. So I didn't miss a beat. I just kept right on walking into the room, as if I hadn't seen anything.

It's been years since I actually cried over a case. Not since my own days as a cop when I was first working Louisville's west end. In those days I used to come home every night, pop a beer, and bawl over everything I'd seen during the day.

Of course, it was always after I'd put my daughter, Hannah, to bed so I didn't scare her. And—let's face it—I was probably doing some pretty heavy self-pity back then, too. It was right after the divorce. My ex had already married his twenty-something girlfriend, and he was rapidly getting behind on his child-support checks. I guess the prospect of being a single parent didn't exactly thrill me.

Funny, it seems as if all that happened last month maybe, but it was over seventeen years ago. Seventeen years. Lord. How time flies when you're not having fun.

After a week or so of boo-hooing every night, I'd decided that if I was going to cry every time I came across a sad case, I'd be dehydrated in a month. So I quit that nonsense.

Now that I think about it, that right there was probably the biggest reason that I finally ended up quitting the force. After a few years of walking around, not reacting, I started wondering if I was turning into a robot. Robocop—that was me.

Right now being a robot didn't seem like such a bad idea. Grieber closed the front door behind us, and he started moving around the room. You'd think, watching him, that he was just wandering around aimlessly. Unless you noticed his eyes. His eyes were darting from one object to another, like a carnivore hunting for prey. Grieber was looking for something, anything, that might've been missed earlier.

"I don't know, Bess," Grieber said with a sigh. "The guys downtown are pretty thorough."

He picked up a silver-framed, color photograph from the mantel. I glanced at it and immediately looked away. It was a duplicate of the photograph I'd seen in my office a couple days ago. The photograph of the little girl and her mother. In the photo, the little girl is holding the doll with the yellow yarn hair. She's looking straight at the camera with a shy smile.

That smile reminded me of my daughter at that age. Hannah will be twenty-one this year—the same age I was when she was born. She's almost legal drinking age here in Kentucky, and yet, I still think of her as my baby.

My baby was about to finish her undergraduate degree in Pre-Law at Centre College in Danville.

Grieber was putting the photograph back where he got it. I moved across the living room toward the open door on my right, took a deep breath, and then entered the bedroom. There was, as expected, another tape outline on the floor in here, right in front of the bed. I barely glanced at the outline. Instead, I started scanning the room.

Grieber came in right behind me. I'd hoped Captain Fleenor would've given me Miller or Hanrahan to escort me over here. But beggars can't be choosers. The captain had made it clear this morning that he was doing me a monumental favor to let me view the crime scene at all. Asking for Miller or Hanrahan would've been pushing it. Too bad, though. Miller and Hanrahan didn't know me as well as Grieber. I probably could have a nervous breakdown right in front of those two, and they might not notice if I didn't want them to.

Grieber, on the other hand, was another story. I'd worked with him the three years I was on the force, and as far as I could tell, he never missed a trick. Even after I got burned out and started working for a big detective agency out in Oldham County, I still kept running into Grieber. On one case or another.

These past five years alone, since I opened up my own agency—Bess Mackey Investigations—I bet Grieber and I have run into each other on as many as twenty cases. So Grieber knows me all right. And he sure as hell knows when I'm faking it.

Now, as he moved around the living room, Grieber gave me a long look. "You okay?"

I shrugged. Real casual. I tried for a smile. "Sure," I said. "It's rough when it's a kid. That's all." I moved farther into the bedroom, toward the dresser to my right, away from Grieber.

"Yeah," he said, "this one's a rough one, all right." Grieber has three daughters of his own. No sons, just daughters. All of them, thank heavens, take after his wife, a pretty brunette. Grieber, on the other hand—with his beefy brow, his double chin, and his pockmarked cheeks—would make a mud fence look good. Grieber was now looking at the manila folder in his hand. He started to hand it to me, but I shook my head. I knew what it said. Sarah Elizabeth Wakefield, age five, died of a gunshot wound to the chest. Her mother, Alanna Shields Wakefield, thirty-two, died the same way. Death for both of them was, according to the report, "probably immediate."

It was the word *probably* that bothered me. Did that poor baby have time to suffer? To be frightened? I blinked the thought away and began to concentrate on the bedroom. There was another ugly stain on the floor in here. The stain was right beside the bed, again just inside the tape outline on the floor. Above the outline, a long brown smear moved down the cream-colored wall beside the bed. I swallowed and looked away again.

"Stuart Wakefield's fingerprints are all over the place, according to this report," Grieber said. He shrugged and added, "Doesn't mean a thing, though. Wakefield said he'd been here several times to visit his daughter and to try to work out a reconciliation with his wife."

"Did they find any other prints?"

Grieber shook his head. "Nope. There's just the husband's and the sister's." He paused, cleared his throat, and added, "And the victims, of course."

I gave him another quick nod and started opening drawers. There was a photo of Wakefield turned facedown in the top drawer of the bed stand. I held it up so that Grieber could see it. He shrugged his beefy shoulders again. Unlike a lot of people, when Grieber doesn't have anything to say, he doesn't say anything. It's one of the things I like best about him.

I turned my attention to the ornately carved antique dresser positioned in the middle of the wall to the left of the bed. A faint scent of lilac sachet still clung to the lacy undergarments in the top drawer. Most of the things in the drawer were silk. Evidently, Alanna Wakefield had had expensive tastes—and the money to indulge them.

If I myself ever have more money than I know what to do with, I plan to buy some silk lingerie. Of course, it'll probably look pretty ridiculous on somebody in her nineties.

I glanced back over at the stain on the floor, and for a moment I felt intensely glad that Alanna Wakefield had been able to pamper herself.

I felt under the neatly folded cashmere sweaters in the second and third drawers. There was a sweater in nearly every pastel shade you could think of. I lifted each sweater, looked under it, felt around the edge of each drawer. I had no idea what I was looking for. Finally, I finished with all the drawers, stood up, and turned around. Grieber had been right. There was precious little chance that we'd find anything new. He knew it, and I knew it.

That didn't keep me from looking, though.

Next, I went through the large double closets. Both closets were filled to capacity, and everything in them seemed to have a designer label. I started going through the pockets of Dior suits, but in my mind I was still seeing that doll out there in the living room.

The doll made it seem more real somehow. Up until I'd seen the doll, I almost could have made myself believe that this whole thing was nothing more than a tragic story some woman had told me two days ago.

Two short days ago. It seemed like a lot longer.

In Louisville's Yellow Pages, there are twenty-seven detective agencies listed besides mine. I checked it out. Twenty-seven. Those are pretty good odds that Rebecca Shields would not end up sitting across from me one day.

She did, though. Rebecca walked into my office about nine o'clock on Monday, looking as if she'd spent the last ten years of her life crying.

As it turned out, it had been closer to ten weeks.

"My sister and my niece are dead," Rebecca had said bluntly. "And the police are going to let their murderer go free. I—I can't accept that."

It has been my experience that the police are never all that anxious to let the guilty get away with their crimes. "What makes you think the police are—"

Rebecca answered me before I'd finished my question. "They're now talking to acquaintances that my sister hadn't seen in years! And yet, I've told them all along who did it. They just won't listen!" Her voice was shaking. She got up and walked over to the window.

My office is on the tenth floor of the Grossman Building in downtown Louisville. The Grossman is an old stone Victorian building that the real estate people who rented my office to me described as "updated." After I moved in, I realized that "updated" was Realtor-speak for "painted." The elevators in the Grossman Building constantly break down, the windows still open by means of pulleys, and the narrow hallways always smell faintly of mildew. The rent, in fact, is just about the only thing attractive about my office.

Rebecca actually stood there at my ancient office window and looked out as if there really was something out there to see besides bedraggled pigeons and an ugly iron fire escape.

She was an attractive woman. In her early thirties was my guess. With hair frosted an icy blonde, she was dressed in a pale blue cashmere sweater and pale blue wool pants that exactly matched her pale blue pumps. Even in her distress, she'd taken the time to apply makeup impeccably.

I gestured toward a chair. "You say you know who killed them?"

Rebecca ignored my gesture and walked over to the other window. It offered an identical view. The same fire escape and pigeons from a slightly different angle.

"Of course I know who did it." Rebecca's tone was impatient. "It was Stuart. Alanna had just left that jerk. Finally! After years of his running around, his lying, his cheating, his temper tantr—"

I cut in. She sounded as if she might go on in this vein for some time. "They were divorced?"

"Separated." Rebecca turned then from the window to look straight at me. A fashionably dressed woman whose tidy, comfortable life had been suddenly, unspeakably disrupted. In her blue mascaraed eyes I saw grief and anger—and something else. Surprise.

I stared back at her. It looked to me as if, up until the deaths of her sister and her niece, Rebecca Shields had thought herself immune from such things.

At one time I guess I'd thought I was, too. I'd thought such horrors happen to other people. The years I'd spent as a cop had destroyed that notion. I'd soon realized I'd never been immune. I'd just been lucky.

"Alanna and Stuart had been separated just two weeks. Alanna was going to build a new life for herself and Sarah. She had so many plans. So many . . ." Rebecca's voice broke, and she started rummaging through her purse for a tissue.

I would've offered her one, but a box of Kleenex is the one thing I keep forgetting to buy for my office. I'm not sure why. Maybe, subconsciously, I do it on purpose. To subtly discourage people from crying in front of me. Maybe my subconscious has decided that if *I* don't get to cry, nobody else gets to cry either.

I waited until Rebecca had found her own Kleenex in her purse before I spoke. There didn't seem to be any way to say this delicately. "Do you really think that your brother-in-law killed his wife and his own child?"

Rebecca stopped sniffling then, and said, her voice suddenly as cold and hard as ice, "I don't *think* it. I *know* it." She knotted up the tissue in her hand. "Besides, Sarah wasn't Stuart's child. Not by blood, anyway. Sarah was adopted. I don't think Stuart ever really regarded Sarah as his daughter."

I didn't know what to say to that one.

"It was Alanna who wanted a baby, Alanna who talked Stuart into putting their name on an adoption waiting list when they couldn't have a child of their own." Rebecca dabbed at her eyes with the balled-up tissue. "I think Stuart always considered Sarah to be Alanna's child. Not his."

My throat started to hurt. What a terrific situation for little Sarah to be in. "All this doesn't mean he committed murder," I said. "Do you have any proof?"

Rebecca shook her head. "That's what I need you for."

I started to get up. "I don't know. To be honest, all this sounds pretty flimsy. If the police haven't found anything, I doubt—"

That was when she handed me the photograph. Another copy of the one Grieber had just shown me, of the little girl and her mother. And the doll. I'd taken one look, and for a brief second I'd seen Hannah.

"Sarah loved that Chatty Patty doll," Rebecca said. "She was always giving it little kisses. It was one of those dolls that talk, you know."

"I know," I said automatically, but I didn't know. Once, when Hannah was little, I could've told you the name of practically every doll on the market. Mainly because Hannah had wanted every one of them. Once Hannah reached twelve, though, I'd pretty much lost touch with dolls. I figured Chatty Patty must be a new one, because I'd never heard of it.

Once she'd shown me the photo, Rebecca began to talk very fast. "I'd just given Sarah that Chatty Patty doll. For her birthday. She was just five, you know. Just a baby really. She loved that doll. She carried it around with her everywhere."

Rebecca seemed to be talking just to fill the air around her. Hannah does the same thing when she's upset—she talks and talks and talks. I asked her about it once, years ago. Hannah must've been about thirteen at the time. She'd told me, "When you're talking, Mom, you don't have to think so much."

It made sense to me.

Rebecca drew a ragged breath. "I think Sarah fell in love with that doll the minute she saw it. She was just so delighted. Her birthday seems like years ago, but it was only a little over a month ago. September 15. Not long ago at all."

I swallowed, staring straight at Rebecca. My expression must not have changed all that much, though, because she went right on. "Look, I don't expect miracles. I just want you to talk to Stuart. Just see what you think, okay?"

She signed one of my standard contracts and wrote me a check, and I went through all the motions as mechanically as if I really were that robot I used to be afraid I'd become.

When Rebecca Shields left my office, I realized I was still holding the photograph she'd given me. I sat there behind my desk, staring at it for a long, long time. Staring at it, and thinking.

A lot of baby girls, no doubt, were born in this area on September 15 five years ago. Quite a few of which could've ended up being adopted. Birth dates didn't really mean a thing. It was just a coincidence, that's all.

A coincidence.

But that night I called Hannah. I guess maybe I had to. I had to hear her young voice, so happy, so absorbed in her studies. "Mom, everything's going great," she said. "I just made an A on my calculus exam and my polysci quiz!" Her familiar laugh sounded in my ear. "Is everything going okay with you?"

Well, tomorrow I've got to go and see some guy who might've wiped out his family. "Everything's just fine, sweetheart," I said. "I'm busy, as always."

"As always," Hannah echoed.

The next morning—could it have been just yesterday?—Stuart Wakefield kept me waiting outside his office for twenty-five minutes. Twenty-five minutes of looking at umpteen design awards lining his walls. Rebecca apparently had neglected to mention that her brother-in-law was a nationally recognized architect. I sat there, counting design awards and shaking my head. Rebecca's murder theory was looking more and more unlikely.

Wakefield's secretary was a Miss Sturgill, according to the nameplate on her desk. Miss Sturgill was a woman in her fifties doing everything in her power to look twenty years younger. She would've succeeded if the office had been lit by candlelight.

Under the fluorescent light in Wakefield's office, however, you could plainly tell that the red of her hair was clearly a shade God couldn't give you, but Clairol could. Her makeup was so thick, it cracked at the corners of her mouth when she smiled.

Apparently, judging from how often her makeup cracked during the time I was there, Miss Sturgill loved her work. All the time she was filing papers, typing, answering the phone, she continued to smile.

I don't care how many less muscles they say it takes to smile rather than frown, that much smiling has got to be an effort. It made me weary, just watching her.

When Wakefield finally appeared, I realized why Miss Sturgill loved her work. She looked at Wakefield with transparent adoration.

I have to admit Stuart Wakefield was something to look at. Tall and slim, with black wavy hair, brown eyes, and a square jaw, he looked as if he'd just stepped out of the latest Spiegel catalog. His white shirt had Ralph Lauren's little horse embroidered on the left pocket, his gray gabardine slacks looked freshly pressed, and his tie was a geometric print held in place by a diamond stickpin.

I stared at the diamond pin. It had to be twice the size of my wedding ring. The ring I hadn't worn in seventeen years and currently kept in the back of my jewelry box.

Wakefield shook my hand warmly. "Sorry for the delay. I've gotten behind in my work, since—" He didn't finish, just left the word hanging. *Since.*

I followed him into his office. Seated opposite him in a large dark green leather chair, the first thing that really impressed me was how white his teeth were. Very, very white against that deep tan.

"First," I said, "I want to apologize for the intrusion. I'm Bess Mackey, a private investigator." I handed Wakefield my identification. He looked hard at my license—too hard, as if maybe he was trying to commit my license number to memory. "I've been retained by Rebecca Shields," I went on.

Wakefield was in the process of handing my ID back to me, but his hand froze momentarily at the mention of Rebecca's name. Apparently, he was well aware of what his sister-in-law had been saying about him.

I suppressed a sigh. This was not going to make questioning him any easier. I took my ID and put it back in my purse. "I just need some information," I said.

Wakefield now looked guarded, wary. "Yes?" One word. Obviously, he was now not about to say anything more than he absolutely had to. Oh my, yes, Rebecca must've made her suspicions abundantly clear. Terrific.

"Do you know of anyone who might've had a reason to harm your wife—or your daughter?"

He shook his head. "No, no one." He ran a tanned hand through his dark waves and then added, "My wife was a wonderful woman, Bess. Everyone loved her. And little Sarah, well, she was just a joy."

It always makes me feel uncomfortable to suddenly be on a first-name basis with a total stranger. Salesmen are always doing that—dropping your name into every other sentence. Now it made me wonder what Wakefield was selling.

"Rebecca tells me that you and your wife were getting a divorce?"

Something flickered in his eyes. "Rebecca is mistaken, Bess. Alanna and I would never get a divorce. We belonged together." Irritation had crept into his voice, but he caught himself immediately, assuming an expression of regret. "Oh, we quarreled occasionally, like all couples do, but we always made up."

"But weren't you, in fact, separated?"

There was, once again, a flicker in his eyes, but it was gone as quickly as it came. He waved his hand. "We'd had a little tiff, that's all. Alanna needed to get away by herself for a while to think things through. She was planning to move back the following week." He looked away. When he looked back at me, tears glittered in his eyes. "I loved her very much."

The way he said it didn't quite ring true. The words, the tears—it all seemed, somehow, staged: The Bereaved Husband, Act 1, Scene 1.

At the same time, I wondered if I might not be jumping to conclusions. *Really, Bess,* I told myself, *it's the nineties. Men could display genuine emotion these days without it being an act.*

"Rebecca also tells me that Sarah was adopted—"

Wakefield interrupted me. "Sarah may have been adopted, but ever since the day Alanna and I brought her home from St. Joseph's, we felt as if she was our very own."

My breath actually caught. St. Joseph's. He'd said *St. Joseph's.* This time something must've shown in my face. Something Wakefield misread. He answered as if I'd asked a question. "St. Joseph's is a facility located about sixty miles from here. It's what, I suppose, years ago would've been called a home for wayward girls, Bess. Sarah's natural mother was a teenager. Unmarried, of course."

Of course. My heart began to pound.

Stuart Wakefield didn't have to tell me about St. Joseph's. A little over five years ago I'd gotten to know St. Joseph's very well. You couldn't forget that gray stone façade. Someone had tried to soften its old exterior by placing stone cherubs on each side of the porch. It hadn't worked.

I hoped my voice sounded natural. "How old was the baby when you adopted her?"

Wakefield looked at me. I could see the question in his eyes: *Why on earth does she want to know something like that?* But he answered, anyway. "She was three days old. Born September 15."

Wakefield's expression now silently said, *See what a devoted father I was? See? I even remember the kid's birthday.*

I, however, was too distracted to be impressed. I closed my eyes for a split second, and I could see Hannah again.

On September 15, five years ago, I'd been with her the whole time, holding her hand. Watching her writhe with each contraction.

Hannah at sixteen, just a baby herself. She never did tell me who the father was. We'd talked about everything else, but she wouldn't talk about him. All she'd ever said was, "He doesn't believe me, Mom." She'd been sobbing then. "He thinks it isn't his baby."

I'd wanted to kill that anonymous boy.

Hannah and I had talked about what to do for months. Deciding what would be best. For the baby, for everybody. I'd just opened my own agency, and Hannah hadn't even graduated from high school yet. How were we going to manage a baby? Those were the things I told Hannah, but I think even then I'd known what the bottom line was: I was thirty-seven, I didn't want to raise another child, and I knew Hannah couldn't do it alone. "There are couples out there just waiting for a baby to love," I'd told her.

All this flashed through my mind while Wakefield went on. "When we found out there was a baby for us, Alanna and I were so happy. We'd been on a waiting list for years, and then suddenly, we got this phone call." He actually smiled, as if for a moment he'd forgotten what had happened.

But then, almost as quickly as it appeared, his smile faded.

I was on my feet by then. What I suddenly wanted more than anything else was to get out of there, to go somewhere that I could think. "I guess that's all for now. I do appreciate your taking the time—"

But Wakefield wasn't ready to let me go. He continued to sit. "I want you to know that Rebecca's accusations are absurd. If you'll ask around, you'll see that the very idea that I, of all people, could be capable of—"

"I will be asking around," I said quietly. "You can count on that."

Wakefield went on as if I hadn't even spoken. "There is absolutely nothing to put me in that apartment that evening. Nothing. And I have a witness who'll testify that I was with her all that evening."

"Oh?"

"Miss Sturgill will testify that she was with me." He looked toward the doorway, and I realized he was indicating his secretary. I just looked at him. That woman would swear Stuart Wakefield was on the moon if he told her to do it.

"I see." That was all I said, but Wakefield evidently read a little more into those two words than I actually meant.

"No, you don't see," he said, sounding angry for the first time. "We were here. Working. The entire evening."

I continued to just look at him.

"So there's no way whatsoever that Rebecca can prove her ridiculous charges. You can tell her that for me."

It occurred to me that he had not actually said that he did not do it. All he'd said was that Rebecca couldn't prove it.

At that moment, however, I was mainly concentrating on getting as far away as I could from Wakefield's tanned smile as fast as I could. I'd already turned and taken a step toward the door when Wakefield added, "I don't suppose it has occurred to you to wonder why Rebecca is doing this? Why she wants to divert suspicion to me?"

That stopped me. I turned back toward him. "Why do you think?"

Wakefield spread his hands in a gesture of complete openness. "Because if everybody's concentrating on me, they won't be looking anywhere else."

I stared at him. "Where else should they look?"

Wakefield's mouth did this odd pinching thing before he answered. It looked as if he'd bitten down on something bitter. "How about taking a look at the person I was dating before I dropped her and started dating Alanna? At the person who was always coming around making trouble for me and Alanna? Telling Alanna the most outrageous lies, trying to break us up? At the person who, when Alanna and I adopted little Sarah, was so jealous that she didn't come around and see our new baby for weeks?"

If this was some sort of quiz game, I wasn't going to play. "Who are you talking about?"

Wakefield flashed those white teeth. "Rebecca, that's who." He leaned forward. "Rebecca's always been jealous of her sister. She's always wanted what Alanna and I had together. What she's never been able to have for herself." Wakefield cleared his throat, his eyes narrowing. "So, the next time you're listening to Rebecca's accusations, you might want to ask her: *Where was she the night Alanna and Sarah were killed?*"

Could he be right? Had Rebecca brought me into this investigation because she was afraid the police might be homing in on her? Was my function merely to divert suspicion away from her?

All of this was a lot to think about on the way back to my office. It was almost a relief, in fact, to have something else to go over in my mind, other than the thing I most didn't want to concentrate on.

It wasn't until I got back to my office that I started to shake. I guess maybe it took that long to really hit me. I sat at my desk, staring at my phone, and I just shook. As if I were having chills. I guess I must've stared at that phone for a half hour yesterday afternoon. A phone call—that's all it would take. Dial a few numbers, and in no time at all, I could find out the identity of little Sarah Wakefield's natural mother.

I've traced adoptions before; and it's gotten a lot easier lately, ever since Kentucky passed an adoption search law. Even without the search law, I'd gotten pretty friendly with one of the state social workers with the Cabinet for Human Resources in Kentucky. I could call her up, and I'd probably find out what I wanted to know in a matter of minutes.

The problem was, though, did I really want to know? I mean, what did it matter at this late date? Would knowing change anything?

It was while I was staring at my phone that it rang. I must've jumped a foot before I picked up the receiver.

"Well?" I recognized Rebecca's voice. "Did you talk to him? What do you think?"

"I saw him," I said. "He had some interesting things to say."

"Interesting? What do you mean?" Was I imagining it, or did Rebecca suddenly sound wary? Just like Wakefield earlier.

I cleared my throat. "Well, for one thing, he said that you and he had dated once."

There was a sound on the line that I thought for a moment was static. Then Rebecca said, "That's right. We did. But after I'd gone out with him for a few months, I saw through him to what he really was. I saw his lies, his cheating. And I ended it. That's when he took up with my sister."

Well, now, this was a slightly different version than what Wakefield had told me. I wondered which was the truth.

"He said you were so upset when he and your sister adopted Sarah, that you didn't come around for weeks."

Rebecca didn't hesitate. Had she already carefully planned what she'd say if anybody ever brought this particular subject up? "Of course I wasn't happy to see Alanna adopt a baby with that man! I'd been trying to get her to leave that asshole, and then all of a sudden she's making herself more dependent on him! And not only herself, but a baby as well!" I could hear Rebecca take a deep breath. "So I guess this means you believe him? That he's mesmerized you, too, just like he's mesmerized every other woman he's ever come into contact with!"

My first impulse was to say something equally as angry back to her. But years as a cop have taught me to always confront anger with absolute calm. To defuse the situation. "As a matter of fact," I said evenly, "I've decided to look into this case a little further."

"You are?" Rebecca's voice instantly went from angry to elated. "Oh, that's great, that's—"

I interrupted her. "I intend to find out exactly who killed your niece and your sister."

"Oh, that's wonderful!" Rebecca said. "Thank you so much!"

I listened to her and wondered. Would she pay me good money and sound this happy if I were investigating a crime she'd really committed herself? Surely not. Unless, of course, she was that confident she could get away with it.

Or that confident she could pin it on somebody else.

Rebecca then hung up and left me sitting there at my desk, once again staring at my phone.

Somehow, while I was talking to Rebecca, the question I'd been considering before she'd called had become something else. It had gone from "Did I want to know the truth?" to "Could I stand not knowing?"

I left my office for the day about an hour later—without making up my mind. On either question.

That, of course, was yesterday. Today, walking in here and seeing that doll in Alanna Wakefield's living room did not help me think any clearer. If anything, it only made things worse. Seeing that photo again, that little Sarah's shy smile, so like Hannah's. It reminded me, of course, that it wasn't just me involved in this. Shouldn't I find out the truth for Hannah?

Grieber and I had finished looking around Alanna Wakefield's apartment, but neither of us seemed to want to admit it. We both wandered back out to the living room and stood there in the middle of the room, looking around. There really wasn't anything else left for us to do.

I didn't want to, but I couldn't help myself. I looked back over at the doll. Grieber's glance followed mine.

"Chatty Patty," he said. "This year's Cabbage Patch doll."

I didn't even try to conceal my surprise. "You know dolls, Grieber?"

He smiled. "I have three daughters, you know." He looked back over at the doll, and his smile froze. "My youngest has a Chatty Patty. She plays with it all the time. Drives me nuts." He started fishing in his pocket for keys. "The damn thing talks back to you, repeating whatever you just said to it." As he spoke, Grieber was beginning to move toward the door.

I stayed where I was. Leaving would be admitting that I'd given up. It would be admitting that the apartment had nothing to tell me. I turned back toward the doll. "How does the thing work?" I asked. I was filling the air now myself. Like Rebecca and Hannah.

Grieber was almost at the front door now. "You press one of its hands, talk to it, and then you press the other hand and it'll repeat what you just said." He had his back to me, his hand now turning the doorknob. "My six-year-old drives me nuts with her Chatty Patty. It's jabbering all the time."

"You mean, the doll is like a tape recorder?" I looked back over at the doll. "So that if Sarah was playing with it, when—" My breath caught in my throat. "Grieber, is it possible she could've been holding the doll when whoever did this came to the door? Rebecca Shields told me Sarah always had the doll with her. . ."

One thing about Grieber, he catches on fast. He turned, starting to move after I did, and still managed to beat me to the doll.

Lord. Was it possible that the Crime Lab could've overlooked examining the doll? I could see, even as Grieber picked the thing up, that there were no stains, none whatsoever, on the doll's clothing. And yet—I didn't want to picture it, I even tried to blink the image away—and yet, couldn't the impact have knocked the doll across the room? To where it was lying now, its head against the wall? It might've been flung there. . .

Grieber was holding the doll now, squeezing its right hand. My heart started pounding so loud, I was afraid I wouldn't be able to hear anything. But I heard, all right.

For a second there was nothing but a gentle whirring sound. Then Grieber and I both listened to what the doll had to say.

And we looked at each other.

Twenty-five minutes later Grieber was still holding the doll when he and I walked into Stuart Wakefield's office. Rebecca Shields had apparently arrived just seconds before us. She was still standing in front of Miss Sturgill's desk.

This time Rebecca was dressed in navy blue—slacks, sweater, shoes. All a perfect match. I'd called her from a pay phone just outside of her sister's apartment not twenty minutes ago, and yet Rebecca's champagne hair looked perfectly coiffed, her makeup once again impeccably applied.

When I introduced her to Grieber, Rebecca's voice shook a little when she said, "Glad to meet you." You might've thought, however, that she was not saying this to Grieber, but to the doll in his hands. That was where her gaze was directed.

Rebecca's eyes looked very wide.

Today none of us had to wait any time at all. Of course, this might've been because Miss Sturgill, no doubt, went in and told Wakefield that there was a big, beefy guy waiting to see him—and that this particular guy was out in his lobby playing with a doll.

Miss Sturgill showed us in, giving Grieber a faintly worried glance as he walked by her. We were all seated before Wakefield looked up from the blueprints he was studying. His eyes narrowed when they lighted on Rebecca. "So what's all this about?" As he spoke, his eyes traveled to what Grieber had in his hands.

Grieber held the doll out in front of him, so that both Rebecca and Stuart Wakefield could get a good look at it. "I'm Otto Grieber with the Louisville Police Department. I believe you've both already met Bess Mackey. She and I needed to talk to the both of you about some new evidence that's just come up in our investigation into the deaths of Alanna and Sarah Wakefield. We thought it might save some time if we talked to you both together."

I gave Grieber a quick, sideways glance. Grieber can be amazingly articulate under pressure.

Wakefield's eyebrows went up. "Oh?" he said.

"I've got a doll here that we believe Sarah was holding the night she died," Grieber said.

Wakefield's eyes flickered to the doll.

"This is a very special doll," I added at this point. And then, slowly, I began to explain exactly how the doll works. All the time I was talking, I was watching Rebecca's and Wakefield's reaction.

They both just sat there. Unmoving. Their eyes on the doll.

Grieber handed Chatty Patty to me. "Now," he said, his eyes flickering from Rebecca's face to Wakefield's and back, "I want you two to hear what this doll has to say." As casually as if he were changing the channels on a TV set, Grieber slowly reached over to press down on Chatty Patty's right hand. Rebecca stared.

And Wakefield's eyes showed the whites all around.

"No!" The word seemed torn from Wakefield's throat.

Grieber stopped in mid-action and looked at Wakefield.

"No," Wakefield repeated. "No. I can't hear that again. I—I just can't." Wakefield started to cry then.

While Rebecca and Grieber and I all watched, Wakefield sat there behind his expensive desk and sobbed. He started mumbling about how he hadn't meant to do it. About how he hadn't realized that it was Sarah who'd answered the door.

About how he'd just blindly shot the second the door opened. And about how it wasn't really his fault.

I stopped listening when Wakefield got to that part. If it wasn't his fault, whose was it? Wakefield was still crying when Grieber read him his rights and led him away.

Rebecca was crying by then, too. "The doll recorded it all?"

For an answer, I pressed Chatty Patty's hand. Once again, just like in Alanna's apartment earlier, I heard a gentle whirring noise.

And then there was the voice of a little girl. "Lullaby, and good night—" Sarah Elizabeth Wakefield sang. Such a clear, sweet little voice. "—and roses and—and—" At this point Sarah must've forgotten the rest of the words to her song because she stopped and giggled.

After that, there was only silence.

Rebecca blinked. "Thank God Stuart is a damn coward," she said.

I nodded.

And yet, who was I to talk? I, too, was a damn coward. Like Stuart Wakefield, I was afraid of what I might hear.

Rebecca actually gave me a hug before she left. I tried to respond warmly—my heart did go out to her—but I guess I was already thinking about what I was about to do.

As Rebecca went out the door, I reached for the phone. And, just as I'd thought, in a few short minutes, I had my answer.

For a very long time after that, I couldn't stop crying. I cried for Alanna, and I cried for Hannah, and I cried for all the women who've ever had to make difficult choices. Mostly, though, I cried for little Sarah Elizabeth Wakefield, born September 15, 1994, to an unwed teenager named Tara Louise James.

Ode to a Dead Gardenia

by Elizabeth Daniels Squire

Elizabeth Daniels Squire writes mysteries set in North Carolina. She is an ex-reporter who has covered everything from murder trials to floods. Born into a newspaper family involved with the News and Observer *in Raleigh, North Carolina, she knew the workings of that newspaper intimately as a member of the board. Squire's grandfather, a controversial editor and publisher, received death threats. Her* Kill the Messenger *is about a family-owned newspaper and the murder of the publisher. A winner of the Agatha Award for best mystery short story, Squire also writes a series about an absentminded sleuth who uses her memory tricks to solve murders.* Forget About Murder *is the latest in that series.*

"Edgar Allen Poe would have loved this house, and especially the garden," I said to my cousin Robert, the English professor. The place depressed me so much that I had to say something halfway cheerful.

"Yes, Poe would have felt absolutely inspired by this garden," Robert said bitterly, as he brushed away a trailing frond of wisteria hanging down from a smothered tree. "He would even have liked the mystery that may ruin all our lives."

As we walked toward it, the graceful lines of the big old house with fluted columns across the front made it seem to cry out for help. It must once have been white but now was splotched dirty gray. A window shutter hung at an angle, and several were missing, and all around the house were the remains of a generous garden now grown up in tangles. The house stood almost in the shadow of an office building on one side, and I'd noticed a sign in front of the house on the other side which said FUTURE SITE OF THE LOOMIS BUILDING. Too bad that nice looking house, which even had a swimming pool, was going to be torn down.

"Raleigh is growing fast and our Aunt Camellia keeps getting higher and higher offers for her house," Robert said, pointing at the old mansion. "It's on a huge lot, and the last offer was over two million dollars."

I whistled.

"But as I told you, even though we are all broke, Aunt Camellia says that while she's alive she'll never sell. She says there's a reason. But when we ask why, she clamps her mouth shut." Robert sighed. "Even though she's seventy-three years old and has such bad arthritis she can hardly climb the stairs. Even though she can't afford to keep the place repaired. And then there's the problem of Cammie. She'd like to help with that, too. Cammie is her namesake and her goddaughter and her heir. But right now Aunt Camellia doesn't have a cent to spare."

I'd just seen Cammie when we got the key to the house. She wrenched my heart. She was beautiful, dark-haired, maybe forty years old, and confined to a wheelchair with multiple sclerosis. That sometimes goes into remission even after years, but they couldn't count on it. Cammie had given me a warm smile and held out her hand. The hand shook slightly, but the smile held steady. "Robert says that maybe you can help us."

Well, I am a newspaper reporter. I have even stumbled across the solutions to murders occasionally up in the mountains where I live. But this mystery about the house, God willing, was nothing like that.

I'd held Cammie's hand so firmly that it didn't shake. "I'll do what I can," I'd said. Behind her, on a shelf, was a wedding picture of Robert with Cammie all in white, both beaming. That was the past. Also a picture of Cammie in her wheelchair with three little children smiling up at her.

Now Robert was working two jobs to pay for sitters and nurses so Cammie could stay at home with him and the kids. He even moonlighted driving an armored truck because that paid well—because it was dangerous work, I thought with a shiver.

A brier from the edge of the path scratched my leg. "Aunt Camellia hasn't given you a clue about why she won't sell?" I asked.

Robert pulled a brier loose from a trouser leg. "Once, she said her husband, Claude, wanted to sell that house, and she'll never do what he wanted to do. That's crazy, now that he's dead." He sighed. "And she won't even consider a mortgage because the bank might foreclose. That's what happened to the people who owned the house before her husband bought it."

"Is she losing her marbles?" I asked.

Robert shook his head. "She's eccentric but she's sharp as a tack. She's in the hospital today for tests—that's why I have the key to feed the cat. But it's physical stuff. She's been having dizzy spells. She'll be out tomorrow."

I hoped he'd told me the whole story. People can sometimes ignore ugly things when they convince themselves that it won't matter and will make life smoother.

The red-brick path led to the front door—a double door with paint peeling like all the rest of the house. He unlocked the door and let us into a hallway with rooms on both sides and a sweeping circular staircase to the next floor.

"Wow," I said, "this must have been something!" Now, the white paint was dingy yellow and flaked. This certainly seemed like the house of somebody who didn't care. And yet I saw that even if the house might be in bad repair, it was scrupulously clean.

The high-ceilinged rooms to the right and left of the hall, and two more across the back of the house, were empty. "Aunt Camellia has sold most of the antiques," Robert said.

Huge mirrors over the mantels showed only us, looking puzzled. We went up the circular stairs and, on the next floor, found a portrait staring at us, a well-painted man in a Civil War uniform.

"That's Aunt Camellia's great-grandfather," Robert explained. "This house originally belonged to Aunt Camellia's family. They lost it to taxes after the Civil War. Claude managed to buy it back when the new owners lost it during the Great Depression. Some folks said she married Claude for the house, and that's why she didn't mind going off and looking after her mother in Nashville for three months once and leaving him alone. I think she just felt she had to do it. She's big on duty."

Only two rooms upstairs were furnished. One was a bedroom, one seemed to be a study. I thought I heard a footstep in the distance. "Does this house have a ghost?" I asked, half joking and half serious.

"Not that I've ever heard," he said shortly.

We zeroed in on the two rooms Aunt Camellia lived in. These were sparsely furnished with necessities—a bed, a bed stand, and a bureau in one and a desk and a few chairs in the other.

"What are we looking for?" I asked, but Robert said he didn't know. He just felt sure there must be a clue somewhere in the old house. That was his only hope.

I began to have a feeling that someone was following us. Old houses can creak in strange ways. Perhaps it was only that—but I asked, "Did you lock the garden gate behind us?"

He frowned. "No. But we're here. And there's not much to steal."

I kept my ears cocked.

We looked through the clothes in the closet. They were mostly in shades of violet. Obviously her favorite color. All a tiny bit musty. We found nothing, even in the pockets, except for a rumpled handkerchief with lace around the edge.

On Aunt Camellia's old-fashioned mahogany dresser stood a large bottle of gardenia perfume. She must have really liked that scent to have such a large bottle. Or maybe it had been a present from an admirer long ago. The bottle was dusty as if she never used it now. *Odd*, I found myself thinking. Nothing else in the room was dusty.

And why gardenia perfume for a woman named Camellia? Camellias have always intrigued me. My aunt in Charleston had a camellia bush, and the pink flowers looked as if they should be delicate and smell delicious, but they were long lasting and without scent.

We went into the study. "Aunt Camellia writes poetry," Robert told me with some pride. "There are notebooks with her poetry here. And a few magazines where her poems have been published."

The notebooks and magazines were in a pile on a rolltop desk.

I turned to Robert: "I'm going to look through the drawers—okay?"

He looked embarrassed and said, "Considering how worried we are . . ." His voice trailed off.

I looked in the dresser drawers and was surprised to find a legal document in the top right drawer. LAST WILL AND TESTAMENT, it said. I hoped her lawyer had a copy in his safe. Aside from being creaky, this old wooden mansion was probably a firetrap.

"She read us the will," Robert said. "We know what's in it."

Skipping the legal language, the heirs mentioned were her niece Camellia (Cammie) and someone named Jewel Parkham. Cammie and Robert got the house and the portrait of the general. Jewel Parkham got the furniture, "and I wish it could be more."

"Jewel Parkham is the nurse who raised Aunt Camellia," Robert explained when I asked. "She was married to a preacher but her husband died and she went to work for Miss Camellia's father as a kind of housekeeper-nurse. Jewel must be in her mid-nineties by now. Her granddaughter is on the city council: Dorothy Parkham. She's a lawyer, specialty real estate."

I noticed the notebooks on top of the desk, and something made me stop and skim through Aunt Camellia's poetry. A few poems were rather old-fashioned but others were quite fresh. I was impressed. One poem was about gardenias. I would have expected it to be in praise of those lovely white flowers, especially since Aunt Camellia had gardenia perfume on her dressing table.

Even the title was odd: "Ode to a Dead Gardenia."

> If you do not touch me
> I bathe you in perfume,
> which is too sweet.
> I stay ivory as heavy cream.
> If you touch me, I turn dark as a bruise.
> I will be a curse, until you die.

I remembered I'd worn a gardenia to my high-school prom. When I took my corsage off, I touched the flower petals by mistake and saw how soon they darkened.

I shivered and was not sure why.

Now I heard the creaking noise. So loud this time I knew it was more than old-house noise. Someone had followed us! In fact, the door opened and there stood an African-American woman, bowed with age. Her hair was white and she leaned on a cane, trembling.

Robert rushed to get a chair for her. "Jewel!" he cried. "You came up all those stairs." He was tense with alarm, and I could see why.

The old woman all but fell into the chair, out of breath, leaned back and shut her eyes. Her right hand dropped the cane and clutched her heart. "I came up slow," she whispered.

Gradually she began to breathe normally and opened her eyes. "I'm not gone yet!" she announced. "There's spunk in this gal yet."

"But why have you come here?" Robert asked in a worried tone.

"I went to see your Aunt Camellia in the hospital," she said. "My granddaughter took me. I saw your car here and you folks at the door. My poor Camellia is scared sick. She's scared they'll take this house for taxes."

Good grief. If Aunt Camellia's stubbornness meant they took the house for taxes, that would be a real catastrophe.

"I raised that girl," Jewel said. "After her mama died, there was just me. Oh, her father was there, but he was mostly busy. Now I hate to see her so scared. That's why she's sick. She's scared sick. Scared to sell and scared she'll lose this house if she won't sell."

It was incredible to me that seventy-three-year-old Aunt Camellia had a baby-nurse who was still alive and worried about her—who was maybe the only one she felt safe to tell. Tell exactly what?

"This has to do with a gardenia, doesn't it?" I asked. That was a pretty wild guess, but if a gardenia was going to curse her until she died—well, it must figure in.

Jewel gave me a sharp look. "I've never told," she said. "I've been good to that girl and she's been good to me."

"But maybe you could help us understand," Robert said, "if there is anything we can do. This is not like before. We're desperate, and so is Aunt Camellia. My friend here is absolutely discreet. She's helping us."

Jewel gave me another piercing glance. "You're our friend?" she demanded.

"Absolutely," I said.

She continued to look me up and down. Finally she took a deep breath and said, "All right. I'll trust you." Then her words poured out.

"That Lulu woman liked to wear a gardenia behind her ear. Oh, she was good-looking with red hair and the kind of curves men want. And she was spiteful. Said she didn't like women, only men. I'd come over to get the house back in shape the day before Miss Camellia was coming back from seeing to her mama in Nashville. I heard that Lulu woman talking to Mr. Claude. Used to be that folks like her treated us blacks like we weren't there. They'd say anything in front of us or with us in the next room. Forgot we were around. It was downright interesting." She smiled a wry little smile.

"Mr. Claude told that Lulu woman that he couldn't see her anymore—that everything was finished. Had to be.

"That woman said she wouldn't let him loose. She said she'd tell Camellia what they'd done and Camellia would leave him. She'd see to that."

"And were you there when she confronted Camellia?" I asked, fascinated.

"No," she said. "That mean-talking woman disappeared and nobody missed her. Some said she'd gone to Knoxville.

"But I worked for Miss Camellia. Even if she was grown she still needed me. And I needed the work. My daughter was in college at Shaw. I was so proud of that. The day after they said that woman left for Knoxville, I found a dead gardenia lying in a corner of Camellia's room. So dark and bruised, you'd hardly know what it was. I picked it up and Camellia saw me and turned pale as a ghost. I said, 'You killed that woman and I don't blame you.' I had to know.

"Well, she gave up and told me. That girl came by at night when Mr. Claude was out at a meeting and told my poor Camellia what she and Mr. Claude did and began to tell her all the details of what they did, like no lady ever would, and my Camellia slapped her. That hussy went wild and choked my Camellia. But Mr. Claude had come home. They didn't even hear him. He hit that Lulu with the poker from the fireplace. Hit her right on the head where it crushed that gardenia. That's why it was all black when I found it."

"He killed her!" I gasped.

She gave me a speculative look. "He saved Camellia."

But suddenly I wondered, *Was all this a lie to cover whatever really happened?* Loyalty shone strong in Jewel's face. Loyalty to the child she raised, even if it wasn't her own child.

I thought I heard the stairs creak again. I should have said, "Is someone coming?" But I wanted Jewel to finish her story so badly that I told myself it was nothing.

"Mr. Claude told Camellia she was no good at telling a lie. That girl never was. So he told her he didn't want her to know what he did with the body. She had to swear to stay in her room. She says she did it. She swore not to look out the window, and she didn't. But she did look at the clock. He left about ten o'clock. He came back before eleven. She figured he must have buried that body somewhere in the garden."

"But that would have been crazy!" I said.

She stared me down. "I guess Mr. Claude did what he felt he had to do. The next day he signed up for a cruise to send my poor Camellia away from here. Her and her sister. To be out of a question-asking place, if anybody missed that Lulu. Before they left, he must have managed to get that Lulu's bags from the motel where she was staying, ready to move in with Claude as soon as she scared Camellia off. Must have got rid of the car, too."

"But then," said Robert, "why on earth would Claude want to sell the house? Someone might find the body."

The old woman laughed. "It was Camellia who said Mr. Claude wanted to sell. I never heard that man say a word about it when he was alive. After he was gone, she said he'd wanted to sell."

I looked out the window into the tangled garden. I didn't believe the body was there. And in a shallow grave, at that, if he took less than an hour to bury it.

"Was Claude smart?" I asked.

"Absolutely brilliant," Robert said. "He was a contractor, but he also made and lost three fortunes in real estate. Unfortunately he lost the last one just before he died."

"Then the body is not in the garden," I said, "unless he thought he had some really foolproof hiding place."

"Don't matter if the body is in the garden," Jewel said. "Miss Camellia believes it's there. She'll never sell. And I don't know what she'll do about the taxes."

The door opened again. Oh, boy, someone had heard the whole story and it was my fault for not speaking up.

A young African-American woman in a stylish gray silk suit and red pocketbook and heels hurried into the room. "Good morning," she said to us. "I'm Dorothy Parkham." She turned immediately to Jewel. "You should have told me about this house, Grandma," she said. Ah, the councilwoman. The real estate lawyer. She'd followed her grandmother here.

"That was none of your business," Jewel said. "Miss Camellia helped your mama get an education. So your mama could help you. But I knew if I told you her secret, you'd try to make her sell this house no matter what."

The councilwoman smiled. "Not by blackmail!" she said. "But it sounds like she's in trouble! She says she won't sell it while she's alive. But she knows it'll be sold when she dies. What difference does it make?"

"When she's gone," Jewel said, "they can't ask her questions. Like I say, that girl can't lie."

The councilwoman sat in the one remaining chair and tossed her head. "I have a client who wants to buy this house," she said. "I think I know how to persuade Miss Camellia to sell it."

"Oh, Lord," Jewel cried, and her hands flew up in front of her as if to ward off trouble. "What have I done?"

But Robert was interested. "How can you make Aunt Camellia want to sell the house?" he asked.

"This piece of land will be worth more every year. This town is growing like crazy," the councilwoman said. I could see by the twinkle in her eye that she was pleased with herself. "Now, Grandma, you stop looking that way and have faith. My client wants this property for an investment. He can buy on the basis that Miss Camellia lives here until she dies. He can begin to pay her for the house while she's alive. She can live in that house and be comfortable!" she said.

Jewel burst into tears. "Lord be praised," she gasped.

Robert stepped forward and grasped the granddaughter's hand. "I can't tell you what this will mean to us all!"

"Us all, including me," the councilwoman said. "I'll get a good commission."

"But what should we do about the murder?" I asked.

They all said it together: "What murder?"

On my next trip through town, I called Robert to see how things were going. "Oh, you'll have to come by," he said. "Aunt Camellia has invited Cammie and me for tea to see what she's doing to the house and garden. And, yes, she's also helping us, God bless her. Meet us there at three."

I found that changes had already started. I walked around the house and admired them. The blinds were rehung straight and a crew of men was pulling down a small ugly porch on the back which didn't seem to go with the house. Obviously a later addition. The flower beds by the house were weeded, though the edges of the huge garden were left wild. Oddly, that was an attractive effect. The front door was painted, but the rest of the house was still gray with age. One thing at a time.

Robert met me at the door and led me to a room on the first floor, easily accessible to Cammie in her wheelchair. There, around a small table with a lace cloth, were Cammie and Miss Camellia and Jewel. I bet Jewel appreciated the lack of stairs almost as much as Cammie did. She beamed and winked at me. Miss Camellia, in a lavender dress that complemented her gray-blue hair, poured tea from a silver tea service she'd managed to hold onto because, she said, it was her great-grandmother's. The very tea set they'd buried to hide it from the Yankees. I guess that really did happen sometimes.

"We are all beholden to Jewel," Robert said, "for figuring out a way to save this house."

"Jewel is so smart," Miss Camellia said, smiling so her wrinkles looked like many laugh lines. "She asked her granddaughter if there wasn't a way to get money for this house while I still lived, a way that guaranteed that I could stay here. And that smart girl came up with a way."

Jewel winked at me again. So Camellia didn't know her secret was out.

"Robert showed me your house while he was feeding the cat. It's a lovely house," I said. "I notice you are very fond of gardenia perfume."

"Oh, that," she said. A faraway look came into her eyes. "You know, nobody is perfect, and long ago my husband gave that perfume to another woman. I kept it there to remind us to work at being true to one another."

Oh, boy! I bet that husband walked the straight and narrow path.

So everything was finally all right then, and everything was going to be all right now. I was glad.

But just then, a workman in old overalls broke in without a by-your-leave.

"Ma'am," he said to Miss Camellia, "we've found something."

I worked to keep my face blank. Miss Camellia blinked, startled.

"Under that old porch, we've found a great big old block of cement. Must be eight feet long. And thick. Not going to fit in the flower beds you want by the house." Now the workman's eyes lit up. Did he suspect as I did that a body was in that cement? I felt cold.

No one said a word. Our poker faces did us proud.

"Now, my brother is pulling down that house next door," the man in overalls said. "He's got his heavy stuff there today. He's filling the pool. Now, the easiest way to get rid of this ugly block of cement—unless it's something you want—is to get him to drag it over to the pool."

I'm proud to say not one of us let out a sigh of relief.

Miss Camellia smiled graciously. "Yes, tell your brother that cement block is his for fill for the building next door." Maybe she couldn't lie, but she could sure keep her cool.

I told myself we were camellias, not gardenias. We would endure.

"Clackin' the Bones"

by Noreen Ayres and A. B. Robbins

Texas resident Noreen Ayres is the author of several novels featuring Smokey Brandon, the ex-stripper, forensic specialist for the Orange County (California) Sheriff's Department. This is one of several stories written as a collaboration between Ayres and Robbins.

Ben Weems had it in mind to bust out but I wanted no part of it.

"Alls we do is make that door," he said, voice as soft as a singer who knows how to make a crowd weep. "Walk right out, like we helping Virgil. Y'all don't take care of your own selfs, somebody else be scratching your balls." His eyes gleamed bright as a beetle's, and it was hard to tell if it was from rousting me or from the concerns of his young heart.

"I got nineteen days left of my thirty," I said. "I can do that spinning on a knuckle."

Over by the far wall, two inmates were sitting at a table, slapping cards down and calling each other good-natured names while they spent their dream jackpots. We were thirty-nine of us stashed temporarily in the basement of the old civil courts building downtown because the main jail was full-up and the municipal work farm was overflowing. So this was jail, a building that looked pretty much like all the other ancient brown brick buildings downtown, the rooms dim or glaring with fluorescents.

"Gotta get me on home, see my boy, Cisroe, so's he don' forget his daddy's face." He focused on the TV set across the room where fists were flying between guests on the stage of a talk show, the audio cutting in and out because of swear words.

I scooted my plastic chair forward and said, "You bust out and they gonna *pile* on the time."

"Some people make out okay in lockup, Mistah Perkins," he said, polishing the bridge of his nose with a finger. "Some don't. I be one of them don'ts. Trouble always gon' find my address. I be collecting more time whether I goes today or whether I stays."

"Negative thinking don't help a man no matter where he's

putting his shoes at night," I said.

Ben was twenty-eight to my near-sixty, and I thought I knew a thing or two I could impart, but I could see my advice was about as welcome as warts. The judge had laid a month on me, but I knew sometimes you can get out in twenty days and I was already fifteen down. Ben only had a couple of more months himself.

But stubborn stands with stupid sometimes. Ben had a way about him that would keep him from drawing back his hand from a snake hole. These same impulses tossed him in the slam in the first place: One unthinking day he walked into a convenience store and pointed nothing more dangerous than a big black finger at the clerk, demanding what lay in the till. Later he explained the deed by saying he had a nervous breakdown, when what it seemed to be was that he loved a gorgeous woman who was down on him for a better living all day long.

"Mistah Perkins, I feel better you come out wit' me."

"No can do, son."

"You not on de train, den?"

"Not me, son." Ben was fixed on me for no good reason I could get, except for one. I own a barbecue joint called Kozy Krib, down in Fifth Ward. I don't run it anymore myself, I have a reliable lady who does. When Ben was young, *Little* Ben is how we knew him. He grew to double-man size over one summer, but the name didn't change with him.

"It's simple as a cat hopping over a caterpillar," Ben said, trying one more time.

"You got Owens for company, Ben. You don't need me."

"Owens is on the bumper. He don't have no spot in the car."

"Owens is a good man."

"Owens is a screw-up."

"That don't make him a bad man."

"Listen," Ben said, impatient but respectful, "we goin' out right around fi'-forty-five. You change your min' . . ."

I smacked him on the knee with my palm as I stood up. "'Preciate it anyway, son."

What brought me to this dreary place was a false conviction for possession of stolen credit cards. They were found in the back of the till at Kozy Krib and in the garage of my own house over in Fourth Ward near Waugh and West Gray, out of which I offer my PI services. Now, I didn't put those cards in either place and I was pretty sure I know who did. Even so, I wouldn't say, and the gavel did come down.

The worst thing against me was a prosecutor named Johnnie Hardwick, who'd been looking to bust my ass for at least five years. He had a pretty daughter named Toby. For a few months I dated her. She was twenty years my junior, white to my black, and had a cocaine problem before I met her. Her daddy wanted to believe she had acquired the habit under my influence, but that was false as high makeup on a whore.

I have an attorney named Bridge Jones I figured would be getting me out of the mess some way. But then Hardwick went and baited me in the courtroom after the judge offered probation and deferred adjudication. I didn't want any damned adjudication except vindication. I stuck a finger in Hardwick's face and told him he was sorrier than a warthog 'cause a warthog you can shoot and eat. For good measure I flapped my jaws at the judge, who I knew to be soiled around the edges most of the time; I flapped my yap and he gave me thirty and warned me for more. A man can be more years smackin' sandals on the planet than Little Ben and be just as dumb-acting sometimes.

The worst thing about it all was I had made a promise to a lady named Joanette to help her track down her mama before the tumor in Joanette's lung would have its quick and lethal way, and the unfulfillment of that task made me blue at times. I let Joanette know of my situation right away and told her to get another PI, but she wanted to hang in there with me. I prayed I might get my sentence cut to weekends, the judge having a heart after all, but it was not to be.

At mess that evening I was fretful for Ben. I knew that if he took the break and was picked up again or surrendered on his own he'd be doing mop-and-pail into the next century. It's not my way to tell a man a thing more than twice, because such argument only packs the ground and there's always a chance he'll change his mind on his own once a seed is planted.

Ben truly did love his boy. Ben knew it was his and he fell in love with it the minute it hit the birthing table. "Couple o' days off to see my son," he said. "That's all I need and I be all right."

It got to be about 5:40 and the inmates were already moved off into the area along one wall where they hold mess. The trusties were lined up by the carts with the big pots of food on them, and the one guard on duty had stepped outside the door to see the papers of somebody who had rapped on the window square.

When I got to the mashed potatoes, Virgil plopped a spoonful on my plate and leaned forward and said, "Ben's in the hat." I stared into Virgil's eyes. He followed mine as I moved on, then turned back to scooping for the next man.

I was not sure what I had just heard. Virgil was from the neighborhood same as me and Ben, and he would want to look out for any of us. I moved on down the line, then went to a table and set my tray down and sat before it and listened for what else might be said as I ate.

Then I saw Mel Owens and Fortunato Marquez moving with their dirty plates toward one of the bus-carts, and Ben Weems rising from his seat at the end of a far table to do the same. He set his plate on the stack, then grabbed the cart by the handle and moved off down the hall toward the elevators, according to plan, like he'd been asked to take the cart to clean-up.

Mel Owens took a cart as well, even though it wasn't half-full, and that seemed to confuse Fortunato, so he returned nervously to his table. A giant man with a goatee, two layers of butterscotch-colored flesh at the back of his neck, and eyes like dark holes poked in dough got up from his table and followed Mel and Ben Weems. The big man was Derek Fortier. He had attitude visible from any angle. He was racked for a misdemeanor same as all of us, but a misdemeanor doesn't necessarily mean a man ain't a killer in his bones; luck and lawyers are how it goes.

A johnny at my table said quietly, "Green light for Weems." Green light I knew. In the hat, I didn't. But it was all the same: Someone was going to shank Ben Weems.

My feet took full purchase of the floor and I was out and over the bench and across the room, casting a quick eye on a trusty bouncing against the wall as if he had music on. I put a fist to my stomach and made a face for his benefit as if my digestion didn't get in line with inmate food, and in a moment my long stride had me closing on Butterscotch, who was on the heels of Mel and my friend Ben Weems. I didn't know what I was going to do to save Ben's life.

I have never been much of a physical man. In the army I was taught some moves, but that had been decades ago. Now I would try to talk the situation down without even knowing what I was going to say as I would step in Fortier's way.

I realized a perfect place for a hit would be the *L* of the hallway to the Men's room or the Men's room itself. The guard couldn't be everywhere at once, and right now he was nowhere as far as that was concerned. And if either of those locations didn't work, there was an alcove of six-foot-high black file cabinets that cut off the line of sight by the drinking fountain.

Looking to the right at the end of the hall, I saw that Ben and Mel Owens had made it to the elevator. The doors were closed and the UP light was on. Fatso Fortier glanced back at me as he headed for the stairway. I was sure the door would be locked, had to be locked, after all. It wasn't, and Derek Fortier blew through it like nobody's business. Before it closed, I followed him through. He knew I was behind but maybe thought I was only intent on sidewalk-parole.

The first-floor door opened onto a wide hallway. Fortier moved along with the exiting crowd. None of us wore anything that would make us stand out from the general population. As low-risk misdemeanor types, we had respite from the usual orange jumpsuits because of the shortage. We wore white T-shirts and blue jeans. If a person were to see four of us in a cluster and in a hurry all dressed the same, he might draw a conclusion; but no one did. The female officer at the metal detector near the entrance was focused on her job scrutinizing the people coming in, caring less for all the people leaving out the door intent on beating end-of-day traffic.

All four of us now, fugitives the minute we stepped outside.

Mel Owens and Ben Weems were far ahead, crossing the street at the intersection and entering a parking lot jammed with cars waiting to pay the ticket taker. Fortier was behind them a good thirty yards.

A strong wind whipped the branches of the big oak tree out front of the building. I clipped along after Fortier. Little Ben never even looked over his shoulder, though Mel did, nervous enough to tip off a blind man.

Fortier must have figured he wasn't going to catch up to Mel and Ben, so he jogged across the opposite street, disappearing from sight as a Metro bus pulled away. When I saw him again, he was walking like a man with no doubts or fears or evil on his mind. At that moment I doubted myself once more. Fortier's going one way, Ben's going the other. Could be I read the situation wrong. Maybe I should just do an about-face back to jail to see if anyone missed me. Or go on home and call Bridge Jones to help get me out of the deep mud I just now stepped in. If, however, my first sense of things was true, then Fatso Fortier and Little Ben were going to wind up together, and the outcome I did not want to imagine.

As I walked south on Milam, the wind hurled leaves and spun chips of debris in little swirls. From a Thai restaurant several blocks down I phoned Kozy Krib. "Fernetta, it's Cisroe." Fernetta is waitress, manager, busboy, and busybody, been in my employ long enough to have packed on 128 good pounds since we met.

"You out already, Cisroe? I real happy for that."

"I want you to look up Ben Weems for me in the phone book, will you? You remember Little Ben?"

"He still come in here wit' that pretty wife o' his."

"Get his auntie's number for me. He's not in Information."

"His auntie don't hear so good, might not come t' the phone. I knows, 'cause for when I was gettin' up help for the church auction."

"Look quick anyway, will you?"

"Okay, hold on. Sometimes these mens they put the phone in their wife names, they credit is bad. I look anyways." When she came back, she said, "Somebody musta thrown them old books out, Cisroe. An' I din' put my address book in my handbag today. Must still be on the sink where I was digging for sumpin else."

"Damn. Is Aibrey there?"

"He in the back, at the pit."

"I know it's dinner hour, but I need you to come get me off of Milam and Tuam. Just tell Aibrey you be back in a while." Fernetta's face would be darkening about now. Her brow would be coming down to meet her nose and she'd be casting eyes right and left. "Don't think about it, Fernetta," I said. "Just do it. Leave now."

When I slipped into Fernetta's car I told her to head for my street. I pulled myself low in the seat, and as we drove I observed the black limbs of oak trees on the dark blue sky file by, and felt like a kid again on my uncle's farm out in Dime Box, sleeping on his army cot in the tall grass.

Fernetta tried asking me what this was all about, but I said it's best she pretend she was transporting her grandchild to nursery school, 'cause that's about how foolish I felt busting out of a perfectly good jail.

It was a quiet night, traffic-wise. I had Fernetta let me out around the corner from my house, then told her to get on back to work. I passed through Mr. Buehler's backyard and heard his bullfrogs belch and then go quiet at my approach, and I went on into my own yard straightaway, opening the latch of a little gate flanked by yellow roses which I planted last June. They were beautiful in the moonlight.

In the kitchen I went to the refrigerator, held the light-button in, and got out some bottled iced tea. I took it to the darkened living room and sat in the rocker and punched the button that dialed my lawyer. "Bridge, this is Cisroe. I did a foolish thing and I need you like I never needed you before."

"Foolish *and* stupid it seem to me," said Fernetta's voice over my shoulder. "I got it figured out." She was framed in the doorway looking puffed enough to go bear hunting with a willow stick. I shushed her and motioned her to sit, but she stood there with her big handbag adding to her fearsomeness.

Fernetta listened to me go through the whole thing with Bridge. When she heard enough she said, "Cisroe, what you done!" shaking her head the whole time as she walked out the door to go back to work. "Land, and I think my *boy* is stupid sometimes!"

Bridge chewed on me a while, then told me to get over to his office.

"Can't do that, Bridge. I'm sure Ben don't know a hit's been called on him. I got to find him and tell him, if nothing else."

He relented but told me to call him every thirty minutes on the cell phone, said he'd think of how to mend the punched wallboard.

I went to change my clothes and then came back to the refrigerator and took out two slices of onion and some rounds of liverwurst that had been there since before my incarceration. Trusting they were still good, I pressed an onion slice on each side of the wurst and bit into the pile as I went down to my basement. There, I removed a cinder block from the wall behind a stack of storage boxes, unwrapped my .38 snubby, checked that the cylinder was full, and tucked it in the back of my belt under my shirt. A year had gone by since I had held the gun in my hand but it still felt familiar. I've never had to use it. I hoped that would continue to be the case.

Sometimes things happen so quick you feel it's rolling by on a movie screen and you're just there in the dark watching along with all the other fools. I left my house knowing every car coming my way was the police hunting me, and I dodged next door to Mr. Buehler's place to get his old blue Escort. Part of a deal Mr. B. and I had was I could borrow his car anytime he wasn't using it; say, if I needed it for a surveillance. Once inside Buehler's car I felt better, wrapped in steel and partway hidden from looking eyes.

I was betting Ben wouldn't be dumb enough to go home and stay there after busting out. I also knew that having his wife and baby with him circumscribed where he could go.

Domino games go on in the wards twenty-four hours a day. I figured somebody at one of them would know where Ben was. Only problem was, if I could find out, so could Fatso Fortier. I hit the game on Hazard first. A bunch of the guys I knew from earlier days were there, clackin' the bones. As well, there were some newcomers barely older than Fernetta's son, a couple of gays, and a couple of white kids from over the Montrose area. No money showed on the table, but you knew it was there somewhere. In the front room, cigar smoke made it seem like the couch was smoldering with hidden fire.

Josie Marfin got up from his game and took me out back to talk. Fortier had been there asking about Ben Weems. Josie had no news about Ben, but about Fortier he said, "He just now left," cutting his head toward the street.

"Say where he was bound?"

"Axed if the game was still operating over on Lyons. I said far as I know. Then he split."

"You see a car?"

"Only reason I saw what he came in is he banged into Climone's bumper and the two of them had a few words before he got away. Old gray Merc. One busted-up right front fender."

I took out for Lyons Avenue. It was Troyce Givens's game, but I didn't have to get all the way there before I saw Derek Fortier coming out of a Stop 'n' Go after paying for his tank. There was the gray Merc, there was Fortier, and I was sitting at a light that was stuck on red for at least a minute. I saw Fortier get in, but he paused there for some reason. When the light changed I thought, *Okay, the army taught me the best defense is a good offense.* I barreled in and pulled up slightly behind him, jumped out quick, and cut around the back of his car. His left arm was on the window ledge, half-out, and the other hand was stuffin' his face with MoonPie.

I pulled his arm out and grabbed hold of his pinkie finger, splaying it to the angle I know causes a man's scrotum to shrink to the size of chickpeas. Leaning next to his ear, I said, "Listen, bro, you leave whatever complaint you got on Ben Weems to the trash man."

His eyes went bloodshot and moist from pain. "I am the trash man, jack. An' you best mind your own bidness."

"Today Ben Weems is my business. Be that way tomorrow, too."

"Get out of here, old man."

Lifting the finger again, I said, "Your ass better not be found anywhere near that boy, son, or you will deal with me." I gave his pinkie an extra inch-and-a-half of bend, whacked his elbow on the window opening, and got my ass out of there.

My cell phone gave off beeps telling me I had a message: Fernetta. But it was coming on to 9:00 and I hadn't checked in with Bridge. I did that first. He had left a recorded, private message for me on his private line, said he was meeting D. A. Johnnie Hardwick at the River Oaks Country Club for a game of tennis and a little chitchat, and if I get this message, to check back with him about 9:30.

Then I called Fernetta. She found her little address book and called Ben's auntie. Ben was there with his wife and baby. "I told him you be calling or coming by," she said. "I be doing all that for you, Cisroe, an' serving bahbecue too." I knew she was grinning and fixing to ask me for a raise.

When I got to Ben's auntie's, he was sitting on the porch-swing holding his tiny young son in his huge arms and talking drivel talk. I called his wife, Lolene, out of the house and told them both what Derek Fortier had in mind. Lolene grabbed up her baby out of Ben's arms as if to protect him right then and there. "Don't worry, baby," Ben said. "I ain't gonna let nothing happen to you and lil' Ben."

"Uh-huh you won't," Lolene said. "I'll kill you myself, you do." She was gorgeous in yellow pants and top, even in her murderous tones.

Ben gave Lolene a glance, shrugged as if to say it ain't no big deal really, then turned to me with a tale about how he had gone into Fortier's bunk and made off with two of his MoonPies. "Wouldn'ta been so bad if I took one, but I took *both* of 'em," he said, grinning. Lolene's eyes rolled and she shook her head at another Ben story. I wasn't going to challenge his story in front of her, but I knew whatever grudge Fortier had against Ben it wasn't about purloined MoonPies.

I knew a place belonging to an old client of mine, by the Jewish Community Center off Braeswood. The man lived most of the time in New York and didn't like to rent out, so it was always vacant and he let me know where to find a key. I could stash Ben and family there. I didn't figure this would take long to settle anyhow. I'd either have Ben back in protected custody or Fortier skewered on a plank. I drove the family there and called Bridge. He said he was at his office and I should get over there a.s.a.p.

When I walked into his office my jaw dropped. Hardass Hardwick, Boy District Attorney, was there sipping a Courvoissier, bouncing his knee as he sat in front of the brass NO SMOKING sign tacked onto the front of Bridge's desk.

"Let's get the small stuff out of the way first," my lawyer said.

Hardwick let Bridge go on about the future of things, but he obviously wasn't enjoying any of it.

Bridge handed me a folder. It contained my arrest documents, mug shots, the whole shebang. The next envelope he handed me had the heft and feel of the belongings I surrendered when I was booked in—wristwatch, pocketknife, billfold, keys, breath candies, condoms, and drugstore pen. If a man gets hit along the roadway, the contents of his pockets might easy tell the whole package of his life. It came to me then that Bridge must have called in a favor. My man. I was a fugitive no more.

The conversation got around to the others who took sidewalk-parole. Mel got snagged within the hour, trying to pick a pocket on Main Street for bus fare to get out of town. The cover for Ben Weems would be that he and his wife and child had just disappeared, because in a way they had. Bridge would work on a fix for that with a judge who is known to be reasonable. "Johnnie here tells me Derek Fortier is under suspicion for murder, drugs, prostitution activity, and bookmaking, but the investigators can't get anything on him except for some misdemeanor crap."

"Like the rest of us in the basement-hotel, huh?" I said, giving Hardwick a sly smile to make him hate me more. But I wound up thanking him as I left, and Bridge, too, of course. I said it had been a long day, and I'd best be going on home. Bridge narrowed his eyes. "Have a good night's sleep, Cisroe. At home," he said, as I closed the door behind me.

Soon as I got in my car I had another call waiting from Fernetta. "That boy o' mine did it *now*," she said. "That Willard, I swear. He's gone."

"Did what, Fernetta?"

"He was in on that credit card stuff 'n' all. I wormed it out of him. You went t' jail for something Willard did, and I want to say I am sorry as the day is long, Cisroe." She said her son, along with his pal Rodney, was waiting to tell me the story himself, and I could accept his apology if I would.

The boys were sitting in a booth at Kozy Krib when I got there, slunk down and looking like their ears had been chewed on by Jimmy Boyd's Rottweiler. Fernetta was behind the counter, keeping a hawk's eye on them.

I no sooner stepped in when the door opened right behind me and I turned to see Deacon George P. Johnson of the Full Gospel Assembly Church, the same "Deacon Johnson" who had a chance at one of the U.S. heavyweight titles a few years back; but that's another story. The deacon saw the restaurant was empty except for us, turned, locked the door, flipped the OPEN sign around, and walked over to the booth where the boys were.

In no time they told us about needing money immediately to buy a trumpet and a trombone. They were in the school band and were asked to join a hot neighborhood group, and their schoolboy horns wouldn't cut it. That's when they went to see what they could do for Derek Fortier to earn some money. Right away Fortier started them on errands and had them use my property for stashing stolen credit cards.

Then they filled in another piece of the puzzle: Lolene, that lovely, had been Derek's biggest moneymaker in Galveston . . . until she met her black knight in shining armor, namely one Ben Weems. Ever since, Fortier was looking for a way Ben could make that loss up to him. Little Ben latching onto MoonPies might have been the straw that bore through the two-by-four to Fortier.

We heard a ruckus out back, a clattering. By the time I rose, Fernetta was already out the door to check. "Lord, Cisroe! Get on out here!"

Under the light by the back door, a blood-soaked Ben was stumbling over the 55-gallon steel drums used for trash. "Cisroe," he said, "I found that sumabitch."

"Look like he found you better, boy."

Clutching his side, Ben said, "Stabbed me, Cisroe."

Deacon took charge. We lifted Ben up, put him in the back of Deacon's pickup, and ferried him over to the whiskey doc on Navigation. Doc cut away Ben's blood-soaked shirt and went to work.

I took out for the house on Braeswood, as Lolene had not answered the damn telephone and now I was worried for her besides needing to bring her to Ben. When I got there, *she* wasn't. I had a fright that Fortier had found her. Would he harm her, and the baby? Or just use them to get to Ben?

I rang up Fernetta again, this time at home. She was fairly gasping with concern, saying she had ordered the boys home after the deacon and I left with Ben, but they went out a window. "What I gonna *do* wit' them boys, Cisroe? They's gonna turn out just like they daddies, both of 'em."

"You want me to go looking for them, hon?"

"Oh, I do, now. You find 'em, you whoop on 'em good for me, Cisroe, you do that?"

I had her tell me where they hung out, then cruised a couple of streets and made a few stops, and then by hunch I swung on over to Kozy Krib again. The back door was open a crack and light was creeping through. Inside, I found them, both kicked back and copping beers. They were scared and goofy all at once when I came in, but when they saw I wasn't about to shoot 'em for the theft of my brews, in short order they told me they had a surprise for me. They had gone to where Fatso Fortier was hid out from the authorities and lured him back to Kozy Krib under the pretense Ben Weems was there. They gained entry by use of a key I keep hid that only Fernetta and Aibrey are supposed to know about. In the dark, they told Fortier that Ben was in the walk-in cooler putting meat away as a favor for Fernetta. When Fortier stepped in, the boys took a deep breath, shoved him into the corner, bolted out, slammed the door, and stuck the pin in the metal loop. The boys were scared all the while, they said, but still managed to high-five. And there he was, whimpering in the cold up to about a minute ago. Maybe he's stiff by now.

I hid my shock and said, "We'll take care of him in a second," then asked if Fortier had Lolene and the baby with him.

"No, sir. He was alone at his hideaway when we got there," Rodney said.

"Yeah," said Willard. "We just went on in and asked him how many dollahs it was worth to know where Ben Weems was. That got his attention good. He won't hurt us. We know too much on him." Willard puffed himself up, like his mama does when she's in a snit, and said, "Know a whole lot on him, man, it help you out."

The boys knew everything about Fortier that Johnnie Hardwick and the whole D.A.'s office had been looking for, going on two years now. Little-pitchers-have-big-ears type of thing. Now I had the plan. Fortier was pounding now on the cooler door and making his muffled roars, but I sat back in the booth and called Bridge Jones and told him it was time for one more deal. "This one gets Ben and the boys off with a minimal sentence," I said. "And we give Johnnie-Boy Hardwick a chance to put Fortier on a plate with an apple stuck in his mouth."

"Keep talking," Bridge said.

When I hung up, I went to the cooler door and shouted to Fortier that I had cut the cooler power and he should just hang tight another hour. He swore and threatened but, goodness, the acoustics were so bad through the thickness that I sure never heard what all he said. It might not have been good for the boys to see me so heartless, but I figured I'd show them my better side some other day.

Under their guidance I drove them to Fortier's not-so-secret clean-house, a new townhome he managed to buy under a phony name, and there watched as the boys rounded up incriminating pieces of evidence they had learned of during their sherlocking, including the weapon that would link Fortier to a homicide. I opened a briefcase containing 380-grand of cash money I would bet IRS agents would be happy to inquire about. Leaving the 380-grand was the hard part. The boys just shook their heads, seeing me pack up that green and put it away. "Past your bedtime, boys," I said and took them to Fernetta, who promptly phoned the deacon to come sleep on her couch.

Back at Kozy Krib, again I spoke to Fortier through the cooler door. I said I'd let him go if he forgot about Ben Weems and Lolene, and who shoved him in there.

I knew he'd lie to the Pope about this time, but I opened up the door and let him out. He was a humbled man—as they say, for the nonce—a little blue around the gills, and shaking so much his flab blurred. The murderous thoughts I knew he had against me now were held in check by the snubby hanging in my hand. I knew he'd head straight for his supposed secret house, and I knew D.A. Hardwick would be waiting for him with a few of Houston's finest when Fortier turned the lights on in his living room.

And so it was.

Straightaway, Bridge Jones set about to make a deal with Hardwick that the boys and Ben would be paroled to Deacon Johnson for a year: tougher service than anything the state could lay on them all.

Next day, when I got back to the whiskey doc's to check on Ben, he was holding onto his little baby, talking drivel talk, and there was Lolene, looking at them both with loving eyes. Fernetta and the boys were present too. I told them what the deal was with Deacon Johnson. The boys looked like they didn't know whether to spit, shit, or polish Mars.

Fernetta came over to me and hugged me with her big mama arms, lifting me clean off my feet. "Cisroe," she said, "you some kinda man."

In twenty years that's the first time she hugged me straight on, and I marveled inside that it felt so good, but I said in my gruffest voice, "That's enough, woman. Put me down!"

"You all talk, tough guy," she said, and if I didn't know better, I believe she winked at me in a way that would give a healthy man ideas.

Under Siege

by Jeffrey Marks

Jeffrey Marks is the editor of this anthology as well as a contributor. He has written articles for every major mystery magazine and served as a judge on the TAD award for scholarly mystery work given at Magna Cum Murder. He has also written a biography of Craig Rice that appeared in a French edition. He has published a number of short stories in anthologies and magazines, including "Talked to Death" which won the Barnes and Noble Award. His latest anthology, Canine Christmas, *is a winter 1999 Ballantine release.*

A shot rang out amidst the clustered tents, audible over the slap of raindrops on canvas. Whiskey splashed out of Grant's flask. His fingers fumbled the ties on his tent as he stuck his head out the flaps in anger. What the hell was going on? The Union expected him to win a war with troops that didn't know which end of the gun to point. This latest batch from Ohio were worse than usual. They regaled him with stories of seeing Rebs in their hometowns as if these yarns made them battle ready. Grant rued his Ohio birth after two weeks of this green regiment.

He sputtered out a few curses and went back inside. He took another swig and sat down on the edge of his bunk to untie his shoes for bed. Vicksburg wasn't a luxury resort. He smiled for a second, imagining Julia and the uppity Dent clan camped in the wilds of Mississippi. They'd be worse than any recruit. She'd be wanting to invite Bowen, their former neighbor and current nemesis, over for tea. As if Bowen's leading the Rebs against Grant's siege of the river town made no difference in social rank or protocol.

A man tapped on the canvas and stuck his head in the flap. "Excuse me, sir. There's a problem with one of the men."

Grant rolled his eyes. Was he expected to be a nanny? One of the recruits needs changing. "What seems to be the problem, Captain Turner?"

Turner was a good man. From Ohio, like Grant, and a longtime military man. He stood tall and thin, but with a softness in his mouth and chin that told his character. And his hands, with their long fingers and soft pads, looked more like a woman's than a soldier's. Turner was easy on the recruits, pampering them like a nursemaid more than making men from boys.

"One of the men is dead. Private Walters." Turner had taken a shine to Walters, both being from the same small town and all. He'd seen them huddled around the fire, trading stories on more than one night.

"No problem there, Captain. Bury him. Shot himself while cleaning his weapon?" Grant went back to unlacing his boot. That would make ten in the year since the campaign started. Grant knew Walters vaguely and had been impressed with the recruit's ambition. Could he be that wrong about character?

"Not to my line of thinking, sir. The gunshot looks intentional."

Grant stood up and tripped over his laces. "Turner, think about what you're saying. Murder? Here? It's unheard of."

Turner shook his head. "Not murder. Suicide. Death by his own hand."

Grant pressed his lips into a thin line. "What makes you so sure about this, Turner? Could it have been an accident? Happens all the time with those rifles."

Turner winced. "Why don't you come and look for yourself, sir? I think you'll see."

Grant snatched up his rain slicker and donned it over his shirt. The rain hadn't let up any as they sloshed through the puddles of the warm Southern night. Turner led the way to a small tent on the outskirts of the encampment. He held the flap open for Grant to enter.

Immediately, he understood why the captain had been so courteous. Nothing to do with protocol. In the blood-speckled light of the lantern, the tent resembled the worst of battlefield carnage.

Walters's remains lay next to his cot. A bullet had smashed his face at close range, eating away flesh and bone, pushing it inward. Brain tissue splattered the far wall of the tent, and a hole whistled out from the canvas. Not a pretty picture of one of their few decent recruits. A single impression remained in the soft dirt by the bed, a mark like the perfectly rounded heel of a small man.

Grant pointed to the spackled second cot. "Where's the man's bunkmate?"

"Douglas is out on patrol, sir. Been there all evening."

Grant closed his eyes for a second. "Get him." Someone needed to clean up this mess.

As Grant turned his interest to the area near the entrance, Turner's knees buckled. He found his way to the ground as Grant watched him. A weapon lay next to the officer and Grant picked it up. He stroked the long barrel and the carefully applied bluing. A gun like this shouldn't be thrown on the floor so casually. "Officer's .44. Why would that be here?"

Turner's face matched the verdant line of grass around him. "That's probably Vail's weapon. He reported it missing yesterday."

Grant rolled his eyes. These men couldn't keep track of their asses if they weren't held in their pants. He started to understand Turner's reluctance to name the crime. Why would the weapon be by the door if it had been an accident or suicide? The gun should have been in the bed or floor or in Walters's hand.

Grant stroked the cool, clean butt of the gun. "Get him in here."

Turner stood up and looked at him with sad brown eyes. "Sir?"

Grant waved him away and went to the tent's opening. "Vail. Get his ass in here now." He brushed his hands on his pants as he stepped inside again. The image of Walters's concave face made his stomach flutter. He remembered the same feeling from his father's tannery. Animal entrails mixed with their blood on the floor. Too bad he'd left his flask back in his quarters. He had a feeling he'd be needing it.

Captain Vail stepped into the tent and his mouth dropped open. Hard to take when it's one of your own. He held the entrance flap of the tent and Grant noticed the front wall of the structure trembling.

"You know anything about this?" Grant bored his steely eyes through the officer, hoping for a quick resolution. The man deserved a proper burial, even if the wound had been self-inflicted. Some here would disagree, citing the Church.

Vail stammered out his answer. "N-n-no, sir. I heard the shot like everyone else."

Grant held up the .44 by the barrel. "Recognize this?"

Vail took a step forward. "That's my gun. There's a chip on the butt. See?" He pointed a tremulous finger at the weapon, scared to touch it. Incautious behavior to mar a service weapon.

"You reported your sidearm as missing?"

"Yes, sir. I noticed it gone yesterday after the incident with the sniper. I followed protocol for a missing sidearm, sir."

Grant winced. He didn't want to be reminded of the sniper. A reb had slipped undetected into their proximity and taken out three men before Walters had shot him. Not a good report to send back to Washington. Lincoln got enough bad press over his promotion of Grant without adding fuel to the fire.

Proper protocol for a lost weapon should have included lynching, but the Army hadn't consulted Grant on the policy.

"Any reason why Walters would have wanted to kill himself?"

Vail shook his head. "No, sir. I told him yesterday that I was putting him in for a bravery medal. He seemed kind of strange about that." Vail kicked at the grass near the wall.

"You told him he would get an award and he goes and shoots himself. What the hell kind of logic is that? Did Walters have any enemies?"

Turner answered from the door, ashen-faced. "Everyone had a good word for Walters, sir."

Grant busied himself in the tent, trying to ignore the jumpiness of Turner, who continued to jiggle one leg. His sidearm jumped with the nervous motions.

He felt the linens of the small cot and slid a hand under a pillow. A piece of paper brushed his hand and he pulled it out. Grant held a photograph made by that newfangled toy Brady used to record the war. If this device caught on, people wouldn't stomach long drawn out battles like Vicksburg. Blue bloods like the Dents didn't have the stomach to see photos of the war.

This likeness was homier. Uncomfortably positioned, this family waited for the end of the silent torture. Walters stood next to a man whose face had been punctured by a bullet hole. The pellet had pierced the face of the family member, leaving the others to stare forward without a son and brother. Trying to pretend like everything was okay.

Grant fluffed the hay pillow, but no signs of a wound. Just the one in the back of the tent caused by the .44. How did photos get bullets through them when the bedsheets weren't disturbed?

"Have you seen this before?" Grant held out the picture to the officers. Vail shook his head quickly, but Turner took his time.

Another man entered the tent. Grant felt claustrophobic, trapped in space with these men and a body. The sentry dripped water on the floor as he waited for instructions. Douglas, Grant presumed. The Ohio farm boy was strapping, six foot tall and a good two hundred twenty pounds. Grant knew he could depend on a man like that in battle.

Douglas took his turn with the likeness. "No, sir. I thought maybe I'd seen it somewhere, but I don't remember Walters having any such thing of his family."

Grant cleared his throat, wishing this investigation were over. "So we're talking a second shot now, gentlemen. Anyone hear it?" The spectacle of the corpse was far too gruesome without the specter of a potential murderer hidden among the thousands of troops.

Vail shook his head. "No, sir. If I might—this looks like a musket-ball entry. The edges of the likeness aren't burnt, so nobody held a gun to it." He gulped hard. "Like they did with Walters." The blue-coat looked greenish now.

"So two guns, two gunmen. One sounds like our sniper." Grant looked at Walters's body, but he found no sign of another wound on him. Not that there'd need to be, but the bullet puncturing the paper hadn't gone through the man.

"Should I round up the troops and have a look?" Vail's face was pasty and he looked eager to leave. The man had missed the action at Shiloh.

Grant didn't relish the idea of another report back to Washington about more snipers. Vicksburg had been long enough without adding treachery to the mix. "Not yet."

He picked up the photograph and studied it again. The rounded hole reminded him of a rifle shot. Just what he needed was another weapon involved.

"Vail, what happened to the sniper's body from yesterday?" Grant turned the likeness over and studied it from behind, noticing the blossom-like shred around the gap.

"Left it where it laid, sir. No use in burying a murderer." Vail's hand played with the tent flap.

"Could you bring me the man's identification please? Immediately."

Vail left before Grant could look up. Turner didn't speak as he sat on the ground; his breathing came hard and loud enough.

Vail returned and held out a bloodied pouch, which Grant snatched. His hands were dark with blood and dirt. "Sorry it took so long, sir. It looks like someone tried to bury the body today."

Grant already knew what he would find inside. He read the papers and nodded in slow bobs, his head heavy from the knowledge. He laid the pouch on the prostrate corpse and turned to the men.

Grant cleared his throat and thought of his reaction if he shot

Bowen. Even if he killed a neighbor, would he go to these extremes? "Gentlemen, this knowledge is to go no further than this room. Yesterday's sniper was a reb by the name of Jamison Walters of Maysville, Kentucky. Just across the Ohio from your home, Turner? I'd say it safe to assume that these men were kin, most likely brothers. Private Walters shot a reb and a blood relative. He hid the evidence—the photo he found on that body—and broods over it for hours. Then he decides to take his life rather than explain to his parents how he received a medal of bravery for killing his family. He even went so far as to give himself the Mark of Cain."

"But what about the gun and the bullet?" Turner stammered.

Grant sighed and pointed to the indentation in the floor. "That's where the recoil kicked the gun into the dirt. Vail's weapon didn't have dirt on it and didn't leave a mark where the chip on the butt should be. I felt that weapon. It was as cold as an Illinois winter. Hence, his gun wasn't fired."

"Then it was murder?" Vail looked at his weapon and studied the marks.

"No, if my guess is correct, Turner palmed the real weapon when he found his friend dead and put the sidearm that you carelessly left outside down by the door. That's why he's jumping around with his leg against a hot weapon."

Turner slumped. "I would never kill Walters. He was my friend."

"But you would save his family from the shame of fratricide. I rule that Walters killed himself in remorse." Grant walked past the two white faced officers. "Could you please bury Walters, Turner? He was a good man who tried his best."

White Trash

by Jeff Abbott

Jeff Abbott is the Agatha award-winning author of the Jordan Poteet series set in a small town in Texas. Although that series has not had a new entry since 1996, Jeff honored this book with a new Jordan Poteet story. Currently he is writing a non-series book and lives in Austin with his wife and baby son.

"I want me a book on poison, Mr. Poteet," a voice rumbled above my head.

I glanced up from gluing in a date-due slip in the latest Jackie Collins opus. Fletus Godkin glared down at me. His eyes were a pale, ghostly blue. Stray strands of oily gray hair lay plastered along his skull. A faint smell of cow dung hung around him, an unwanted cologne.

Fletus in the library was roughly akin to Pat Buchanan at the nudist colony. Neither's going to go and you don't want to see them there anyway.

"Poison, Mr. Godkin? You got you some rats in the barn?" I asked.

"Mebbe so." Fletus wasn't going to elaborate on his pestilence problems. "Where's the book at?"

I started to suggest he consult the card catalog but realized research was probably not Fletus's forte. Plus I didn't want the cards smudged with whatever was on his fingertips. I walked over to the catalog, Fletus following me closely as though the books were dangerous and might attack.

I flipped through the listings, going past the few books on true crime poisoning cases and backpedaling to our library's few chemical references.

"I don't want no thick, hard-to-read book," Fletus said.

"I'll try to find one with lots of pictures," I answered pleasantly. I led the expectant Fletus to the appropriate shelf and pulled off a thin green book.

"Does this look like what you need?" I asked.

He flipped to the table of contents and ran a grimy finger down the listing, pausing partway down. "This'll do. What all I got to do to check it out? Sell you my soul?" He cracked a smile of crooked, ill-cared-for teeth.

It was good for him I didn't drive such a hard bargain, because Fletus needed to keep his soul close to hand. He was dead two days later.

I heard about Fletus barreling home to his Maker from Lucy Todd, a daily patron of the Mirabeau library (being too cheap to subscribe to the Houston paper herself), who toddled in on Thursday morning. She eyed the still-unwrapped *Houston Post* and dropped her bomb. "Shame about Fletus Godkin, ain't it, Jordan?"

"What about him?"

Delighted to be the bearer of bad news, Lucy leaned forward. "He's dead. Nelda over at the police station said they sent an ambulance out there this morning."

My tongue felt glued to the roof of my mouth.

"Heart attack or stroke or seizure, I guess." Lucy wasn't a stickler for technical accuracy.

My palms began to sweat as I thought of myself handing over the book about poison to Fletus. I hadn't noted any suicidal air about the man, but then I didn't know him well. You didn't know a Godkin unless you couldn't help it. More bluntly, they were the epitome of Mirabeau white trash, as my mother used to say.

As soon as one of my volunteers arrived, I asked her to run the library. I made a quick phone call and determined that Junebug Moncrief, our police chief, was out at the Godkins' place. I grabbed my keys and headed out to my truck.

The Godkins lived out in the boonies, right where they belonged. I don't say that out of any snobbery; the Godkins would agree with me one hundred percent. There are certain folks that would feel smothered in a town, even one as small as Mirabeau. The Godkins had, for generations, lived out in the dense woodlands that surrounded Mirabeau, down close to the Colorado River. Most of the residents of Mirabeau could trace their ancestry back to the earliest German settlers in the area; the Godkins had wandered in from Georgia, like many others after the Civil War, looking for a part of the South that wasn't torched. They'd found a niche, squatted on the land for the long haul, and bred like rabbits on hormone treatments, scattering moonshining Godkins all over Bonaparte County. It was not a clan you admired. But they had their own code: A Godkin didn't owe folks money, beat someone up without due provocation, or finish school if he could help it.

I turned my Blazer up a winding dirt road that cut through a dense motte of live oaks. With my window down, I could hear the restless murmur of the Colorado as it wound through the farmland and town. On a gorgeous day like today, I usually enjoyed a country drive, but not an on errand like this. I wondered if I might be blamed for Fletus's death if it turned out he'd swallowed poison. I felt a pang of guilt and then reason set in: How could I have been expected to know he was considering suicide?

A ramshackle house appeared in a curve of the road. A small clearing in the heavy undergrowth showed a house, and in the distance was a dilapidated barn with an attached pig pen. Rusted cars squatted near, broken-down guardians of the homestead. A beige trailer sat behind the house, like someone's idea of guest quarters. An assortment of tricycles and bicycles, the descendants possibly of the rusted cars, lay scattered across the unmown grass. Another trailer, painted an improbable pink, stood a slight ways off, with MARIBETH'S OF MIRABEAU written in huge, cursive, fading letters. Plastic flowers hung limp; even they were not immune to the crushing early summer humidity.

The entire little sad homestead seemed as though it had lost something long before Fletus died. Dignity, perhaps, or a sense of purpose.

I parked next to the Mirabeau PD cruiser. A shiny new Ford pickup, its glossiness highlighted by the dinginess of the grounds, sat next to the cruiser. I didn't think it could be a Godkin vehicle, in that it wasn't Bondoed through, so I wondered who else was here. Perhaps a stray Godkin had accidentally gotten prosperous. I walked up to the house, onto the porch, and knocked on the front door.

It was answered by a tired woman in her mid-forties. Her eyes were swollen and red, and her brown hair had the tattered look of having had anxious fingers continuously running through it.

"I'm sorry, ma'am, to disturb y'all. Is Chief Moncrief here?"

She nodded and when she spoke her voice was surprisingly deep. "Yeah, he is."

"Could you please tell him that Jordan Poteet is here and that I need to speak with him?"

She shrugged. "Tell him yourself. Come on in."

I'd preferred to speak to Junebug privately, but apparently I wasn't going to have the chance. She'd already turned away from the door and gone. I didn't feel like hollering after her into a house of mourning.

I followed the woman into a living room. The grimy paint and wallpaper looked centuries old, and a threadbare couch straddled the floor, spilling its foamy guts. I had settled my opinion on the room when I saw the shiny new 21-inch color television set—with the attached VCR that looked fresh from a box, and the stereo rack with a stack of CDs. Maybe the Godkins were slaves to culture and not to cleanliness.

Junebug was in the kitchen, talking quietly with several people. As soon as he saw me he steered me into a hallway. Despite our long friendship, he did not seem overly pleased to see me.

"What the hell are you out here for?"

"I thought you might like to know that Fletus Godkin checked out a book on poison from the library two days ago." I said. "He asked me specifically for help with research on poison. Is this remotely of interest to you?"

"Geez, Jordan," Junebug said. He stared at me. "He got real dizzy, his granddaughter says, and complained of pain in his stomach and his chest. Then he just collapsed and went into convulsions."

"Sounds like a heart attack, maybe," I said.

"Coroner'll have to say. But hell, now I'm gonna have to have them test for all different kinds of stuff—" Junebug didn't get to finish. A woman's piercingly shrill voice erupted from the living room.

Junebug hurried back to the living room and I followed. A woman in her fifties, her thin, pinkish hair hanging in her face from a collapsing beehive, sat sobbing on the floor, shrieking cuss words at no one in particular. A teenage girl hovered near her, glaring angrily at a blustery, dough-faced man. The man stood by a teenage boy and the dour-looking woman who'd let me in. The woman clutched the boy's beefy forearm to steady herself. His face was red with anger. It wasn't hard to see that sides had been drawn in this family feud.

"Hold it!" Junebug hollered at the top of his sizable lungs, and everyone froze. "Now what's the problem?"

The dough-faced man stared with eyes as eerily pale as Fletus Godkin's. "That bitch murdered my daddy, and y'all ain't doing a thing about it."

"I did not!" Pink Hair screeched. The softly pretty teenage girl—I'd seen her a few times in the library but didn't know her name—

shot a killing look at the fat man.

"You know that's a lie, Uncle Buddy," the girl said. "Papa Fletus was sick."

Buddy Godkin ignored the girl and continued to glare at Pink Hair. "I know you did it, Maribeth. You're gonna pay for killing Daddy."

"Buddy, get ahold of yourself," Junebug ordered.

The other woman stepped forward. "Don't arrest him, Chief, please. Buddy don't work, we don't eat. He's just awful upset."

"It's okay, Yvonne," Pink Hair rose unsteadily to her feet. She wobbled on stiletto gold heels meant for feet thirty years younger. Faded jeans encased her rail-thin legs and she wore, inexplicably, a magenta tube-top. A roll of freckled stomach protruded between top and jeans. "I don't want to press charges against Buddy. He didn't hurt me, he just scared me. He's upset. He and his daddy were just . . . so . . . close." Sugar coated the venom in her voice.

I felt the girl's gaze come to me. "What's Mr. Poteet doing here?" She knew me even if I didn't know her.

I kept my mouth shut while Junebug explained. The assorted Godkins stared at me like I was a two-headed mule being shown off in the traveling freak show. The room got as still as a midsummer's day, where even the mosquitoes are too sluggish with torpor to move. You could nearly hear the muscles tensing in the silence.

"You're saying Daddy took poison?" Buddy sounded even angrier.

Junebug provided the social niceties. "Jordan, this is Mr. Godkin's son, Buddy; Buddy's wife, Yvonne; their son, Cody. This young lady here is Laurie Godkin, Mr. Godkin's granddaughter. And this lady here is Maribeth Hill . . . a . . . er . . . special friend of Mr. Godkin's."

"I was his common-law wife, and I know my rights," Maribeth announced loudly. "They don't include being verbally abused by a no-good slouchcer like Buddy. Now that Fletus is deader than a doornail, I'm empowering myself. I watch *Oprah*, you know."

"Buddy ain't gonna bother anyone anymore, are you, sugar?" Yvonne Godkin looked imploringly at her husband. "He's just upset about Papa Fletus."

That excuse had worn thin with me, so I had to interject, "Buddy being upset doesn't mean he can go around bullying women."

Buddy Godkin looked at me as though he was open-minded enough to bully men if the mood took him. I smiled, daring him to try. Buddy was big, but it was all fat. I topped him at six-foot-two, and I run five miles a day. If I couldn't whomp him, I could outrun him.

"Y'all know where this poisons book is?" Junebug asked the collected Godkins.

"We didn't even know he'd taken out such a book," Maribeth murmured. "I can't imagine why. We ain't had many rats around this spring, what with Buddy working regular." She sniffed loudly, savoring her wit. Buddy mouthed "bitch" deep under his breath. The absence of kindness between them seemed to mirror the absence of care on their land.

"I knew he had the book," Laurie Godkin offered. Her eyes were frank and intelligent. "He showed it to me the other night."

I saw Maribeth stiffen and heard Yvonne's sudden intake of breath.

Junebug turned to the girl. "When was this, Laurie?"

"Tuesday night. I'd been watching TV, but Cody came in and made me change it to some stupid basketball game. So I wandered out to the porch. Papa Fletus was reading, which was weird. I asked what book and he showed me. It was *A Layman's Guide to Poisons*."

"Did he say why he was reading it?" Junebug asked.

"No," Laurie answered. "I thought maybe he was going to get rid of Maribeth, but I only thought that for a second." She smiled the slightest of smiles.

"Get rid of . . . get rid of . . . ," Maribeth stuttered. "But Fletus loved me!" I sensed another performance of self-choreographed histrionics was upon us.

Junebug took me by the arm and steered me straight toward the porch. "Thank you for your information, Jordan. It sure will be useful to us, and we'll return the library book after the inquest into Fletus's death."

With that, I was alone in the warming heat of a Mirabeau spring day. Behind the closed door, Godkins kept yelling at each other.

The next morning, I was pricing CD-ROM drives for the library's two computers when Laurie Godkin appeared in my office door. She was scrubbed and official-looking in a waitress uniform, her dark hair pulled up in a bun underneath a red polyester cap.

"Mr. Poteet? I wonder if you have a minute."

"Sure, Laurie, come in. You on your way to work?" I asked.

Surely she would not be working right after her grandfather's death, unless the Godkins didn't hold with official periods of mourning. She must need the money, I decided.

"Coming back from it," she answered. "In the summers I work the breakfast shift at the Downtown Café, then I go back out and help Maribeth with her customers . . . you know, shampoo, sweep up, run the cash register. But Maribeth's too overwrought to be doing hair."

"I'm so sorry about your grandfather, Laurie," I said.

"Thank you. I wanted to know if he was acting odd when he came and got that book on poisons."

"I don't know what constituted odd for your grandfather, but I wouldn't say he was acting disturbed or suicidal." I leaned back in my chair. "If he *had* been, I might not have loaned him the book."

"He didn't kill himself and he didn't have die from seizure. Someone murdered him."

"Why are you telling me this?" I asked.

"Junebug Moncrief isn't listening to me. He knows Papa Fletus had been sick for a while, checked out a book on poisons, then left a suicide note. I'm afraid he thinks that wraps it up, that Papa Fletus thought he was terminally ill and took an easy way out. I don't believe that for a minute."

So there was a suicide note; this was news. "What did the note say?"

Laurie pouted. "Said he was tired of being sick all the time. That he would miss us all." Her face screwed up, as though tears might come. "But I know he didn't kill himself."

"Laurie, suicide is terribly hard on a family."

"Please don't talk down to me." She straightened her thin shoulders. She couldn't have been more than seventeen; in a few years I thought she would slip from awkwardness and become a stunning beauty. She already had the self-assurance that would attract good men. "You and everyone else think this is suicide, because he checked out that book and Maribeth found that note. But he wouldn't kill himself. The only financial planning he ever did was getting life insurance. He has a policy for fifty thousand dollars. But the insurance company won't pay if he killed himself. I need that money to go to school, Mr. Poteet. I want to get the hell out of the river bottom, make something of myself, see the world. You can understand that."

So it was money, not grief, that drove this strange young girl.

"But he left a suicide note."

"Doesn't matter."

"Tell me why."

"Well, Papa Fletus, Maribeth, and me all live in the big house."

That dump was a big house to her, I thought.

"Uncle Buddy, Aunt Yvonne, Cody, and the little ones live in that trailer behind it. Maribeth has her beauty parlor in the other trailer. She gives the cheapest perms in town."

That I believed.

"So yesterday morning, Papa Fletus comes out of the kitchen, saying he's sure not feeling well. I figured he was having just another sick spell, so I suggested he go lie down. He wasn't feeling better after a while and I offered to call the doctor down at the free clinic. Maribeth told me not to bother, that Papa Fletus would be fine. After about five minutes he—" she stopped and steadied her voice "—he got up and fell over on me, moaning something fierce. Holding his stomach. He tried to stand but he faltered. He started vomiting real bad, so I started hollering for Maribeth. He was dead five minutes after that."

"You said he'd been sick already for a while. What kind of symptoms did he have?"

"He hadn't been feeling good the past few weeks. I made him go to the clinic once. The doctor said it was kidney trouble, but he couldn't find signs of cancer or nothing. Papa Fletus complained he wasn't peeing very much, no matter how much beer or ice tea he drank. Yvonne told him all that liquid was just absorbing Maribeth's greasy cooking. I just figured he had a bladder stone. And he had bouts of stomach flu, throwing up, feeling dizzy. He'd also get these funny red pinpricks on his skin, kind of like a rash. Yvonne and I asked him to go back to the doctor, but he said it was wasting money."

"If he was so sick, why didn't the murderer just wait for him to die?"

Laurie shook her head. "I don't know."

"Who would have a reason to kill him?"

"I'm afraid I've already given you mine—that insurance money for college." She shrugged. "But I wouldn't kill him for it. I couldn't go to college from prison, could I?"

I smiled. She struck me as the most intelligent of the Godkins, and that might make her the leading suspect if Fletus was murdered and the method required an ounce of cleverness.

"Well, there's Maribeth, obviously," Laurie said after a moment. "She and Daddy Fletus had been together about fifteen years. He never would properly marry her. But they usually got along fine. Till about six months ago, when Maribeth met Gary Armbrister."

"Who?"

"He delivers beauty supplies to her salon, from some place over in Bavary. Nice-looking fellow for an old guy, got big arms and all his hair. It was easy to see he was sweet on Maribeth. And she liked him plenty, too."

"Why wouldn't she just leave Fletus since they weren't married?"

"By common law they were. She'd have a right to what was his. And he funded her business and still owned most of the equipment and trailer."

"What about Yvonne and Buddy?"

"Papa Fletus and Buddy fought a lot. Usually when they were drunk, but more lately just over the littlest things. Buddy got told a few weeks back he might get laid off—he works at that junkyard over off Highway 71, between Mirabeau and Bavary. I think Buddy figured he'd just live off the rest of us. Papa Fletus told him if he was too lazy to work he'd cut him out of the will."

"How much would that have been worth?" I couldn't imagine Fletus Godkin's legacy to be more than a six-pack, those ramshackle trailers, and maybe a few hundred in the bank.

"Well, our place faces right onto the road, and we own the land all the way down to the river. It's several acres, even though we didn't do anything with it. Then there's the insurance money. It'd be a lot to someone like Buddy."

I didn't doubt that. A three-dollar lottery ticket would probably get Buddy salivating.

"And Yvonne, she was awful upset with Papa Fletus lately, just 'cause he wasn't gonna give them a dime to live on if Buddy lost his job."

"What about Cody?"

She snorted. "That Cody is a zero. All he thinks about is that drop-dead ugly girlfriend of his." Laurie sniffed derisively. "His girlfriend works at that same beauty supply company in Bavary that Gary Armbrister delivers for. You think she'd scare off the customers."

I steered the conversation back toward Cody. "How'd he get along with his grandfather?"

Laurie's face grew pinched. "Fine. Papa Fletus knew Cody'd

never amount to spit, but Cody's a boy, so he can't do much wrong. As long as Cody didn't get a girl pregnant, he was solid with Papa Fletus. He'd already gotten in trouble once for getting kids fake IDs, but Papa Fletus only whipped him a few licks."

"So if I'm hearing you right, your best suspect is Maribeth."

"I like Maribeth," Laurie said. "She's okay to me, she's just got an awful mouth. You saw that at the house, her taunting Buddy right after his daddy died."

"So Maribeth works, you work, Buddy tries not to work; what about Yvonne and Cody?"

"Yvonne's busy taking care of all those little ones. They got three babies, so I guess Uncle Buddy's not lazy all the time. Sometimes she does housecleaning for ladies in town, when she can get Maribeth or me to baby-sit." She frowned. "Cody's just interested in driving his fancy new truck, raising hell and test-driving rubbers with that slutty girlfriend of his."

So the sparkling new pickup I saw was Cody's. "You haven't always lived with your grandfather, I take it?"

She shook her head with real sadness; her dark eyes, not Godkin eyes, stared down into her lap. "No. My folks died two years ago. My father was Papa Fletus's youngest son. We lived over in Brenham. Daddy worked for the Blue Bell creamery. They died in a car crash, so I came to Mirabeau to live."

"I'm sorry, Laurie."

"I'm sorry, too. I hate it here. My daddy did well working at the creamery. My mom worked a good job as a store clerk. We were happy." Her gaze met mine. "I'm not like the other Godkins, you know. We'd gotten away from them; from living like trash, surrounded by junked cars and smelling of pigs. But I guess you don't ever get as far away as you like."

"So you want to prove your grandfather was murdered, so you can get the insurance money?" I wanted this girl, who'd seen so much suffering, to have a more noble motive.

"You think I'm a little bitch, I guess." Laurie stared back down at her hands. "Yeah, I want the money. Papa Fletus said I could have some of it when he told me about the insurance policy. He laughed and said I'd be the first Godkin to go to college."

She wouldn't have college money without the insurance—but I found myself wondering where the money for all that electronic gadgetry in the Godkin living room came from. And Cody's new truck.

Laurie cleared her throat. "This is gonna sound strange, but I was wondering if you'd come out to dinner tonight at our house. As my guest."

I was stunned. "Are you sure y'all are up for company? I mean right after your grandfather died?"

"Life goes on. I worked today because I have to." Laurie stood. "Please? It'll be at seven."

"Is it okay with Maribeth and the others?"

"I don't care if it is or not. I'm cooking tonight, so I'll ask who I please." She smiled and I wished I were a teenager again. "Please, Jordan. Maybe you can figure out who killed him."

"All right."

It was only after she left that I realized if she was right, I'd be dining in the company of a poisoner.

I'd treated myself to a good long think after Laurie left. Fletus Godkin had been sick for weeks, then checked out a book on poisons, wrote a suicide note, and suddenly keeled over dead. I couldn't blame Junebug for thinking suicide. Except that if Fletus Godkin had been terminally ill and decided to conduct self-euthanasia, I didn't believe for one moment he'd swallow poison. No man around here would. He'd shoot himself first. Most of the men in Mirabeau have guns, and if one of them were going to check out from this life early, he'd want his last touch to be that cold metal friend, firmly in grasp and pressed against his temple. Messy, but quick, and a lot more macho than poison would be.

If Fletus had been murdered, his illness with those quirky symptoms—not urinating, vomiting, lethargy, and a pinprick rash on his skin—didn't sound like a coincidental malady. He had clearly not picked up an exotic ailment while visiting Bora Bora. It sounded like slow poison.

Had Fletus suspected he was being dosed with some toxin? Is that why he had checked out the book on poison, to see what was being introduced into his system? There were murderous motives aplenty, what with most of the Godkins in dire need of money and Maribeth with a new admirer. So why the suicide note? It would not have been in any of their interests to fake the suicide; no beneficiary would collect. So Fletus must've written the note. Had he indeed killed himself?

But I assumed for the moment that Godkin had been poisoned. So where would the poison have been acquired? Buddy worked at a junkyard, surrounded with rusting hulks with God knows what kind of toxins readily at hand. Yvonne undoubtedly kept cleaning solutions for her maid service. Maribeth certainly worked with chemicals in frazzling innocent hair, and her boyfriend worked at a beauty supply shop, as did Cody's girlfriend. Mousse as poison? I laughed then felt terribly ashamed. Maybe Laurie was simply doping him with the blue plate special from the café she worked at.

I looked up the checkout log for *The Layman's Guide to Poisons*. It had not been an especially popular text in Mirabeau. But it had been a little more popular, I saw, on thc outskirts of town.

It'd been checked out and returned six months ago by Maribeth Hill.

I hadn't even known Maribeth had a card. I checked our card records; she'd applied for the card the day she'd checked out the book, and she hadn't checked out any other library materials. I swallowed the lump in my throat.

Funny how we leave a paper trail behind us, and don't always notice.

A few hours later, I had a fair amount of evidence against Maribeth Hill. I'd called the librarian over in Bavary and found they also had a copy of *The Layman's Guide*. We'd done some over-the-phone checking of symptoms in the text's appendices and come up with a few interesting facts.

Bromate poisoning. You hardly ever hear of it these days because bromates aren't used much anymore. They were in perm solutions back in the seventies, but for the most part they've been phased out of most hair-care products. But not all.

Bromates do nasty things to you. It's harmless on your hair, but get it in your gut and the hydrochloric acid that's busy digesting your breakfast grits turns bromate into hydrogen bromate. It corrodes human tissue. You suffer from vomiting, abdominal pain, oliguria (meaning you don't pee), and little red pinpricks on your skin. Eventually you go into convulsions and die. Usually die from a strong enough dose in five to twenty minutes. Fletus died in agony I can't easily imagine.

Maribeth must've been sneaking a highly watered-down bromate solution into Fletus's milk or water or beer. Probably a little dab soured his whole week. I could see it; she checked out the book, found a poison she had readily at hand, and began dosing it out, hoping it'd look like he had only a little time left before giving the final amount.

And Laurie was living in that house with that woman. It chilled my blood. I had no proof, though. I could tell Junebug what I'd found and let him pursue justice. Let the coroner test Fletus's remains for bromates. After dinner, though. I had to find out more, find out why that suicide note was there. That niggled at my mind like a child yanking a mother's apron. Something else Laurie had said lurked in the back of my thoughts, trying to get my attention because it rang odd. But my head hurt and I left the library to go to my guaranteed-to-fry-a-nerve dinner date.

The Godkins didn't dress much for dinner, or for mourning. When I arrived the adult Godkins lolled on the sagging front porch of the house, staring at me.

I nodded toward Buddy and Yvonne; they glanced away. Maribeth finished dabbing a garish red on her lips and tried to play hostess. I offered her a pecan pie I'd bought on the way and she made an attempt at graciousness.

"I'm so glad you could join us, Mr. Poteet. I was a little surprised that Laurie invited you, but you're welcome here." She pressed my hand into hers and I willed my palms not to sweat.

"Thanks, Ms. Hill. I'm not sure why Laurie wanted me here, maybe since I saw Fletus a couple of days before he died."

"I don't want to be here sitting at a table with you, Maribeth," Buddy growled. The air felt heavy with tension. Maribeth turned and walked away to the other end of the porch, keeping her back to Buddy. Buddy stayed put; apparently he had no other dinner plans, threats aside.

I excused myself and walked back to the kitchen with the pie. Laurie was pulling fried chicken out of a sizzling skillet. Usually, when a family suffers a death, their kitchen is choked with food brought by friends and neighbors and churchmen. This kitchen was bare save what Laurie cooked.

She glanced at me. "Did you find out anything?"

I told her what I had learned.

She stayed calm but bit her lip. "You're very smart."

I shrugged. "I just checked into the same kind of books as your grandfather did. I guess I found what he didn't. But nothing can be proved until the autopsy."

Laurie shook her head. "I know she did it, I know it." Determination steeled her young face. "This is like one of those old mystery novels, right, where everyone gathers in the parlor to hear who killed the victim?"

I shook my head. "If you're planning on doing that, Laurie, count me out. I didn't come here for a family scene. And even if I am right, we don't have hard evidence against Maribeth."

"But we know what to look for now," Laurie whispered, her eyes aglow. "Products with bromates in them. Some container she used to mix the solution." She turned back to a pot of black-eyed peas and stirred them dreamily. "You've given it to me, Jordan. I can make her pay for what she did."

My gut squirmed. I wasn't pleased at the prospect of seeing Laurie confront Maribeth, but neither was I comfortable with the thought of just leaving. I didn't want Maribeth turning on Laurie. Or worse, Buddy would probably just strangle Maribeth with his bare hands before she could be arrested. And still unanswered was the reason for the suicide note.

We returned to the porch to summon the others to supper. Cody Godkin's polished pickup squealed into the yard, spewing mud and gravel. He jumped out of the truck and trotted toward the house, giving me a suspicious stare as we went in to eat.

We sat down to a meal where I hardly tasted anything but I will never forget. Laurie was an excellent cook, but I had no taste for the crispy chicken, the peas, and the potato salad. Loss didn't seem to impair the Godkin appetites. Buddy shoveled the food in like a coal man on an old train. Cody's food got no chance to cool, and Yvonne ate as daintily as a buzzard. Only Maribeth picked at her food, which made me highly nervous. I'd feel better about Godkin dinners if she were devouring it.

I tried to make conversation by complimenting Laurie on her cooking.

"Laurie just does *everything* well," Maribeth said icily. "I suppose now she'll be gone next year, off getting to be even better than the rest of us." She slurped at her tea.

"I was better than you before I got here," Laurie retorted. Laurie had been Maribeth's defender the first go-round, but now I could tell all bets were off.

Maribeth frowned. "You might think so, missy, but you're not. You're just as much a part of this place as I am, as Fletus was. Maybe you won't be using that insurance money you're so eager for."

Yvonne glanced up from her tattered chicken. "We need that money, too, y'know. Buddy's gonna lose his job."

"Sell Cody's truck," Laurie replied. "Y'all could live off that and food stamps till hell froze hard."

"I can't sell my truck!" Cody wailed, mortally wounded at the thought. "Papa Fletus gave me that truck, it's the onliest memory of him I got."

"Jealous!" Maribeth snapped at Laurie, bits of chicken flesh flying from her lips. "You're nothing but jealous, pretending to be my friend at first and now turning on me."

"You killed him!" Laurie shot to her feet. She didn't scream; her voice was icy in practice, as though she'd long rehearsed this speech. "You killed him. I finally know. All of Papa Fletus's symptoms were from what Jordan found is bromate poisoning. And where do you get bromates? From that old cold perm gunk you smear on women's hair!"

The silence was sudden and heavy. Maribeth stared uncomprehendingly at Laurie, an errant chunk of fried chicken dangling from the corner of her scarlet lips.

"Why . . . why would I kill my darlin'?" Maribeth stammered.

"For Gary Armbrister," Laurie answered.

"You murdering bitch!" Buddy hollered at Maribeth. His fat forearms jiggled in anger.

"Gary? I don't give a crap in a cone about Gary Armbrister!" Maribeth found her voice. "What on earth made you think that, you little nut? And how would I even know about this bromate crap?"

"You checked out the book on poisons, the same one Fletus did," I said softly. "I found the record of it in the library."

Maribeth looked at me with utter incredulity, as though I had turned to her and asked her opinion about some fine nuance of particle physics. In Swahili. "I don't even know where the damn library is."

Buddy lurched toward Maribeth, but Yvonne and Cody seized his arms and pulled him back. Maribeth scampered to a corner of the room, keeping a wary eye on Buddy. Laurie gloated: "You might as well confess it now, Maribeth. All of the evidence is going to be in."

"I don't know what you're talking about!" Maribeth screamed, and in that moment, I believed her. I had no reason to before, but I did now. A jumble of images played in my mind: Cody's new truck, Laurie's parents dying in a car wreck, Buddy shuffling home from a lost job to a waiting Yvonne, all the shiny new electronics in the decrepit living room, Cody in trouble with the police, and Fletus's mild reaction.

"Excuse me." I stumbled into the hot kitchen and found the phone. I called the library; my volunteer was just locking up for the night. I asked her for one favor and waited on the line. She returned and basically told me who killed Fletus Godkin. I thanked her and hung up. Then I called the police and spoke quickly to Junebug.When I returned to the dining room, a crying Yvonne and a stern-faced Cody still held Buddy down. Maribeth sobbed, frozen. Laurie held the back of her chair as though needing help standing.

"I don't like being played for a fool," I said frostily. "So, Laurie, maybe you should tell them why you killed your grandfather."

I saw the cool reserve in her eyes looked more like cold calculation. "What?"

"You heard me. I think I know why you did it, and now I think I know how." I stepped toward her, cutting off her closest exit from the room. "You've been slipping a diluted bromate solution into your grandfather's food. It made him feel terribly sick, even to where maybe he thought he was terminally ill. But then he got suspicious. He checked out a book on poisons and figured out his unusual mix of symptoms pointed toward bromate poisoning. He came to you for help, because you were the smartest one in the family."

I paused, clenching my hands into fists. "You'd set it up beautifully, Laurie. You'd picked a poison that pointed real hard at one member of your family. Then you manufactured that lie about Maribeth and Gary Armbrister. I don't think there was a single thing going on between them."

"You're lying!" Laurie screamed. Maribeth, stunned into silence, moved behind the girl.

"You needed him dead for the insurance money, so you could attend college. That bothered me no end, and I couldn't figure out why. You'd told me that your parents had done well in Brenham—so why would you need your grandfather's insurance? What happened to the insurance when your own parents died?"

Laurie's eyes hooded and she stared down at the floor. Soft sobbing came from Maribeth; silence from the other Godkins. I glanced at them.

"I know where it went. You bastards took it from her. Or Fletus took it and handed it around. Spending it on a new truck for Cody, on all that electronic crap in the living room, and God knows what else. He took your future so you killed him."

"I wasn't going to be like them," Laurie screamed. "I wanted out! I didn't want to scrub floors or slop pigs, stuck in this damn river bottom for the rest of my life. That's not what my parents worked for. That was money he stole from me . . . mine . . . mine . . ." Her voice collapsed into sobs.

"So you killed him for his money. Tit for tat. And you framed Maribeth for it. You picked a poison she had access to, suggested she had a romantic interest in another man, and made it look like she'd checked out a book on poison when you'd done it yourself."

"How?" Maribeth asked weakly.

I glanced at Cody. "Ask Mr. Fake ID here. He's already gotten in trouble once for getting kids IDs to drink with. Getting Laurie a fake ID to use as 'Maribeth Hill' to get a library card was easy. I called the library and asked them to pull the file for Maribeth's library card. According to it, she was born in 1983. The real Maribeth couldn't pull that off."

"But Daddy wrote that note . . ." Buddy managed to say. The Godkins were all staring at the baby of the family, as though she'd suddenly sprouted leathery wings and a tail.

"Yeah, he did write it but he didn't tell Laurie about it. I think Fletus thought Maribeth was trying to kill him, so I guess he wrote it as part of a plan. Maybe he planned to leave that note and vanish, fake his own suicide, escape his poisoner, and watch from a distance as to how you all acted. But before he could do that, Laurie gave him his fatal dose. She probably panicked when she saw him reading the very book that had told her about bromates." I'd gone into this white-trash mess to help her and she'd nearly played me for a fool.

"You used me, Laurie. That note made it look like he'd killed himself, so you wouldn't get one lick of insurance money. You were in the damned uncomfortable position of having murdered him and then needing to prove he was murdered. So you roped me into your plot to frame Maribeth."

Laurie swallowed, a slow, elegant gesture. She wasn't going to cry or scream anymore. She looked at me with eyes like playground marbles left outside on a cold day. "You can't prove any of this."

I heard the distant whine of Junebug's siren. "Yes, we will, Laurie. You said it yourself. All the evidence is going to be in."

And her shoulders, too young for all this weight, slumped as the truth of my words hit home.

With This Ring

by Margaret Maron

Margaret Maron went home to her North Carolina roots to write her ninth novel, Bootlegger's Daughter, *her first to feature Judge Deborah Knott. The result was publishing history.* Bootlegger's Daughter *made a unique and unprecedented sweep of the top mystery awards, winning the Agatha, Anthony, Edgar, and Macavity for best novel. Deborah Knott's adventures continue in* Southern Discomfort *and* Shooting at Loons. *Maron is also the author of seven exquisitely crafted and beautifully written Sigrid Harald novels, which are now being reissued. Coming soon is her eighth Sigrid Harald novel, Fugitive Colors. A nonseries novel, a prequel to* Bootlegger's Daughter, *is* Bloody Kin. *Maron is a past president of Sisters in Crime and a past national director of Mystery Writers of America and is active in the American Crime Writers League. She lives on the family farm near Raleigh, North Carolina. Maron again visits Colleton County and Judge Knott in this delightful and oh-so-southern tale, "With This Ring."*

"Detective Bryant," said Dwight's voice when he finally picked up his extension at the Colleton County Sheriff's Department.

"Can you still button the pants of your army dress uniform?" I asked.

"Say what?"

"I was out at your mother's last week." I let a hint of mischief slip into my tone. "She said that picture of you at the White House was taken only three years ago, but I reckon you've put on a few pounds since you came home and started eating regular."

As if a district court judge has nothing better to do with her time than call just to needle him about his thickening waistline, Dwight bit like a largemouth bass suckered by some plastic feathers and shiny paint.

"Listen, Deborah," he said. "I bet I can fit into my old clothes a lot better'n you could fit into yours."

I reeled him in. "It's a bet. Loser pays for the tickets."

"Wait a minute. You want to back that mule up and walk her

past me again?"

"The Widdington Jaycees are putting on a charity ball for Valentine's Day," I explained. "I know you don't own a tuxedo, but—"

"You and that Chapin guy have a fight?" Dwight growled. "Or don't he know how to dance in a monkey suit?"

For the life of me, I can't understand Dwight's attitude. It's not like Kidd's the first man he's ever seen me with, and it's certainly not like he's interested in me himself. Our families have known each other five or six generations, and Dwight's always treated me like he's one of my older brothers. One of my *bossy* older brothers. Unfortunately, small-town social life resembles the Ark—everything two by two. So when I need an escort and don't have one on tap, I just call Dwight, who's divorced and still unattached. By choice, he says.

Yet ever since I met Kidd Chapin down at the coast last spring, Dwight's done nothing but snipe at him. Dwight's a chief of detectives; Kidd's a game warden. Both like to hunt and fish and stomp around in the woods. Wouldn't you think they'd mesh together tight as Velcro?

Oil and vinegar.

I've decided it's a guy thing and nothing worth bothering my pretty little head with.

"Kidd has to be at a conference down in Atlanta that weekend. Look, if you don't want to come dancing and help me act the fool, fine. I'll call Davis, see if he's free that night."

Davis Reed's a good-timing, currently unmarried state representative from down east, and Dwight hates his politics. (Hey, I'd never actually sleep with a Republican, but that doesn't mean I won't let one buy me dinner.)

"Act the fool how?" Dwight asked cautiously, and I knew I had him flopping in my net.

"It's a bridesmaids ball," I said. "Everybody's supposed to wear something we've worn in a wedding."

"What's so foolish about that?"

"Dwight Bryant, have you ever *looked* at one of those dresses?" I was torn between amusement and exasperation.

Men.

But that's not fair. Why should I bad-mouth men when it's women that keep putting four to eight of their best friends into some of the most ridiculous dresses known to polite society?

Was it a man who thought it'd look really darling to send us down the aisle one Christmas wearing red plaid taffeta over enormous hoop skirts and carrying tall white candles?

Lighted white candles that dripped wax all down the front of our skirts?

No, that was Missy Randolph.

Was it a man who put us in skin-tight sheaths of bright pink satin so that the bride looked like a silver spoon surrounded by six Pepto-Bismol bottles?

No, that was Portland Smith.

"What about this one?" said Aunt Zell as we prowled the far end of her unheated attic, where several long gowns hung like ghosts from the rafter nails, each Cinderella fantasy shrouded in a white cotton sheet.

"You girls were just precious in these picture hats."

"The hats were okay," I conceded, shivering in the February chill, "though that shade of lavender made me look downright jaundiced." It was the scratchy lace mitts. My wrists itched for a week. And Katy's parasol kept poking all the ushers in the eye.

"Such a pretty garden wedding," Aunt Zell sighed as she pulled the sheet back over that gown. "Too bad they split up before the first frost. Now where's the dress you wore when Seth and Minnie married? You were cute as a june bug in it."

"That was a flower-girl dress," I reminded her. "And have you ever seen a flower girl who wasn't cute as a june bug?"

Here in Colleton County, if a groom has a sister, she will be in the wedding even if she and the bride despise each other. For the record, I never exactly despised any of my brothers' brides (some of the boys got married before I was even born), but scattering rose petals can get awfully tiresome after you've done it four or five times.

The attic was too chilly for lingering, and I quickly narrowed my choices down to two.

The ball committee promised us prizes in various categories. If total tackiness were a category, surely the dress I'd worn in Caroline Corbett's wedding would be an automatic winner: moss green lace over a moss polyester sateen that had already started mutating toward chartreuse before the first chord of Mendelssohn was ever played. The neckline dipped so low in front that only a cluster of green chiffon roses preserved our maiden modesty. Droopy shoulder flounces were tied up with dangling sateen ribbons that had tickled my arms just enough to keep me slapping for a fly or a mosquito. Accessories included a floppy picture hat big as a cartwheel and a wicker basket filled with more chiffon roses. What finally decided me against wearing it to the ball were the tiered net petticoats that shredded panty hose and legs indiscriminately.

Besides, the frosty air made bare-armed summer frocks look even more inane than usual. I was drawn instead to a wintry blue velvet concoction.

Janelle Mayhew's idea of Victorian began with a high, tight white lace collar, descended to pouf sleeves that had to be stuffed with tissue paper to hold their balloon shape, and was topped (or should I say bottomed?) by an enormous bustle. The white plumed fan had barely begun to molt, and it ought to amuse Dwight. Besides, the dark blue velvet, bustle and all, actually flattered my sandy blonde hair and turned my blue eyes sapphire. As a thirty-something judge, maybe it'd be more dignified to go for pretty instead of comic.

More politic, too, because Janelle and Glenn Riggsbee were Widdington Jaycees and certain to be at the ball. Their restaurant has prospered over the years, and they contributed to my last campaign by hosting a big reception for me out there in the country.

The old-fashioned dress had been a little on the loose side twelve years ago; now it needed a whalebone corset with power lacing. Even with a girdle, I was going to have to sit up straight all evening and remember to laugh no harder than Queen Victoria.

When Dwight came to pick me up that Saturday night, he was wearing a borrowed black tuxedo and the fuchsia sateen cummerbund and clip-on bow tie that had been dyed to match the bridesmaids' dresses when he ushered for a friend in D.C.

"Aw, and I was really looking forward to your sword," I teased.

"Mama could've let out the pants," Dwight said sheepishly, "but she said she'd rather pay for the damn tickets herself than try to get that dress jacket to fit."

Before he'd write me a check for the cost of the tickets, he rousted Aunt Zell from upstairs where she and Uncle Ash were watching the news and made her swear she hadn't added a gusset of blue velvet in my side seams.

"No gloating, okay?"

"I never gloat," I told him, tucking the check away in my beaded evening bag.

He and Aunt Zell both snorted.

Widdington's about thirty-five minutes east of Dobbs, and we drove over with Avery and Portland Brewer. Portland is Uncle Ash's sister's daughter and therefore Aunt Zell's niece by marriage, which makes us courtesy cousins. Not that a family connection is needed. We laugh at the same things and have been friends since junior girls class in Sunday school.

When Dwight opened the rear door of their car, she twisted around in the front seat and said, "Oh, shoot! I told Avery I just knew you were going to wear that pig-pink thing Mother made y'all buy for our wedding."

She had a winter coat draped over the droop-shouldered horror of Caroline Corbett's green lace. In Portland's case, the polyester underlining had gone past chartreuse, right on into an acid yellow. "I'm competing in the 'Most Unusual Color Combination' category," she giggled.

"Where's your hat and garden basket?"

"In the trunk," said Avery. "The brim's so wide she couldn't fit in the car."

Before the interior light went off, Portland noticed my pearl earrings. "I thought we wore red-and-blue rhinestone hoops with that dress?"

"We did. That's why Elizabeth thought you stole the ring, remember? When she caught a flash of sparkling stones in your hand?"

"She just said that to throw suspicion off herself," said Portland. "I still think she's the one who took it."

"They never did get it back, did they?" asked Avery as he waited for a pickup to pass before pulling away from the curb.

"Huh?" said Dwight.

"Oh, that's right," I remembered. "You were probably stationed in Panama or someplace when Janelle Mayhew married Glenn Riggsbee. This is the dress Portland and I and their three sisters wore in their wedding."

"All five of you?" he asked dryly. "No wonder you can still squeeze into it."

I fluttered my ostrich-plume fan under his chin. "Why, Rhett, honey, you just say the sweetest thangs. Don't y'all pay him no nevermind," I told Portland and Avery. "He's still pouting 'cause he couldn't get into his little ol' dress uniform."

"You said you never gloat," Dwight reminded me. "What ring?"

Avery sailed through the last stoplight in Dobbs and headed east along a backcountry road. As we drove through the cold winter night, stars blazing overhead, we took turns telling Dwight about Janelle's tacky engagement ring and how it had disappeared in the middle of her wedding to Glenn Riggsbee.

"It all began with Elizabeth and Nancy—Glenn's two sisters," said Portland. "Both of them wanted the ring he gave Janelle."

Dwight might not've gone to college, but he knows about Freudian complexes. "Isn't that a little unnatural?"

"We're talking greed, not Greek," I told him, "and strictly speaking, it really began with Glenn's great-uncle."

Glenn Riggsbee was named for his mother's favorite uncle, a larger-than-life character who ran away from home at fifteen and went wildcatting in Texas back in the twenties. Unlike most kids who go off to seek their fortunes and slink home a few years later hoping nobody'll notice their tails dragging in the mud, Great-Uncle Glenn hit a gusher before he was eighteen, married a flashy dance-hall blonde before he was twenty, and lived high, wide, and handsome for the next fifty years.

He and his wife never had children, so when she died and the big money ran out, he came back to Colleton County, bought a little house next door to his niece, and settled down to bossing Glenn and his sisters around like they were his own grandchildren. Portland and I never even heard of him till our good friend Janelle Mayhew started dating Glenn, but we heard plenty after that because Janelle was terrified of him.

With good reason.

True, he'd been a Daddy Warbucks to Mrs. Riggsbee and her children when he had lots of money, lavishing her with expensive treats and setting up trust funds so Glenn and his two sisters could go to college in style. And yes, he continued to be generous with the dregs of his fortune, helping Glenn buy a first car, for instance, or doling out to the girls some of his late wife's gold and silver baubles.

But in old age, he was just as opinionated and short-tempered as he'd been in his youth. Any help he gave was on his terms, and any gifts he gave came with stretchy elastic attached. For such a renegade, he had a surprisingly wide streak of conservatism.

He had expected both of Glenn's sisters to become schoolteachers and to stop work once they had babies. When Elizabeth majored in accounting and had a chance to buy into a new insurance brokerage firm soon after graduation, he refused to help. Said it wasn't fitting for an unmarried woman to be in a position to boss around married men.

The same thing happened when Nancy wanted to become a minister. A woman preacher? The very concept shocked him to the core. "Be damned if I'll bankroll such blasphemy!" Somehow he found a legal loophole that let him tie up Nancy's college trust fund until she tearfully promised not to take any theology courses.

As a male, Glenn was, theoretically, free to major in whatever he wanted, but you can imagine Great-Uncle Glenn's reaction when he finally realized that Glenn planned to use his shiny new degree in restaurant management to turn an old dilapidated farmhouse into a restaurant.

"A restaurant out in the middle of the country? Stupidest damn thing I ever heard of," he snorted. "Don't expect me to help finance it."

In vain did Glenn point out that I-40 was going to dot the county with housing developments full of wage-earning commuters happy to pay someone else to fix supper.

Nor did it open Great-Uncle Glenn's wallet when he heard that Janelle was taking cooking courses at the local community college. Indeed, he took to wondering audibly if she was good enough for young Glenn. After all, what kind of trashy mama did Janelle have that wouldn't teach her own daughter how to fry chicken and make buttermilk biscuits?

While it's true that the Mayhews were even poorer than the Riggsbees, they were by no means trash, and Janelle was always a hard worker. She also has lovely manners and yes-sirred and no-sirred Great-Uncle Glenn till, when Glenn said he was going to ask her to set a date, the old man went to his lockbox at Dobbs First National and gave Glenn the platinum-and-diamond ring he'd bought to woo his dance-hall wife.

We'd never seen anything quite like it: a huge rose-cut yellow diamond surrounded by forty tapered baguette diamonds, sapphires, and rubies in a ballerina mount.

Dwight interrupted our story: "What's a ballerina mount?"

"Picture a big yellow golf ball surrounded by a red-white-and-blue ruffle," I said.

"Sounds sort of ugly to me," he ventured.

"It was beyond ugly," Portland assured him.

"But the diamond was what they call a flawless fancy yellow and was supposed to have been insured for eighty thousand dollars," I recalled.

"Supposed to be?"

"That's why I'm sure Elizabeth took it," said Portland. "Where else did she get the money to buy a partnership?"

"Circumstantial evidence," Avery murmured. Like Portland, he's an attorney, too.

"Not entirely," she argued. "See, Dwight. Elizabeth hadn't bought in with Bob McAdams yet, but she'd been working there a couple of years and she was supposed to have written up a policy for the ring once it went from Great-Uncle Glenn's lockbox to Janelle's finger—"

"But Elizabeth assumed the Mayhews had household insurance," I said. "And since Janelle was still living at home to save money for the restaurant, Elizabeth thought that would protect it up to the wedding."

"That's what she claimed," said Portland, "but even if the Mayhews did have insurance, no piddly little renters' policy would ever cover an eighty-thousand-dollar ring. Uh-uh, Deb'rah. She knew there'd be hard-nosed investigators swarming all over the place if Janelle flied a claim for eighty thousand. No policy, no claim. No claim, no serious investigation."

"No policy?" asked Dwight from the darkness beside me.

"Elizabeth dated it to take effect at twelve noon, which was when the ceremony took place and when Janelle's residence would officially change from her parents' house. The last time anybody saw the ring was at eleven-thirty when Janelle stuck it in her makeup bag in the choir robing room next to the vestibule."

I took up the tale. "And before you ask, no, nobody was seen going into that room between the time we finished dressing until after the ceremony. Miss Louisa Ferncliff directed the wedding and she was right there in the vestibule the whole time, making sure the ushers knew whether the guests were bride's side or groom's and then sending us down the aisle spaced just right. If anybody'd gone back in, she'd have seen them."

"Who was last out of the robing room?"

"Janelle and me," Portland answered. "Her sister Faye was maid of honor and I was matron of honor. Deb'rah went first, then Nancy, Elizabeth, Faye, and me. The room was empty after Janelle and I went out to the vestibule and I pulled the door shut."

"So who was first back in?"

I shrugged. "All of us. There was a receiving line with the parents right after the recessional, then we all went to put on fresh lipstick for the formal pictures, and that's when Janelle discovered the ring was gone."

"And the only ones in the robing room the whole time were you six?"

"Are you kidding?" said Portland. "Both mothers were in and out, as well as Miss Louisa, the photographer, the minister's wife—"

"Don't forget Omaleen Grimes," I said. "She was dating one of Glenn's ushers, and she acted like that gave her a right to stick her nose in everywhere."

"But between the time Janelle took off the ring and the time she realized it was gone?"

Portland and I had to admit it. During the crucial time, there were just us five bridesmaids, Mrs. Mayhew, Mrs. Riggsbee, and Janelle herself.

Everybody had been sweet as molasses pie, but Portland and I and seventeen-year-old Faye Mayhew had hovered protectively around Janelle because Elizabeth and Nancy still had their noses out of joint. Glenn Riggsbee was damn lucky to find someone as fine as Janelle, but in their minds—particularly Elizabeth's—their brother was marrying down. The Mayhews were too poor to own their own home, Janelle hadn't gone to college, and on top of that, she had somehow dazzled Great-Uncle Glenn into parting with the last substantial piece of jewelry in his possession.

Both sisters had been allowed to wear the ring on special occasions in the past, and each had hoped that Great-Uncle Glenn would leave it to her someday: Elizabeth because she was the oldest, Nancy because she was the baby of the family and had already been given his wife's garnet necklace. No matter how nice Janelle was to them, it was all they could do to maintain a polite façade, though a stranger wouldn't have known it for all the "sugars" and "honeys" being thrown around the choir robing room that morning.

A moment or two before eleven-thirty, Mrs. Mayhew had set the veil on Janelle's hair. When Janelle lifted her hands to adjust it, the gaudy ring flashed in the pale January sunlight.

"Don't forget to take that ring off before you start down the aisle," said Mrs. Mayhew. "Your finger needs to be bare when Glenn puts on your wedding band."

As if in chorus, Elizabeth and Nancy both offered to hold it for her.

"That's okay," said Janelle.

She slipped the yellow diamond into the same worn gray velvet box Great-Uncle Glenn had given his wife sixty years earlier. It was so old, the domed lid no longer closed with a tight snap, but she tucked the box into her makeup bag. Her eyes met ours nervously in the mirror. "Glenn's ring! Por?"

Portland waggled her thumb and there was the wide gold wedding band that Janelle would slip onto Glenn's finger in less than an hour.

At that instant, Miss Louisa stuck her head in and hissed, "Sst! Mothers! Places!"

The clock above the mirror said 11:31.

We'd been primping and preening since ten o'clock, so you'd think we could have sat with our hands folded quietly and discussed the weather or something, wouldn't you? Instead we all dived back into our own makeup bags, touching up mascara and lipstick, adjusting our bustles, adjusting Janelle's veil, reminding each other how to hold the white plumed fans at identical angles, then a final spritz of hair spray before Miss Louisa herded us all out into the vestibule.

Afterwards, none of us could say who had or hadn't touched which makeup bag.

But that was later, when Sheriff Poole questioned us.

At the beginning, Janelle was sure the ring must have somehow worked its way out of the loose-lidded velvet box and slipped down among her cosmetics. Then, that it must have fallen out while we all made last-minute touch-ups. Surely on the floor, beneath the dressing table, under a chair.

Nothing.

"Somebody's taken it!" Portland said dramatically.

"Don't be silly," said Janelle, anxiously uncapping all her lipsticks, as if that ring could possibly fit inside a slender tube. Her sister Faye was down on her hands and knees searching beneath the choir robes. "We were the only ones here and . . ."

Her voice trailed away as she saw Portland and me staring at her new sisters-in-law.

Elizabeth and Nancy both turned beet red.

"If you think for one minute—!" Elizabeth huffed indignantly. "You can search me if you like."

"Me, too!" said Nancy.

"Don't be silly," Janelle said again.

"Girls, girls!" Miss Louisa stood in the doorway. "The photographer is waiting."

"Miss Louisa," I said. "Did anybody come in here during the ceremony?"

"No, of course not, dear. Why do you ask?"

Janelle broke in. "Miss Louisa, could you please tell the photographer we'll be right there?"

As Miss Louisa tottered away on her little high heels, Janelle twisted her brand new wedding band nervously and said, "Look, if one of you took it as a joke—"

Instant denial was on all our lips.

"It's okay if it's a joke," she continued doggedly. "Let's go out like nothing's happened, and if whoever took it will just drop it on the floor, that will be the end of it, okay?" Her voice trembled. "Just don't tell Glenn or our folks, okay? It'd spoil our wedding day. Please?"

Subdued, we promised to keep quiet.

Without looking around, Janelle swept out to the sanctuary and we trailed along after. During the next half hour, as the photographer grouped and regrouped various components of the wedding party, Janelle managed to send each bridesmaid back to the robing room alone. Would Elizabeth fetch her lipstick? Would Nancy be a dear and find a comb? A tissue, Faye? Oh goodness, Por, she'd forgotten her blue garter!

Before she could invent a task for me, the photographer decided to take a shot of the newlyweds' hands, and Great-Uncle Glenn said, "Take me one with her engagement ring, too."

"I'll go get it," I said brightly, absolutely positive that I'd find the stupid thing back on the robing room dressing table.

Wrong.

Nor had it been dropped on the floor as Janelle suggested. I searched every square inch.

After that, a bit of discreet hell broke loose. Mrs. Riggsbee managed to keep Great-Uncle Glenn reined in till after the reception was over. Fortunately, it was only punch and wedding cake in the church's fellowship hall; and as soon as the cake was cut, Janelle and Glenn pretended to leave in a shower of rice. Actually, all they did was drive over to their new apartment, change clothes, and sneak back into the church robing room where Sheriff Bo Poole was questioning the rest of us.

"I'm surprised I never heard anything about this," Dwight said as we entered the outskirts of Widdington.

"They pretty much hushed it up when it was clear nobody was going to confess," said Portland. "Janelle insisted that someone had to've sneaked into the robing room while Miss Louisa was watching the ceremony because there was no way that a sister or friend could have done her that shabby."

I smoothed the plumes on my fan. "Great-Uncle Glenn was furious, of course."

"But Janelle faced him down," Portland said. "She told him it was her ring and she was the one who'd been careless with it and it was her loss, not his."

"Remember his face when Elizabeth admitted that there was no insurance? I thought he was going to hit her with his walking stick."

"So what happened next?" asked Dwight.

"I think Sheriff Poole put a description on the wire, but I never heard that anything came of it," said Portland. "Great-Uncle Glenn died a few months later, and when Janelle and Glenn got back from the funeral, they found the ring in their mailbox. All the little diamonds and sapphires and rubies were still there, but the big yellow diamond was gone."

"No one ever confessed?" asked Dwight.

"Not that we ever heard," we told him.

What we left unsaid was the suspicion that maybe Janelle thought Portland or I had taken the ring because after that, we were never quite as close again.

"I don't care what happened to it!" she stormed when Portland pressed her about the theft a few months later. "If one of y'all needed the money that bad, then that was a better use for that darned old ring than on my finger."

Portland had called me the minute she got back to Dobbs. "She thinks you or I took it."

"She probably heard about our new mink coats and all our trips to Bermuda," I said dryly.

So we dropped it after that. Janelle was still friendly with us when we saw her, but as time passed, those occasions were less frequent. She and Glenn threw themselves into the restaurant, which took off like a rocket from opening day, and Portland and I were both caught up in our own careers back in Dobbs. Anyhow, loyalties always realign when you marry outside your own crowd.

Janelle had made her bed among Riggsbees, and from that day forward, it was as if Elizabeth and Nancy had never acted ugly to her. Or stolen from her and Glenn.

"Well, one good thing came out of it," Portland said, paralleling my thoughts. "Elizabeth was so grateful to Janelle for understanding about the insurance mix-up that they became real friends from then on."

The Widdington Jaycees were holding their ball at the new Shrine club, and as Avery drove into the parking lot, laughing couples streamed toward the entrance.

Heaven knows there was plenty to laugh at. I haven't seen that much organdy, chiffon, and taffeta froufrou since I helped judge a Little Miss Makely beauty contest last year.

Inside, the club was decorated in valentines of every size and jammed to the walls, but friends had saved space at a table for us. While Dwight and Avery went off to fight their way to the bar, lights played across the dance floor and I saw a lot of familiar faces.

And one familiar dress.

Nancy Riggsbee was much heavier now. The seams on her blue velvet had clearly been let out and her bustle rode on hips even more ample than mine, but she beamed with seeming pleasure when she spotted me and came right over.

"Deborah Knott! How you been, lady?"

We kissed air, and half-screaming to be heard above the music and talk, I said, "Where's your fan? And don't tell me Elizabeth's here in this same dress, too? And Faye?"

"No, Faye's living in Boston now and Elizabeth's little girl came home from school sick with the flu yesterday, so I'm here on her ticket. In her dress. Mine was cut up for a church pageant years ago. Mary and one of the Magi, I think. The fans went for angel wings."

So Elizabeth had porked up a bit, too, since I last saw her? Mean of me to be smug about it. To atone, I told Nancy I'd heard about her getting a church out in the country from Durham and how was she liking it after so long in Virginia?

It was too loud for small talk though, and after a few more shouted pleasantries, Dwight and Avery came back with our drinks. I introduced Dwight to Nancy, who said she was going to go find Janelle and tell her we were there.

Fortunately someone got the band to turn down their speakers about then and conversation became possible again.

"So she got to be a preacher after all?" Dwight asked.

I nodded. "After Great-Uncle Glenn died, the others encouraged her to go to divinity school. It was a struggle because he didn't leave much, but Janelle and Glenn pitched in. Elizabeth, too, even though she was scraping every penny to buy into the firm about then."

"Notice Nancy's ring if she comes back," Portland told him. "After the ring came home without the yellow diamond, Glenn had the diamond baguettes set into a sort of engagement ring. They gave Elizabeth the sapphires and Nancy the rubies. Janelle told me that's pretty much what they would've done anyhow if he'd left both girls the ring—sell the big stone and make two rings out of the little ones. In the end, it made three."

I was tired of that stupid ring. The band was playing a lively two-step and I wanted to shake my bustle. Despite his size, Dwight dances surprisingly well, and I didn't mean to waste the music talking about something over and done with. We moved out onto the dance floor and were soon twirling with the best.

A couple of slow numbers followed, then the spotlight fell on the emcee who announced the first category of the evening: Heart and Flowers, i.e., fussiest dress. To the strains of "Here Comes the Bride," nine women glided across the dance floor, as if down an aisle, to a makeshift altar behind the emcee. The clear winner was a stiff yellow net covered with row upon row of tight little ruffles.

Amid the laughter and applause, I felt a light touch on my arm and there was Janelle smiling at Portland and me. She gave us each a hug and said to me, "Nancy said you signed up in the prettiest dress category? I'm so flattered. It was a beautiful wedding, wasn't it?"

She herself was wearing ice blue satin from her sister-in-law Elizabeth's wedding. "That's the only time I was a bridesmaid," Janelle said regretfully. "I was always big-as-a-house pregnant when everybody else was getting married."

One of the Widdington Jaycees dragged her away to help with something, and she made us promise we wouldn't leave without speaking again.

The next category was My Funny Valentine for the most unusual gown, and it was a tie between a Ronald McDonald clown (the bride managed a local franchise) and a gold lamé jumpsuit (the skydiving bride and groom were married in free-fall).

Portland didn't win the Purple Heart Award—the most unusual color actually went to a hot-pink velvet bodice, orange organza skirt, and lime green sash—but she was persuaded to enter Kind Hearts and Coronets for the most accessories and won handily with her huge picture hat, arm-length lace mitts, and wicker basket full of chiffon roses.

In between, as groups of contestants were assembled for their march down the mock aisle, we danced and chatted and filled several bedoilied sandwich plates with the usual array of finger foods found at a typical wedding reception: raw vegetables and herb dip, cheese straws, cucumber sandwiches, tiny hot rolls stuffed with ham and melted pimiento cheese, salted nuts, and heart-shaped butter mints.

Despite all the laughter, wearing the dress brought back memories of Janelle and Glenn's wedding; and seeing Nancy around the room in the same garb only emphasized the feeling. I knew Portland was flashing on it, too, because she kept going back to the missing ring. Faye, Nancy, or Elizabeth. Who had taken it? (Loyally, we'd each long since cleared the other.)

If Faye had eventually lavished money around, we'd never heard of it.

It had to be Elizabeth or Nancy.

"Nancy's a preacher," Portland said.

"That wouldn't have mattered," I argued. "They both felt entitled to the ring. Don't forget, she came up with tuition to divinity school."

"Elizabeth helped her though. And so did Glenn and Janelle. Janelle didn't buy any new clothes for three years, till long after Elizabeth bought a partnership with Bob McAdams. Where did Elizabeth get enough money if not from pawning the ring?"

"I thought Glenn co-signed a loan with her?" said Avery.

"Yes, but—"

"You gals have gone at it all wrong," said Dwight. "From what you've told me, there's only one person who could have taken the ring without being caught or even suspected."

I hate that superior air he puts on when he's being Dick Tracy, but all of a sudden, I realized he was right.

"Who?" asked Avery.

"The woman who directed the wedding, of course.

"Miss Louisa Ferncliff!" Portland exclaimed.

Dwight lifted his glass to her. "The only person alone out in the vestibule while everyone else was taking part in the ceremony. Anybody ever take a look at her lifestyle after the wedding?"

Avery cocked his head. "You know something, ol' son? I sort of remember when she died, Ed Whitbread was the one who drew up her will, and when he came over to file it at the courthouse, seems like he said he was surprised how much money she did have to leave that sorry nephew of hers down in Wilmington."

Portland was looking doubtful. "Miss Louisa?"

I spread my fan and drew myself up in a most judicial manner. "It's unfair to slander the name of a good woman who can no longer defend herself, but"—I used the fan to shield my voice from the rest of the table—"one thing's for sure. Miss Louisa Ferncliff directed just about every single wedding at that church for years. She sure would know that brides take off their engagement rings and leave them somewhere in the robing room, but that was the first ring really worth taking, wouldn't you say?"

"I'll be damned," said Portland. "Miss Louisa!"

She jumped up from the table. "Come on, Deb'rah! Let's go tell Janelle."

Protesting that we had no proof, I followed her around the edge of the dance floor until we found Janelle, who, as one of the ball's organizers, had just presented the Heart of Carolina prize for the most denim or gingham in a bridesmaid's dress.

Quickly, we maneuvered her into the lobby where it was quieter, and Portland laid out Dwight's theory and my supporting logic.

Janelle was flabbergasted. "Miss Louisa stole my ring?"

"She certainly had plenty of opportunity," I said cautiously, "but I don't see how you'd ever prove it. She left everything to that sorry nephew, and what he didn't sell off, he either burned or threw out."

"I don't care!" A radiance swept across Janelle's sweet face and she hugged Portland. "We never once thought of Miss Louisa. I can't wait to tell Glenn. If you could know what it means that we can say it was her and not—"

She broke off and hugged us both again, then whirled away back into the ballroom.

"Well, I'll be blessed," said Portland, standing there with her mouth hanging open. "Not you or me after all, Deb'rah. She really did think it was one of Glenn's sisters."

"Or they could have accused her own sister," I reminded her. "For all they knew, Faye could have been the thief."

"Oh, I'm so glad Dwight finally figured it out. Let's go buy him a drink."

"You go ahead," I told her.

The band was playing a suburban version of "Hometown Honeymoon" when I caught up with Janelle.

"You and Glenn went to New York on your honeymoon, didn't you?"

Surprised, she nodded.

"Is that where you sold the diamond?"

"What?"

"The biggest diamond market in the country's right there on Forty-seventh Street. You'd have gotten better money for it there than anywhere here in North Carolina."

There was a door off to the side and Janelle pulled me through it into an empty office, the club manager's by the look of it.

"You said Miss Louisa must've taken it."

"I said she had lots of opportunity," I corrected. "You had the most though."

"That's crazy! Why would I steal my own engagement ring? It wasn't even insured."

"I think that's exactly why you did it," I said. "You're not really a thief and you wouldn't have pretended it was stolen if it meant the insurance company was going to be defrauded of eighty thousand dollars. But the ring was legally yours, you and Glenn needed money, and that was the simplest way to get it without ticking off his uncle. All you needed to do was go through that charade."

Janelle was shaking her head. "No, no, NO!"

"Oh, get real," I told her. "How else did you and Glenn have enough to get the restaurant off to such a good start? How'd Glenn have enough collateral to cosign a loan for Elizabeth's partnership so quick?"

"Uncle Glenn—"

"Uncle Glenn didn't leave that kind of money. I was nosy enough to look up the records when his estate was settled, even though I never put two and two together. The house went to Glenn's mom, and what was split between Glenn and his sisters wouldn't have bought a partnership in a hot dog stand at the fair. That's why we were so sure one of them took it."

Her eyes fell.

"It was mean of you to let Portland think you suspected us all these years.

Janelle threw up her hands in exasperation. "I didn't want to, but it was the only way I could make her quit talking about it. I was afraid if she kept on, she'd finally figure it out."

That dog-with-a-bone tenacity makes Portland a good lawyer, but it's a real pain in the neck for some of her friends, and I couldn't help grinning.

"Are you going to tell her?" Janelle asked.

"And spoil the fun she and Dwight are having, thinking Miss Louisa did it?"

Janelle giggled and I had to laugh, too. "You know, I bet Miss Louisa would love it if people remembered her for pulling off a slick jewel theft."

Better than not being remembered at all, I judged, then clasped Janelle's hand. We both looked down at the circle of diamond baguettes that sparkled modestly above her wedding band.

"It really was the tackiest ring in the whole world," she said.

"Something that trashy deserved to get itself stolen," I agreed.

As we stepped back into the room a few minutes later, someone yelled, "Here she is!" and immediately pushed me into the final lineup of the evening. Queen of Hearts. The prettiest dress of weddings past.

Nancy, in her sister's dress, had entered this category, too, and there was a truly gorgeous Scarlett O'Hara confection of pale green organza, plus a couple of sophisticated black silks, but none of them had a fan of white ostrich plumes and none of them was as shameless at working a crowd.

The prize was a five-pound, red satin, heart-shaped box of chocolates.

I won by a landslide.

Presidential Material

by Dean James

In collaboration with Jean Swanson, Dean James is the award-winning author of the reference book By a Woman's Hand. *With Jan Grape and Ellen Nehr, he edited the Edgar-award nominated* Deadly Women: The Woman Mystery Reader's Indispensable Companion. *Dean has written a number of short stories, and his first novel,* Cruel As The Grave, *was published by Silver Dagger Mysteries this spring.*

The woman's scream rent the air as she tumbled over the edge of the cliff, falling hundreds of feet to the bottom of the ravine.

Arnold McDuffie sighed with satisfaction. That sure was a tidy end to a problem.

He clicked the TV off with the remote. If only his problems could be solved so easily. He put away the remote and hit a button on the console on his desk. A panel slid down, covering the TV set. He swiveled in his chair, surveying his office. All the comforts of home, and then some. There were advantages to being the President of McDuffie's Department Store chain. This office was one of them. A nice place to hide away from his wife when he didn't want to go home and listen to that voice.

He sighed again. What was he going to do about Ida Lou? Things just hadn't been the same since old man McDuffie had popped off eight months ago. Arnold grinned. At least the old SOB had gone happily, carousing with some floozie and stuffed to the gills with rich food and wine, his heart giving out right in the middle of his favorite activity.

If nothing else, Arnold had admired the old man's capacity to live life to its fullest, ignoring the way his two daughters constantly tried to reform him.

But because Ida Lou couldn't do anything with her father, she had long ago set her sights on turning her husband into the healthiest, most attentive husband on the face of the earth. It wasn't enough, Arnold complained bitterly to himself, that he'd given up his own name thirty-seven years ago so there'd be a new generation of McDuffies to uphold the family tradition. Nosiree Bob, he'd given everything he had to the McDuffie family and their string of forty-eight department stores across the Southeastern United States. You'd have to look hard to find a suburban mall in Tennessee, Georgia, or Alabama that didn't have a McDuffie's as one of its flagship stores.

Arnold did take some pride in the fact that he had been a major player in the chain's expansion over the last thirty-seven years. As long as old man McDuffie had had enough money to indulge himself in women, wine, cigars, and rich food, he couldn't have cared less about expanding the business. Yep, Arnold was the one who had built the business into a multimillion-dollar empire across the South.

And what had he gotten for it, when the old man died? A lousy seventeen percent of the stock. Which meant, even though he was the President of the company, he couldn't do diddly without both his wife and her sister voting with him. Old man McDuffie had left each of them seventeen percent. If the old bastard weren't already dead, Arnold could have strangled him.

At least Ida Lou usually went along with him when it came to anything to do with the business. Together, they could bulldoze the perennial thorn in his side, Penny McDuffie, into seeing things his way.

But lately Ida Lou had begun to pay more attention to Penny, and that was getting dangerous. He had to come up with some way to control both women completely. He couldn't stand the thought of the two of them taking over the business and pushing him out by getting the rest of the board to vote with them. No way he was going to let that happen.

Arnold got angrier, the more he thought about it. Penny thought the blasted Internet was the solution to everything. She was forever and ever going on about "e-commerce" and becoming an "e-tailer." *What the hell is an e-tailer?* Arnold wanted to know. Did they really need to sell kitchen goods and children's clothes and women's shoes over the damned Internet? Sales at McDuffie's stores had been slipping a bit, the last couple of years, but Arnold couldn't see where putting up a website was going to do a blasted bit of good.

He never should have talked the old man into giving Penny a job fifteen years ago. *Well,* he thought, *that's the price you paid for having an affair with her. Look what it brought you.* But maybe it wasn't too late to do something about it. But what could he do?

Thoughts of the board meeting coming up in three weeks' time made his stomach hurt. Penny had been working on her proposal for the website she planned to put before the board, despite Arnold's opposition. He was planning to counter her proposal with one of his own, for expansion of McDuffie's Department Stores into Mississippi and Louisiana with new stores in Jackson, Shreveport, and New Orleans. He had to have Ida Lou's support on this one. What would he have to do to ensure her support?

He looked at his watch. Almost seven-thirty. Well, if he didn't head home now, Ida Lou would be on the phone any minute, wanting to know why he wasn't at home with her, to have dinner with her and their two children.

Arnold shuddered. How he was supposed to eat, without choking on every bite, while he had to look at the faces of his wife and children, he didn't know. First off, there was Ida Lou with the makeup that made her look like a retarded raccoon. He'd tried, as tactfully as he knew how, to suggest that Ida Lou's beauty consultant, Madame Tyffani, didn't know what the hell she was talking about. But Ida Lou insisted on wearing stuff on her face that made her look like she should be foraging in garbage cans instead of running around in Nashville society. Arnold Jr. he could hardly bear to think about. Why would a good-looking seventeen-year-old boy want to run around in black clothes all the time, with his blond hair dyed black, a ring through his eyebrow and one in his nose, his fingernails painted black and wearing black lipstick, for goodness sake? Arnold wanted to puke every time he looked at his son.

At least his daughter, LouAnn, looked normal. She wore decent clothes, bathed regularly, and was respectful to her father. But why did she think she wanted to become a nun and go live in Africa? Their family wasn't even Catholic. Arnold didn't get it, couldn't figure out what he and Ida Lou had done wrong all these years for their two children, the sweetest babies you ever did see, to turn out like this.

And now, on top of everything else, Ida Lou was on him all the time about working on their marriage. Arnold knew things could be better between them. He couldn't remember the last time he'd made love with Ida Lou. But he just couldn't tell her she was so thin now the thought of having sex with her turned him off completely. She was so proud of having lost all that weight, he didn't have the heart to tell her how bad she looked. He missed the plump and pleasant girl he'd married.

Still, what was he going to do? He stood up from his desk, gathering up his keys and briefcase. He was about to turn off the lights from the console on his desk when his eyes lit upon a brochure Ida Lou had forced on him several days ago. Colorful pictures of a resort hotel near Gatlinburg beckoned him. Frowning, he picked up the brochure.

He glanced through it, for the first time paying attention to the particulars.

Maybe, just maybe, he thought, smiling a little as he tucked the brochure into the inside pocket of his jacket. This could be the answer he had been looking for. He switched off the light and headed for home.

Ida Lou McDuffie looked across her favorite table in one of Nashville's most exclusive restaurants and frowned at her younger sister.

Really, Penny ought to be ashamed to let those dark roots show like that. No matter how hard she tried, she just couldn't get the girl to take more pride in her appearance. No wonder she still wasn't married, and she'd be fifty next year.

"Really, Penny, would it hurt you to go to the beauty shop more than twice a year?" Ida Lou chided her.

"Since you go practically every other day, Sissy," Penny responded sweetly, "I don't see where I need to. You more than make up for me. By the way, isn't it time for another facelift?" *Really*, she thought, *why doesn't Ida Lou just give up?* Not every woman was desperate to have some man hanging on her. Just look at poor Arnold. There was a word to describe Arnold and the way he let Ida Lou push him around, but Penny was too much of a lady to think it, much less say it aloud.

Ida Lou ignored Penny's attempt at an insult. "Why don't you get yourself fixed up a little, and you can come along with Arnold and me to this weekend retreat at that hotel in Gatlinburg?" Her face glowed with happiness. "Arnold and I are going to spend some real quality time together, isn't that wonderful? I can't imagine why he suddenly decided to do it, but I'm not looking my sweet ol' gift horse in the mouth, I can tell you right now."

"And why should I want to intrude on all this matrimonial bliss?" Penny asked, one eyebrow raised in disdain.

Her sarcasm was lost on Ida Lou. "Because it might rub off on you, that's why! You could ask someone to come along. Who knows? You might actually find a man to marry, after all this time."

"And just who am I going to bring along on this little Fantasy Island trip of yours?"

Ida Lou frowned, considering. "I know! How about that new Vice President Arnold hired two months ago?"

Penny almost choked on her wine. "You mean Mr. Charles Truesdell Stanton the Fourth? 'Just call me Chuck.' *That* new Vice President?"

Ida Lou nodded. "Why not? He sure is handsome, and I've noticed lately he seems to like you." Her tone implied she couldn't imagine why, but there you were.

"Ida Lou, have you lost what tiny little mind you have? Chuck may be thirty-five, at the most."

"Now, Penny," Ida Lou said placatingly, "I know he's a bit younger than you"—both sisters managed not to gag over this gross understatement—"but you know there are some men who like the mystique of older women."

Penny snorted into her wineglass.

"Don't be difficult," Ida Lou said. "This is a good chance for you. He's a nice man, and you just never know what might come of it."

Penny stared down at her plate. She was trying hard to suppress memories of Chuck, his head tilted, listening attentively to one of her ideas. Maybe that sparkle in his eyes meant something after all. Why else had he been paying so much attention to her the last few weeks?

Arnold never paid any attention to her ideas for McDuffie's. Once upon a time, she had thought she and Arnold were going to be a team, but that didn't last long. She had spent many an hour imagining the look on Ida Lou's face when Arnold asked her for a divorce. But it had never happened.

Maybe if she got Chuck on her side, the new VP for Sales might help her start to make some changes. Arnold would be less likely to argue with a man, particularly with a man like Chuck, who had a Harvard MBA.

Penny smiled, her mind suddenly made up. "Why not?"

Satisfied, Ida Lou sat back and motioned for the waiter. "I think this calls for some dessert. I haven't had anything sweet for six months. How about chocolate cheesecake?"

Back in her office in the McDuffie Building, Penny punched in Arnold's private extension number on the phone.

"Ida Lou just invited me along on your big romantic weekend," she said when Arnold answered.

Arnold smiled, thankful that Penny couldn't see his face. "Why on earth would she do that?" He worked hard to hit the right note of honest puzzlement.

"She wants me to bring a man along," Penny said. "Chuck Stanton."

Arnold swore under his breath. He hadn't counted on that. Oh, well, he could work with it. "Why not?" he said, chuckling lightly into the phone. "He seems to like you, and if Ida Lou gets bored, we can always play bridge or tennis, if nothing else."

"It doesn't sound like much of a romantic getaway for two, if you ask me," Penny said, "but if it's okay with you, and Chuck will go along with it, I guess it's fine."

"Good," Arnold said. "We'll leave on Friday." He put down the phone. This was working out pretty well, after all. Gave him another option, depending on how he was feeling at the moment. Yep, things were gonna work out just fine.

Charles Truesdell Stanton the Fourth eased his long, lean, and muscular frame into the chair across from Penny's desk. Penny tried not to stare at him. He surely was handsome, and he was well-built, too. She tried not to imagine what he looked like under that expensively tailored suit. She sighed.

"I like your hair that way," Chuck said, smiling at her. "You must've just had it done." He settled back into his chair, completely at ease.

Penny patted her new short cut, the mousy brown color "enhanced," as Madame Tyffani called it, with highlights of red. She had to admit that she did like the way she looked, and it had seemed a small price to pay to get Ida Lou thinking more positively about her proposal for the website.

"Thank you, Chuck," Penny said, hoping her voice sounded calmer than she felt. "It doesn't hurt to try something new once in a while, does it?"

Chuck favored her with a long look, and Penny did her best to halt the blush she could feel creeping up her face. "Not at all, Penny," he said. "Not at all."

He might have spent years back east, Penny thought, but he never had gotten rid of that sexy Mississippi drawl. She uncurled her toes and tried to relax.

"If you don't have any plans for next weekend," Penny began, watching Chuck's face closely, "I'd like to invite you to join Arnold, Ida Lou, and me at a retreat we're going to near Gatlinburg."

"There's nothing I couldn't rearrange," Chuck said, "and I sure do appreciate being invited. But what kind of retreat is this?"

Penny waved one hand in the air. "Oh, you know, we've got that big board meeting coming up, and we've got to decide on which proposal to put before the board. Either the website idea, or the store expansion in Mississippi and Louisiana."

"I see." Chuck nodded. "Now, seems to me like you and Arnold have been disagreeing just a tiny little bit over all this. And since I'm just a Vice President," he flashed a grin, "I'm kinda wondering what input you expect me to have."

Penny smiled, as charmingly as she knew how. "Why, Chuck, you know Arnold has come to value your opinion very highly, even though you've been with McDuffie's only a couple of months. I know an ambitious and energetic man like you can see the future of our business as clearly as I do. We both know Arnold is just digging in his heels because he doesn't understand the technology the way we do," she shrugged, indicating Arnold's foolishness.

Chuck smiled again. "I know what you mean, but this is also a good time for building new stores. There's a lot to consider."

Penny nodded, holding on to her patience. "I'll grant you that, but I think any man with his eye on the future"—here she stared directly into Chuck's eyes—"and his future position with McDuffie's, once Arnold retires, surely ought to know which proposal has more to offer. In the long run."

In response, Chuck gave her one of those smiles that made her itch all over. "I think I'm going to look forward to this retreat," he said, standing up.

Honey, you don't know the half of it, Penny thought as she watched him walk out of her office.

Arnold stood on the deck of the cabin, staring out at the mountainside, and drew on his cigar. At least Ida Lou wasn't fussing about his smoking, for once. When Chuck had politely asked Ida Lou if she minded his smoking—outside, of course—Ida Lou had simpered and sent Arnold out with him.

"Glad you could come along, Chuck," Arnold said, surprised to find that he meant it. At first, he had thought Chuck's presence would complicate matters, but eventually he realized he might be able to work it to his advantage. "And thanks for the cigar."

Beside him, Chuck Stanton also exhaled a cloud of smoke, and the two men grinned at each other.

"You're welcome, Arnold," Chuck said. He gestured with his cigar. "This is some place y'all found for a retreat."

Arnold chuckled. "This was all Ida Lou's doing. You're right, though, it *is* beautiful."

Their cabin, a large guesthouse which slept six, was several hundred feet up the mountainside from the main building of the hotel. Stands of trees, brilliant reds and yellows with their fall foliage, shielded them from sight of the rest of the guests. They even had their own private trail up the mountain. Which suited Arnold just fine.

"What's on the agenda?" Chuck asked. "Maybe y'all discussed that on the drive here. Sorry I couldn't come with you, but I had a couple of things to deal with before I could leave."

"No problem." Arnold was in an expansive mood. "You're here now, so just relax and enjoy yourself. We're not going to talk about business at all, tonight. Plenty of time for that tomorrow and Sunday, before we head back to Nashville."

"Sounds fine to me," Chuck said. "No need to think about that board meeting until we have to, right?"

"Right," Arnold grinned back at him. Chuck had done everything yesterday but come right out and say, when they had spoken in Arnold's office, that he supported Arnold's ideas for expansion. After this weekend, it wouldn't matter much anyway. He'd be completely in control.

He drew again on his cigar, enjoying the rich smoke. Yep, he was finally going to be completely in control.

Arnold complimented Ida Lou on the meal.

Ida Lou made a pouty-face and said, "Now, honey, you know I ordered it all from the hotel kitchen."

Which is why it was actually edible, Arnold wanted to say.

Instead, he said, "I know, dumpling, but your choices were outstanding."

He dropped his linen napkin on the table and stood up. "How about we men clean off the table, and then we'll take you ladies on at bridge?"

"I was hoping to play with Chuck," Ida Lou said, then blushed when she realized how that sounded. "I mean, I just know he's wonderful at bridge, and you and Penny always play together anyway."

"Now, dumpling," Arnold said, gathering up dishes and following Chuck into the kitchen, "let's not be cross." The kitchen door swung shut behind them.

"Yes, dumpling," Penny said, "let the men play together." She giggled.

"You've had too much wine," Ida Lou hissed. "You be careful with yourself, missy."

"Oh, stuff it," Penny said. "You're really starting to get on my nerves, Sissy."

Ida Lou sniffed. "Just remember, if it wasn't for me, you wouldn't even be here. Especially with that gorgeous hunk of man making eyes at you."

Penny giggled again. "Yes, he is being quite attentive, don't you think?" Maybe she hadn't misinterpreted all those sly looks, after all.

Arnold and Chuck came back for the rest of the dishes and silverware.

"You're right, honey," Ida Lou cooed. "You big ol' men can play partners, and Penny and I'll just wipe up the floor with you."

A few minutes later, the four were seated around a card table. Arnold quickly discovered that Chuck was every bit as skilled at bridge as he'd expected. Chuck, however, hadn't expected to feel bare feet, one from either side of him, rubbing up and down his legs. Despite the constant covert attention, he managed to concentrate enough so that he and Arnold were victorious, rubber after rubber.

Finally, at midnight, Ida Lou called a halt. "I guess us girls just weren't up to it tonight, after all." She threw down her cards in disgust. "I don't know about y'all, but I'm ready for bed."

"Yes," Penny said, gazing quickly at Chuck. "I'm *more* than ready for bed."

Arnold stood up. "Come on, dumpling." He held out his hand, and Ida Lou grasped it. He pulled her out of her chair. "Let's get upstairs." He winked at Chuck. "And I don't want to hear any tiptoeing back and forth down here, okay?"

Neither Penny nor Chuck responded to this sally, although Penny's face flushed red. Instead, they wished each other a prim good night and headed to their bedrooms, on opposite sides of the cabin.

Half an hour later, when the lights had been off upstairs for a good fifteen minutes and the sounds of snoring drifted down,

Chuck opened his door cautiously. He moved, making only the slightest of sounds, across the floor to Penny's bedroom.

He knocked softly. Moments later, the door opened. She smiled hugely, then opened the door for him to slip inside. Chuck dropped his robe to the floor as Penny shut the door.

About ten minutes later, a shadowy form tiptoed down the stairs and crossed the floor to Chuck's bedroom door. Turning the knob carefully, the figure opened the door and slipped inside.

Moments later, mumbling under its breath about a "damn slut of a sister," the figure climbed the stairs once more.

Arnold was the first up the next morning. He came softly down the stairs and paused at the bottom, listening. Whistling softly, he proceeded into the kitchen, where he started a pot of coffee, then popped a bagel into the toaster.

Within the half hour, the rest of the party were awake and dressed and in the kitchen, helping themselves to bagels, cereal, coffee, and juice.

"What are we going to do this morning, honey?" Ida Lou asked after she had finished her half-bagel smeared with low-fat margarine and sugar-free strawberry preserves.

"I thought we might take a hike up the mountain," Arnold replied, setting down his coffee cup. "All that fresh air will be good for us, even though it's a mite colder than I expected."

"I don't see why we can't just stay here," Penny grumbled. "Why do we have to go traipsing up the mountainside?"

"I thought it might give us all a chance to reflect, and to think about the board meeting," Arnold said, holding on to his temper. Trust Penny to be difficult!

"I don't see what good that's going to do," Penny said.

"I think it's a good idea," Ida Lou said. "Getting back to nature is good for healing the soul. And spending time together like this will bring us closer, won't it, honeybee?" She batted her eyelashes at Arnold.

"Sure thing, dumpling," Arnold said in his most long-suffering tones. He turned to Penny. "Maybe we could talk some more about your idea for a website." He knew this would have the desired effect.

Penny brightened immediately.

"Besides," Chuck said, smiling, "all that fresh air will sure give us an appetite." He winked at Penny, where Ida Lou and Arnold couldn't see.

After that, Penny couldn't get her hiking boots on fast enough.

Ida Lou had brought along backpacks for all of them, each supplied with several bottles of water and various healthy snacks. As they stood at the beginning of the trail, gazing off up the mountain and shrugging on their backpacks, Penny asked nervously, "What about snakes?"

Chuck laughed. "I don't think you have to worry about them too much right now. It's a bit too cold for them." His breath misted in the cool air as he spoke.

"Fine with me!" Penny said.

"Then follow me," Arnold said, trudging off along the trail.

Single file they followed him, with Chuck bringing up the rear. At first, Penny and Ida Lou chattered, but the higher they climbed, the less inclined any of them were to talk. After about forty-five minutes, Arnold halted in front of a marker and waited for the others to catch up to him.

Breathing a bit heavily, Arnold pointed. "Sign says there's a good observation point over that way. What say we go there and take a little break?"

The others nodded their agreement, so Arnold headed in the direction indicated by the marker. About five minutes later they came upon a rocky promontory about eight feet wide which jutted out over a ravine. Arnold walked cautiously to the edge and peered over it.

"Long way down," he observed, then turned back to the others. Ida Lou had dropped her backpack at the edge of the trees and was squatting beside it, digging for her water. Penny and Chuck stood nearby, breathing deeply of the crisp mountain air.

"Spectacular, isn't it?" Arnold asked cheerfully. "Wouldn't you love to have a view like this every day?"

Penny and Chuck agreed, as they both dropped their backpacks and advanced cautiously the few feet to the edge of the ravine.

Penny laughed nervously. "Good thing I don't have vertigo!"

Chuck laughed with her. "You bet!"

"Good," Arnold said, putting his backpack down by Ida Lou's.

"Then y'all won't mind trying something I thought we might do."

"What's that, honey?" Ida Lou said, putting away her bottle of water and standing up near Arnold.

"Well, I was looking at some of those training videos we have at the office last week," Arnold said, "and I thought one of the things we have to do is build up more trust with each other. You know, trust in what the other one's going to do. That will help us when it comes to the board meeting, to put up a unified front to the other shareholders."

"That's a good idea, Arnold," Penny said, her voice sharp. "But how is that going to help us decide which plan to put in front of them? We can't do both, surely."

"No, you're right," Arnold said. "And we can discuss that later. Right now, I think it's more important to work on trusting each other. The rest will follow." He looked at them each in turn. "How about it?"

"What do we do?" Chuck asked.

"I thought we'd start with Penny and Ida Lou," Arnold said.

"Here's what you do." He walked to the edge of the ravine. "You stand here together, facing each other, then hold out your hands and hold on to each other. Then you each lean back as far as you can, and you trust the other person to hold on to you. It's kind of a variation on something I saw in those videos."

"Isn't that a bit dangerous?" Ida Lou asked, her voice rising in anxiety.

"No," Arnold said. "Look here, let me and Chuck demonstrate. Okay, Chuck?"

"Sure, Arnold." Chuck moved forward without hesitation. He joined Arnold at the edge of the ravine, and they turned toward each other, then extended their hands. Hands joined together, they began leaning backward.

"Oh, Arnold, be careful!" Ida Lou warned. "You're awful close to the edge!"

The men ignored her. The women could see the muscles in the men's arms straining, holding them together. Suddenly Arnold made a swaying motion, and Ida Lou uttered a small scream. Then the men stepped away from the edge, and Ida Lou relaxed.

"See," Arnold said, laughing. "Not dangerous at all. Now, why don't you and Penny try it?"

"How about I try it with Chuck first?" Ida Lou said with a big smile.

"Whatever!" Arnold said. He was in no hurry.

Ida Lou joined Chuck at the edge of the ravine, and they repeated the exercise. Ida Lou uttered small moans of fright the whole time, but Chuck held her with no problem.

"See, what did I tell you?" Arnold said, when they had stepped back from the edge.

"You're right, honey," Ida Lou said. "You always are."

Penny snorted.

"Then how about you and Penny trying it?" Arnold suggested.

"Let me catch my breath a minute, honey," Ida Lou complained. "I need some water. Why don't you and Penny have a go at it, then Penny and I'll try it?" She moved toward her backpack.

Arnold shrugged. "Okay. Come on, Penny." He moved to the edge, and Penny followed, a bit reluctantly.

"Give me your hands," Arnold said, stepping right to the edge. "Just don't look down, and you'll be fine." He clasped Penny's hands in his.

Penny closed her eyes tight and held on to Arnold for dear life as she felt him leaning back. They began to sway slightly.

Ida Lou screamed. "Snake!" She was holding her backpack in her hands, and she threw it away from her, right toward Arnold and Penny.

Startled, Arnold stepped backwards into nothingness. He pulled Penny with him. Their voices spiraling in terror, they plunged into the ravine.

Chuck stooped down to retrieve Ida Lou's backpack.

Ida Lou smiled and thanked him.

"Poor Arnold," she sighed. "What a tragedy. He just never was quite as clever as he thought he was." She hooked her arm through Chuck's. "I don't know if I ever told you this before, Chuck, but by the terms of my father's will, I'll be getting control of both Arnold and Penny's stock in McDuffie's. That means I'm totally in control now."

"You are a sly little devil," Chuck laughed, sweeping her up into a big hug. "You never got around to telling me that."

Ida Lou smiled up at him as he set her down again. They began their long trek back down the mountain. "Now, about that presidency we've been talking about. . ."

A Thief in Monkey Junction

by Deborah Adams

Macavity-winning short story writer Deborah Adams is the author of the Jesus Creek series, set in the small town of Jesus Creek (which seems suspiciously like her own town of Waverly, Tennessee). In setting a new standard for mystery series, she keeps the same town and tells her very Southern stories from the perspective of different townspeople. In this story, she introduces a different town and a different set of problems. Her latest novel, All the Dirty Cowards, *will be published by Silver Dagger Mysteries this fall.*

Miss Virginia Fryar's breakfast was all but spoiled by the sight of the corpse in her backyard. Miss Virginia spotted it as she crossed the dew-wet lawn, carrying a tray that contained her usual morning Danish and coffee.

In spite of reflexes slowed by seventy-three years of life experience, she managed to juggle the tray with its rattling china so that there was little spillage. Setting the tray on her new wrought-iron lawn table, she contemplated the situation.

The late gentleman sprawled across her annuals had a pickax planted firmly in the back of his head. Miss Virginia glared at the body, hoping it would disappear. When it didn't, she eased her delicate frame into a chair and pinched off nibble-sized bits of sweet pastry, popping them into her mouth and chewing thoughtfully.

Miss Virginia recognized the deceased, of course; he was—or had been—the earnest young fellow who'd knocked on her front door the previous day and introduced himself as Perry Hampton, a writer of regional histories.

"I've been told," he'd said, with a dimpled smile, "that you have some fascinating stories."

Miss Virginia's elderly heart beat that much faster and her wrinkled face flushed. These were sensations she'd given up for dead many years before, and now came this handsome boy with an impish grin implying that Miss Virginia might be as fascinating as her stories. Which she was, but no one had noticed for a good long time.

She'd invited him in for ice-cold lemonade and cookies fresh from the bakery, and the two of them had passed a pleasant afternoon together. "Oh, yes," she'd told him. "I've always lived here. Why, I remember when the only business hereabouts was a little filling station. Papa used to take me there to see the monkeys. Of course, back in those days . . ."

Miss Virginia went on to relate her well-worn family tales: the Yankee who'd died on the roof just before the fall of Fort Fisher; the mysterious Gray Man who had saved the Fryar home from a hurricane that leveled all the houses around; even the scandalous escapades of an ancestress who had taken up with Blackbeard the pirate then broken his heart.

Young Mr. Hampton beamed and said, "So there's more than one femme fatale in your family!"

Once upon a time such a comment would have been rewarded with fluttering lashes and an expertly cultivated blush. Miss Virginia was no longer susceptible to such blatant flattery, however much she enjoyed it, and so Mr. Hampton got only a grandmotherly smile for his trouble.

Miss Virginia had shown him family photographs and Bibles, and even taken him to the attic for a tour of six generations' worth of memories. Oohing and aahing over yellowed newspaper clippings that chronicled the lives of numerous Fryars, Mr. Hampton's attention was suddenly and sincerely drawn to a tattered sheet of paper that escaped Miss Virginia's grasp and fluttered to the dusty attic floor.

"What's this?" he asked, retrieving the wayward scrap.

Miss Virginia cocked her head for a closer look. "One of Grandpapa's doodles, I expect," she said. "He was quite artistic, wasn't he?"

"Indeed." Perry Hampton studied the sketched circles and squares and squiggly lines intently for a moment. Then, as if slapped in the face by reality's hand, his gaze returned to Miss Virginia.

"Now what is it you have there?" He indicated the packet of documents she'd pulled from the old sea chest in the corner.

"Well," said Miss Virginia, "my mother was a very thorough amateur genealogist. Would you like to hear about some of my maternal ancestors?"

For an hour or so, Miss Virginia regaled her visitor with tales of her many deceased relatives and the parts they'd played in the social and political scheme in and around Wilmington. Eventually even she grew tired of dead kin, and when her voice cracked from fatigue, Mr. Hampton hurriedly apologized for taking so much of her time.

As he stepped out the front door, Perry Hampton declared himself enchanted by Miss Virginia and her family, and begged an invitation to return, which Miss Virginia graciously offered.

She hadn't counted on his turning up in such an undignified and troublesome position, however.

A shift in the wind's direction caused Miss Virginia to twitch her nose in distaste. She sighed and rose to cross the tidy lawn, looking around to be sure no one traveling down Carolina Beach Road could see her through the ancient iron fence before she squatted by the body.

Running her still-graceful fingers lightly over the earthly remains of Perry Hampton, Miss Virginia found nothing of interest in his soiled tee shirt. (On his first visit, he'd been properly dressed for a social call. His current attire suggested to Miss Virginia that he'd not expected to encounter anyone of worth in her backyard.)

There was a fair amount of dried blood on the back of his head, and an odor she chose not to identify. In the right back pocket of his denims, Miss Virginia found a wallet containing the usual no-nonsense assortment most men carried—driver's license, social security card, and so forth—and five ten-dollar bills.

Miss Virginia replaced everything except forty dollars and tucked the wallet back into the pocket of Mr. Hampton's trousers. She ran her hand into his left back pocket and pulled out a folded piece of tattered and yellowed paper—Grandpapa's doodle!

Obviously Mr. Hampton was not the gentleman she'd assumed he was, for gentlemen didn't steal from elderly ladies—and there was no doubt in her mind that Perry Hampton had stolen the scrap, although she couldn't imagine why he'd want the thing. She wrapped the paper around the four ten-dollar bills and tucked the resulting packet inside her bodice.

As soon as she had carried her breakfast tray back into the house, rinsed the dishes, and set them to drain, Miss Virginia called the police. Then, not wanting to face what was to come without moral support, she made a second call to dear Captain

Lambdin, explaining her dilemma. Captain Lambdin, ever thoughtful and compassionate, promised to start for Miss Virginia's immediately.

"Now, ma'am," Officer Allen said after introducing himself and his partner, "you called in a report about a dead body?" His tone implied that he found this unlikely.

"Indeed." Miss Virginia eyed the two officers, wondering if they were old enough to cope with such a profound emergency. "You'll find him in the backyard. I'll be glad to show you the way if you'll give me a minute."

"Good morning, Miss Virginia!" Howard the mail carrier jiggled all over as he rocked up the steps. "Everything okay?"

"Yes, thank you, Howard." Miss Virginia held out her hand for the day's mail. "There was a difficulty, but the proper authorities have been notified. Now they're here and all is well."

She wasn't about to go into it further. Everyone knew that Howard gossiped like a biddy, and Miss Virginia fairly shuddered at the thought of being the subject of the inevitable speculation to come.

She retrieved her morning's mail, then stepped inside ahead of the openly amused police officers and slammed the door in Howard's face. "We can go through here," she said, leading the way to the back door.

"Let me make sure I've got this straight," said Officer Baxter, who was sandwiched between Miss Virginia and his partner. "There's a dead body in your yard?"

"That's correct," Miss Virginia told him. "Watch your step there. There's a bad spot in the linoleum. I really must have some work done on this kitchen."

Miss Virginia led the officers through the kitchen and out the back door. "He's right over there, in the impatiens." She pointed, lest the officers fail to notice Perry Hampton's lifeless form atop the crushed blooms.

"Holy sh—cow!" Officer Allen whispered. He stepped around Miss Virginia and made his way gingerly across the grass, followed closely by his partner.

"His name, I believe, is Perry Hampton." Miss Virginia held her ground by the back door.

"You knew him?" Officer Allen looked at her in disbelief. "Miss Virginia, you didn't . . .?"

"I didn't kill him, no," Miss Virginia replied. "I merely found him. As it happens, Mr. Hampton had visited me yesterday. He's a writer of regional history books and I was able to provide him with a few anecdotes for his research. I did invite him to visit again—I have quite a few stories left to tell—but I certainly expected him to call ahead!"

"We're gonna have to get the coroner out here, and somebody from homicide," said Officer Baxter. "Hell, I figured at most we'd find a dead dog."

"Watch your language," Officer Allen reminded him, with a nod toward Miss Virginia.

"I can see you have work to do here," she said. "Please make yourselves at home. I'll keep out of your way." With that she melted into the cool dark house, gathered her reading glasses from the desk, and sat down at the kitchen table to open her mail.

The letter on top bore a return address she recognized as that of a distant relative. Miss Virginia put it aside to answer later. She wasn't sure just which relative this was, but that was unimportant. The great disadvantage to living on the coast, she'd decided, was not the effect of salt air on one's skin or tourists or even hurricanes, but rather that one's landlocked kin tended to think of one as a very affordable vacation inn.

In her younger days, when Miss Virginia was still convinced of the basic goodness of her fellow human beings, she had welcomed the assorted cousins, nephews, and twice-removeds. They came in droves, like stampeding cattle, to graze on her food. They thundered through rooms she'd cleaned in their honor and left behind mildewed towels and enough sand to build a full-scale replica of Wrightsville Beach. They gorged themselves at the Oceanic and Buddy's Oyster Bar but never once invited their hostess along or even brought her a doggy bag!

Miss Virginia was tired of boorish relatives who never bothered to send a bread-and-butter note, much less remember her with a small token of affection. Still, it would have been unthinkable to deny family, so for the past few years Miss Virginia had resorted to what she thought of as Mannerly Self-Defense; she replied to all those invitation-begging notes with reports of her lingering and highly contagious illness. No one ever wrote or called to inquire after her health, but they didn't turn up on her doorstep, either.

Miss Virginia deemed her solution a success and made a mental note to add some new symptoms in her reply to these moochers.

The rest of the mail was far more exciting, and Miss Virginia's eyes lit up as she shuffled through it. Two bulb catalogs promised an afternoon of contented browsing. She had recently taken on the task of restoring the landscape around her home, and ordering dozens of exotic perennials gave her a tingle of excitement that she suspected bordered on sin. Fortunately she was too old to worry about her immortal soul, reasoning that, at her age, she could claim senility as an excuse for anything and even God would have to believe her.

The final envelope contained Miss Virginia's new credit card. She'd been preapproved for credit, 6.9 per cent interest for the first six months, and no annual fee. Technically, it was her late mother who'd been preapproved, but Miss Virginia was certain that Mama wouldn't mind that her only child indulged in a wee bit of honest forgery.

Papa had never approved of being indebted to man or business, and Miss Virginia had subscribed to the same philosophy most all her life. Finally, when the Frigidaire and the Buick ceased to function on the same day that Miss Virginia withdrew the last of her savings to buy groceries, she thought for the first time to question Papa's financial strategy.

Thanks to the generous offers of lending institutions across the country, she had since replaced the vital appliances, refurbished the sitting and dining rooms from the Sears catalog, added a central heating and cooling system to the house, and purchased a few unpretentious niceties for herself.

She'd been surprised how easily credit could be obtained. Why, it wasn't necessary to possess good character or assets, it wasn't even required that the credit card holder be either alive or human! So far Miss Virginia had collected four accounts in her own name, one in Papa's, one in Mama's, and one in the name of her dear departed cocker spaniel, Tillie.

No one had noticed that each signature on the many accounts was written in the same hand, and no one had ever asked if Tillie and her parents were alive and well. Miss Virginia certainly would have answered truthfully, for she prided herself on her honestly and high ethical code.

By using her seven (now eight! she noted with glee) credit cards equally, she had kept the monthly payments on each quite low. This allowed her to make the payment on one with her social security, and to use the handy checks provided by credit company A to pay the monthly fee due credit company B, and so on.

The charges for interest did not concern her; Miss Virginia planned to leave that problem for her thankless heirs to handle after her death. The total amount, if there was any justice in the world, would exactly equal what they would have spent on food and hotels during their visits to the ocean.

Officers Allen and Baxter were zealously guarding the body and awaiting the arrival of the coroner when Captain Lambdin finally knocked on the front door. Miss Virginia welcomed her longtime friend with a cup of still-fresh coffee and an offer of pastry.

"Gratefully accepted!" the captain boomed. "Love a Danish in the morning, what?"

Miss Virginia allowed him a peaceful moment in which to take the first bite, then explained the cause of her upset. "There's a dead man in the backyard," she said simply. "The police, of course, have the situation in hand, but all the same—"

"I should think!" the captain agreed. "How on earth did this happen?" He finished his pastry in two bites and gazed hopefully at the remaining sweets on the counter.

"The young man was bashed in the head with Papa's pickax," Miss Virginia explained. "I really should have kept that tool shed locked, but who could have predicted . . .?"

"Quite," the captain agreed. "And what was the deceased doing skulking around your yard at all hours? Just the sort of behavior that leads one to a bad end."

"All I can tell you for certain," she said cautiously, "is that the deceased is Perry Hampton, a writer of—"

"Regional histories!" the captain finished. "Thor's thunder!"

Miss Virginia cocked her head to one side, puzzled. "How long had you known him?"

"Met the lad yesterday, in fact," the captain replied. "Knocked on my door, introduced himself, and said I'd been recommended to him as 'a storehouse of history's facts and follies, a man who knows legends of the sea and the land, of neighbors and strangers.' Pretty speech, eh?"

"Mr. Hampton had many fine speeches, it seems," she said to the captain, "For all that, we are waiting for someone to tell us the young man is dead."

"Ah," replied the captain. "Let's proceed on the assumption that he *is* dead. Have you any thoughts on that?" It was typical of the captain to gather information before forming an opinion. He was a man who enjoyed knowing as much as he enjoyed sharing what he knew.

"Here is what I think," said Miss Virginia. "I believe that Perry Hampton came here looking for more than family history. I don't know what it could have been, but he filched one of Grandpapa's doodles from the attic, then came back here for . . . well, for what remains a mystery."

The two of them finished their coffee in contemplative silence, ignoring the bustle of activity in Miss Virginia's backyard. There would be no end to the rumors, she realized. She'd simply have to hold her head up high and ignore the curious gawkers. That was how Mama had handled the earlier scandal and eventually that had been all but forgotten. Except by Mama, who had created yet another tempest when she'd up and disappeared.

Miss Virginia's sleep was seldom deep or steady, and as might be expected, a body in one's yard did not entice slumber. It was nearing 2 a.m. when she gave up on Morpheus and descended the squeaky old stairs. Hot milk, she'd learned, was of no use at all; a bit of rum was much more effective.

Through the window above her chipped enamel sink, Miss Virginia spotted shadowy movement. "Honestly!" she muttered with disgust. She wrapped a house robe around her slender body before snapping on the yard light, then jerked the back door open and shouted, "Who do you think you are?"

Captain Lambdin spun around at the sound of her voice, dropping his heavy-duty flashlight right on the spot where Perry Hampton's body had lain that morning. "Apollo's apples!" he cried. "You took a good ten years off my life. What are you doing up at this hour?"

While her attic was cluttered and dusty, the same description could not be applied to Miss Virginia's mind, and she said as much to the captain. "The question, sir, is not why I am standing out in the damp air, but rather why are you traipsing about a crime scene? I hope you aren't planning to sell pictures to a tabloid or—"

"Certainly not!" the captain assured her. His pride was wounded; that much was clear. "Although I suppose an explanation is in order."

Miss Virginia felt this statement was throbbing with accuracy and therefore she made no comment, only waited to hear how Captain Lambdin would acquit himself.

"Fortunately, you see, Mr. Hampton came directly to me after his visit here. I say *fortunately* because I am the one person—yourself excluded—who is likely to remember the live oak." The captain gestured toward the far corner of Miss Virginia's backyard.

"The oak?" Miss Virginia asked. It had been a magnificent old tree, steadfast for decades. Half the county mourned its loss when the grand sentinel succumbed to Hurricane Hazel.

"Yes, the very one!" the captain exclaimed. "And so when Mr. Hampton showed me the map, I was able to decipher it based on the location of the tree!"

"Map?" Miss Virginia said. She thought it odd that Mr. Hampton hadn't asked her to look at any map, given that it directed one to her own home—if the captain were to be believed.

"Your grandfather's map!" he explained. "Young Hampton tried to pretend lack of interest, but it was clear he was after the treasure."

"Treasure?" Miss Virginia asked.

"I suppose Hampton thought he'd found Blackbeard's stash." The captain chuckled at such gullibility. "Trash and nonsense, and the lot of 'em fall for it! I expect what we'll find here is the missing Confederate payroll, hidden away by our loyal men who defended Fort Fisher till the end."

The captain's face beamed in the moonlight.

"What is it you're babbling about, Captain?"

"Your grandfather's map, of course. Imagine that boy uncovering it after all these years. And thank goodness he considered me a doddering old fool."

"Captain, if you're searching for treasure on the basis of that doodle dear Mr. Hampton filched, then *you* are a doddering old fool! Why, it's nothing but one of Grandpapa's silly notions."

"Ah . . . but . . ."

"Grandpapa was never a genius," Miss Virginia confessed, "and in his later years he was exceedingly confused. Why do you think we kept him in the attic? Of course, he didn't mind. Just happily whiled away the hours drawing blueprints for his proposed moon base. And maps to imaginary treasure."

She gave him a Look.

The captain's pudgy jowls quivered. "But . . . but . . . if there's no treasure, I killed him for nothing!"

"You killed Mr. Hampton?" Miss Virginia exclaimed. "Captain, what were you thinking? Have you no sense of propriety? Don't you realize what a murder in the neighborhood does to property value?"

"You *will* turn yourself in to the police, won't you, Captain?" Miss Virginia certainly hoped his fine upbringing and integrity would not fail now. Of all the difficult situations she'd weathered in her long life, this was the most daunting.

"Suppose there's nothing else to be done," the captain agreed. He placed a hand over his heart and shook his gray head. "All that digging. The great hopes. Fancied myself a hero of the Confederacy, saving the gold and what from a Yankee."

He steadied himself against the kitchen counter.

"I can see remorse setting in. Something medicinal?" Miss Virginia suggested, reaching into the cabinet for a bottle of rum. "We can both use a calming beverage."

Behind her the captain slid gently to his knees, then toppled face-forward onto the floor. Miss Virginia turned to find him sprawled facedown on the faded linoleum.

"Gracious!" she cried and hurried to the fallen gentleman's side.

Miss Virginia was familiar with CPR, even though she'd never practiced it on a human. The question she asked herself was not about breath-compression ratio, but rather about the wisdom of employing lifesaving techniques. If the captain were revived, he was doomed to face the humiliation of a murder conviction.

Miss Virginia thoughtfully and carefully weighed the options. By the time she'd made her decision, the captain was far beyond caring one way or the other.

Dawn was peaking when Miss Virginia made a complete tour of her house, making sure that all the doors and windows were securely locked. It had taken only a few minutes to cover the captain's body with a good percale sheet, a few more to pack a small suitcase, and she was ready to go. Two dead bodies in the space of a day—well, it was just more than a lady should have to bear. What years were left to her, Miss Virginia vowed, would be enjoyed in the company of strangers, in some foreign place such as Pittsburgh, where no one knew her or her scandalous history.

With her credit cards tucked safely in her purse, Miss Virginia was ready to leave. On the way out of town, she would mail the letter she'd written to those beggarly relatives, extending a warm invitation and suggesting they use the spare key hidden beneath the welcome mat. "Should I be away when you arrive," she'd written, "help yourselves to whatever you find in the kitchen."

Her Good Name

by Carolyn G. Hart

Carolyn Hart is the Oklahoma-based author of two very successful series. The first features Annie and Max Darling of South Carolina who have the enviable job of running a mystery bookstore. As the reader will find in this story, crime is not limited to the shelves in their store. The other series recounts the adventures of Henrie O, a retired journalist and very-much-active sleuth. Henrie's latest adventure is Death on the River Walk.

Annie Laurance Darling willed the telephone to ring.

But the undistinguished garden variety black desk telephone remained mute.

Dammit, Max could at least call!

The more she thought about it, the more she wished that she had gone. Of course, it was undeniably true that Ingrid wasn't available to mind the bookstore, but it wouldn't have been a disaster to close for a few days in November. She didn't let herself dwell on the fact that Saturday had been her best fall day ever. She'd sold cartons of the latest by Lia Matera, Nancy Pickard, and Sara Paretsky.

But there was Max, off to Patagonia and adventure. And here she was, stuck in her closed bookstore on a rainy Sunday afternoon with nothing to do but unpack books and wonder if Max had managed to spring Laurel. Even Laurel should have known better than to take up a collection for Amnesty International in the main hall of the justice ministry in Buenos Aires! A tiny worm of worry wriggled in Annie's mind. She knew, of course, that her husband was absolutely capable, totally in command, unflappable, imperturbable. Annie snapped the book shut and bounced to her feet. But who knew what kind of mess Laurel had—

The phone rang.

Annie leaped across the coffee area and grabbed up the extension behind the coffee bar. She didn't bother saying "Death on Demand." The finest mystery bookstore on the loveliest resort island off the coast of South Carolina wasn't open.

"Hello." She tried not to sound concerned. But maybe if she caught a jet tonight. . .

"Maxwell Darling." The tone was peremptory, cut-through-to-the-bone direct.

Annie's shoulders tensed. She immediately recognized the dry, crackly voice that rustled like old paper. What did the most aristocratic, imperious, absolutely impossible old hag in Chastain, South Carolina, want with Annie's husband?

"Miss Dora, how are you?" Annie could remember her manners even if some others could not. Annie could imagine the flicker of irritation in Miss Dora's reptilian black eyes.

"No time to waste. Get him to the phone."

"I wish I could," Annie snapped.

"Where is he?"

"Patagonia."

A thoughtful pause on the other end, then a sniff. "Laurel, no doubt." The old lady's voice rasped like a rattlesnake slithering across sand as she disgustedly pronounced the name of Max's mother.

"Of course," Annie groused. "And I darn well should have gone. He might need me. You know how dangerous it is in Argentina!"

A lengthening pause, freighted with emanations of chagrin, malevolence, and rapid thought.

"Well, I've no choice. You'll have to do. Meet me at 103 Bay Street, at four o'clock."

Annie's eyes narrowed with fury. Miss Dora was obviously the same old hag she'd always been. And just who the hell did she think she was, ordering Annie to—"A matter of honor." The phone banged into the receiver.

Annie stalked down the storm-dark street, the November rain spattering against her yellow slicker. Clumps of sodden leaves squished underfoot. The semi-tropical Carolina Low Country was not completely immune to winter, and days such as this presaged January and February. Annie felt another quiver of outrage. Why had she succumbed to the old bat? Why was she even now pushing open the gate and starting down the oyster-shell path to 103 Bay Street?

The aged, sandpapery voice sounded again in her mind: *A matter of honor.*

The sign to the right of the front door hung unevenly, one screw yielding to time and weather. An amateur had painted the outstretched, cupped hands, the thumbs overlarge, the palms lumpy. The legend was faded but decipherable: HELPING HANDS.

Annie was almost to the steps of the white frame cottage when she saw Miss Dora, standing regally beneath the low spreading limbs of an ancient live oak. Annie was accustomed to the gnomelike old lady's eccentric dress—nineteenth century bombazine dresses and hats Scarlett would have adored—but even Annie was impressed by the full gray cloak, the wide-brimmed crimson hat protecting shaggy silver hair, and the ivory walking stick planted firmly in front of high-topped, black leather shoes.

A welcoming smile tugged at Annie's lips, then slid to oblivion as Miss Dora scowled and thumped the stick. "You're late. The carillons play at four o'clock."

"Carillons?"

A vexed hiss. "Come, come. We'll go inside. Wanted you to hear the carillons. It's too neat, you know. The shot at precisely four o'clock. Know it must have been then. Otherwise somebody would have heard." Thumping stiffly to the door, Miss Dora scrabbled in her oversized crocheted receptacle. "No one's taking Constance's character into account. Not even her own brother! Blackening her name. A damnable lie." She jammed a black iron key into the lock.

As the door swung in, Miss Dora led the way, a tiny, limping figure. She clicked on the hall light, then regarded Annie with an obvious lack of enthusiasm. "Would do it myself," she muttered obscurely. "But sciatica. With the rain in November."

The parchment face, wrinkled with age, also held lines of pain. Annie almost felt sorry for her. Almost.

The stick swished through the air. "A dependency, of course. Small. Cramped. Cold floors in the winter. Constance had no use for her own creature comforts. Never gave them a thought. Sixty years she took care of the poor and the helpless here in Chastain. Everybody welcome here." The rasp muted to a whisper. "And may her murderer burn in hell."

The hair prickled on the back of Annie's neck. She looked around the dimly lit, linoleum-floored hallway. Worn straight chairs lined both sides of the hail. Near the door, turned sideways to allow passageway, sat a yellow pine desk.

The stick pointed at the desk. "Manned by volunteers, 10 a.m. to 4 p.m., every day but Sunday. Emma Louise Rammert yesterday. You'll talk to her."

The calm assumption irritated Annie. "Look, Miss Dora, you're taking a lot for granted. I only came over here because you hung up before I could say no. Now, I've got things on my mind—"

"Murder?"

Annie fervently hoped not. Surely Max and Laurel were safe! Max had promised to be careful. He was going to hire a mercenary, fly in to the secret airstrip, hijack Laurel from her captors (a potful of money always worked wonders, whatever the political persuasion), and fly right back out. Oh hell, she should have gone! What if he needed her?

"Oh, who knows?' Annie moaned.

"Don't be a weak sister," the old lady scolded. "Asinine to fret. He'll cope, despite his upbringing." A thoughtful pause. "Perhaps because of it. Any event, you've work to do here." The cane pointed at a closed door. "There's where it happened." The rasp was back, implacable, ice hard, vindictive.

The old lady, moving painfully, stumped to the door, threw it open, turned on the light.

"Her blood's still there. I'm on the Board. Gave instructions nothing to be disturbed."

Annie edged reluctantly into the room. She couldn't avoid seeing the desktop and the darkish brown splotches on the scattered sheets of paper. The low-beamed ceiling and rough-hewn unpainted board walls indicated an old, lean-to room. No rugs graced the warped floorboards. An unadorned wooden chair sat behind the scarred and nicked desk. In one corner, a small metal typewriter table held a Remington circa 1930.

Gloved fingers gripped Annie's elbow like talons. The walking stick pointed across the room.

"Her chair. That's the way the police found it."

Propelled by the viselike grip, Annie crossed the few feet to the desk and stared at the chair. The very unremarkable oak chair. Old, yes. But so was everything in the room. Old, with a slat missing.

The ivory stick clicked against the chair seat. "No cushion. Constance always sat on a cushion. Bad hip. Never complained, of course. Now, you tell me, Young Miss, where's that cushion? Right at four o'clock and no cushion!"

Annie was so busy wondering if Miss Dora had finally gone around the bend—which would be no surprise to her, that was for sure—that it took her a moment to realize she was *Young Miss.*

Annie slanted a sideways glance.

Miss Dora hunched over her stick now, her gloved hands tight on the knob. She stared at the empty chair, her lined face sorrowful. "Sixty years I knew Constance. Always doing good works. Didn't simper around with a pious whine or a holier-than-thou manner. Came here every day, and every day the poor in Chastain came to her for help. No electricity. They came here. Husband beat you, son stole your money, they came here. A sick child and no food. They came here."

A tear edged down the ancient sallow cheek. "I used to tell her, 'Constance, the world's full of sorrow. Always has been. Always will be. You're like the little Dutch boy at the dike.'"

The old lady reached out a gloved hand and gently touched the straight chair. Then the reptilian eyes glittered at Annie. "Know what Constance said?"

"No." The dark little room and the blood-spattered desk held no echo of its former tenant. This was just a cold and dreary place, touched by violence.

"Constance said, 'Why, Dora love, it's so simple: "I was hungry and you gave me meat, I was thirsty and you gave me drink. I was a stranger and you took me in. Naked, and you clothed me; I was sick, and you visited me; I was in prison and you came unto to me."'"

Beyond the dry whisper was an echo of a light and musical voice.

Miss Dora's stick cracked sharply against the wooden floor. She stared at Annie with dark and burning eyes. "A woman," she rasped, hard as stone against stone, "who saw her duty and did it. A woman who would never"—the cane struck—"never"—the cane struck—"never"—the cane struck—"quit the course."

Annie reached for the telephone, then yanked her hand back. Dammit, she dreaded making this call. Miss Dora had almost persuaded her yesterday afternoon. Indeed, Constance Bolton's life did argue against her death. Annie studied the picture Miss Dora had provided of a slender, white-haired woman in a navy silk dress. Constance Bolton looked serious, capable, and resourceful, a woman accustomed to facing problems and solving them. Her wide-set brown eyes were knowledgeable but not cynical; her mouth was firm but not unpleasant. Stalwart, steady, thoughtful—yes, she had obviously been all of these and more.

Yet—Annie glanced down at the poorly reproduced copy of the autopsy report on Constance Maude Bolton, white, female, age seventy-two—the answer seemed inescapable, however unpalatable to Constance Bolton's friends. Annie hated to destroy Miss Dora's faith. But facts were facts.

She dialed in a rush.

"Here."

"Miss Dora, this is Annie. I'm at the store. Listen, I got a copy of the autopsy report on Miss Bolton." Annie took a deep breath. "She was sick, Miss Dora. Dying. Bone cancer. She hadn't told many people, but she knew. Her doctor said so. And there were powder burns on her hand."

Gusts of polar wind could not have been colder than Miss Dora's initial silence. Then she growled, "Doesn't matter, Young Miss. Get to work. Think." The receiver thudded with the same force as the cane had struck the floor in that dingy office. "—never—never—never quit the course."

Annie slammed down her own receiver and glared at the phone, then jumped as it rang again.

"Death on Demand."

"The pillow," Miss Dora hissed. "The pillow, Young Miss. The pillow!" and the receiver banged again.

Annie jumped to her feet and paced across the coffee area. Agatha, the bookstore's elegant and imperious black cat, watched with sleepy amber eyes.

"Dammit, Agatha, the old bat's going to drive me crazy!"

Agatha yawned.

"Unreasonable, ill-tempered, stubborn"—Annie stopped at the coffee bar and reached for her mug—"but not stupid, Agatha."

As she drank the delicious French roast brew, Annie stroked Agatha's silky fur and thought about Miss Dora. Irascible, yes. Imperious, yes. Stupid, no. "And about as sentimental as an alligator. So if she knows in the depth of her creaky bones that Constance Bolton wasn't a quitter, where does that leave us?"

If it wasn't suicide, it had to be murder.

How could it be?

Powder burns on her right hand. Constance Bolton was right-handed. A contact wound—star-shaped to the right temple. Bone cancer. And the gun—Annie returned to her table and riffled through the police report—the gun had been identified by Miss Bolton's housekeeper, Sammie Calhoun. A .32 caliber revolver, it had belonged to Constance Bolton's late brother, Everett. It had, as long as Sammie worked there, lain in the bottom drawer of the walnut secretary in the library. She had seen the gun as recently as late last week.

The fact that this gun had been brought from Miss Constance's home was another pointer to suicide.

But if she had been murdered, the use of that gun sharply circumscribed the list of possible killers. It had to be someone with access to the bottom drawer of that walnut secretary.

Suicide? Or murder?

On the one hand, terminal illness, powder marks, a contact wound, a gun brought from home.

On the other hand, Miss Dora's unyielding faith in her friend's character and a missing pillow.

Annie sipped at her coffee. A pillow. There didn't seem to be any reason. She thumped the mug on the counter and clapped her hands. Of course, of course. It could only have been done with a pillow. And that explained why the murder had to occur at four o'clock when the carillons sounded. It wouldn't have been necessary to mask a single shot. But it was essential to mask two shots. The old devil was smart as hell!

Annie pictured the dingy room and Constance sitting behind the desk. A visitor—someone Constance knew well—surely standing beside the desk. The movement would have been snake-quick, a hand yanking the pistol from a pocket, pressing it against her temple and firing. That would have been the moment demanding swiftness, agility. Then it would have been a simple matter, edging the cushion from beneath her, pressing her hand against the gun, and firing into the pillow. That would assure the requisite powder residue on her hand. The stage then was set for suicide and it remained only to slip away, taking the pillow, and, once home, to wash with soap and water to remove the powder marks upon the killer's hand.

Oh yes, Annie could see it all, even hear the tiny click as the door closed, leaving death behind.

But was there anything to this picture? Was this interpretation an illusion born of Miss Dora's grief or the work of a clever killer?

Annie could hear the crackly voice and behind it the musical tones of a good woman.

I was hungry.

Nobody was going to get away with the murder of Constance

Bolton! Not if Annie could help it!

Annie focused on Miss Constance's last few days. If it was murder, why now? Why on Saturday, November 18?

The housekeeper agreed that Miss Constance was sick. "But she paid it no never mind. Miss Constance, she always kept on keepin' on. Even after Mr. Peter was killed in that car wreck up North, that broke her heart, but she never gave in. Howsoever, she was dragged down last week. Thursday night, she hardly pecked at her supper."

Annie made a mental note about Thursday.

She compiled a list of Miss Constance's visitors at Helping Hands the past week.

The visitors were all—to the volunteers—familiar names, familiar troubles, familiar sorrows.

Except on Thursday.

Portia Finley said energetically, "We did have someone new late that afternoon. A young man. Very thin. He looked ill. A Yankee. Wouldn't tell me what his trouble was, said he had to talk to Miss Constance personally. He wrote out a note and asked me to take it in to her. She read it and said she'd see him immediately. They were still in her office talking when I went home."

It took all of Annie's tact, but she finally persuaded Portia Finley to admit she'd read that short note on lined note pad paper. "I wanted to be sure it wasn't a threatening note. Or obscene."

"Oh, by all means," Annie said encouragingly.

"It didn't amount to much. Just said he was a friend of Peter's and Peter had told him to come and see her."

Friday's volunteer, Cindy Axton, reluctantly had nothing out of the ordinary to report.

But Saturday's volunteer, Emma Louise Rammert, had a sharp nose, inquisitive steel gray eyes, and a suspicious mind.

"Don't believe it was suicide. They could show me a video of it and I still wouldn't believe it. Oh yes, I know she was sick. But she never spoke of it. Certainly *that* wouldn't be motive enough. Not for Constance. But something upset her that morning and *I* think it was the paper. The *Clarion*. She was fine when she came in. Oh, serious enough. Looked somber. But not nervy. She went into her office. I came in just a moment later with the mail and she was staring down at the front page of the *Clarion* like it had bitten her. Besides, it seems a mighty odd coincidence that on the afternoon she was to die, she'd send me off early on what turned out to be a wild-goose chase. Supposed to be a woman with a sick child at the Happy Vale trailer court and there wasn't anybody of that name. So I think Constance sent me off so she could talk to somebody without me hearing. Otherwise, I'd've been there at four o'clock, just closing up."

Was the volunteer's absence engineered to make way for suicide—or for an appointment? Constance Bolton, had she planned to die, easily could have waited until the volunteer left for the day. But if she wanted to talk to someone without being overheard, what better place than her office at closing time.

Annie picked up a copy of the Saturday morning *Clarion* and took it to the Sip and Sup Coffee Shop on Main Street.

The lead story was about Arafat and another PLO peace offer. The Town Council had met to consider banning beer from the beach. Property owners attacked the newest beach nourishment tax proposals. Island merchants reported excellent holiday sales.

A story in the bottom right column was headed: AUTOPSY REVEALS CAR OCCUPANT MURDER VICTIM

> Beaufort County authorities announced today that a young man found in a burning car Thursday night, originally thought to have died in a one-car accident on a county road, was a victim of foul play.
>
> Despite extensive burns, the autopsy revealed the young man had died as a result of strangulation. The victim was approximately five feet seven inches tall, weighed 130 pounds, was Caucasian, and suffered from AIDS.
>
> The car was found by a passing motorist late Thursday evening on Culowee Road two miles south of the intersection with Jasper Road.
>
> The car was rented at the Savannah airport on Thursday by a Richard Davis of New York City.
>
> Authorities are seeking information about Davis's activities in Chastain. Anyone with any information about him is urged to contact Sheriff Chadwick Porter.

Annie called Miss Dora. "Tell me about Peter."

"Constance's grandnephew. His father, Morgan, was the son of

Everett, her older brother. Everett died about twenty years ago, not long after Morgan was killed in Vietnam. Peter inherited the plantations, but he never worked them. James did that. The other brother. But they went to Peter. The oldest son of the oldest son inherits in the Bolton family. Peter inherited from his mother, too. She was one of the Cinnamon Hill Morleys. Grieved herself into the grave when Morgan was killed in Vietnam. So Constance raised the boy, and James ran the plantations. When he was grown, Peter went to New York. A photographer. Didn't come back much. Then he was killed last winter. A car wreck."

One car wreck had masked murder.

Had another?

Annie wished for Max as she made one phone call after another, but she knew how to do it. When it became clear that Peter Bolton didn't die in a car wreck—despite that information in his obituary, which had been supplied by his great-uncle James—she redoubled her efforts. She found Peter's address, his telephone number, and the small magazine where his last photograph had been published and talked to the managing editor.

But Peter wasn't murdered.

Peter died in a New York hospital of AIDS.

And Richard Davis had been dying of AIDS before he was strangled and left in a burning car in Beaufort County, South Carolina.

Richard's note to Constance Bolton claimed he was a friend of Peter's. More than a friend?

Maggie Sutton had the apartment above Richard's in an old Brooklyn brownstone.

Her voice on the telephone was clipped and unfriendly. "You want to know anything about Richard Davis, you ask—"

Before she could hang up, destroy Annie's link to Richard and through him to Peter, Annie interrupted quickly. "Richard's dead. Murdered. Please talk to me. I want to find his murderer.

It took a lot of explaining, then Maggie Sutton said simply, "Poor Richie."

"Did you know Richard was coming to South Carolina?"

"Yes. He was sick—"

"I know."

"—and they fired him. They aren't supposed to, but they do it anyway. Before most people with AIDS can appeal, file a lawsuit, they're dead. Richie was almost out of money. His insurance was gone. They only want to insure healthy people, you know. Nobody with real health problems can get insurance. Richie and Peter lived downstairs from me. Nice guys." She paused, repeated forcefully: "Nice guys." A sigh. "It's all so grim. Richie took care of Peter. He died last winter. Last week, Richie told me he was going on a trip and he asked me to feed their cat, Big Boy, while he was gone. Richie said Peter had written a will before he died, leaving everything to Richie, but he didn't do anything about it then. I mean, he didn't want Peter's money. But now he was desperate. And he thought, maybe if he went down there, showed the will to the family . . ." Her voice trailed off.

The family.

The last surviving member of the family stood with his head bowed, his freshly shaved face impassive, his hands clasped loosely behind his back as mourners dispersed at the conclusion of the graveside service on Tuesday afternoon. A dark-suited employee of the funeral home held a black umbrella to shield James Caldwell Bolton from the rain.

The day and James Bolton were a study in grays, the metallic gray of Constance Bolton's casket, resting over the dark pit of her grave, the steel gray of Bolton's pin-stripe suit, the soft gray of weathered stones, the misty gray of the weeping sky, the silver gray of Miss Dora's rain cape, the flinty gray of the stubby palmettos' bark, the ash gray of the rector's grizzled hair.

Annie huddled beneath the outspread limbs of a live oak, a thick wool scarf knotted at her throat, her raincoat collar upturned. Rain splashed softly against gravestones as mourners came forth to shake Bolton's hand and murmur condolences.

Annie stared at the man who had inherited the Bolton and Morley family plantations.

James Bolton didn't look like a murderer.

He looked—as indeed he was—like a substantial and respectable and wealthy member of the community. There was a resemblance to his dead sister, brown eyes, white hair, a firm chin. But where Constance's face was memorable for its calm pity and gentle concern, there was an intolerant and arrogant quality to his stolid burgher's face.

As the last of Miss Constance's friends trod away across the spongy ground of the graveyard, Annie left the oyster-shell path. Skirting behind a stand of pines, she moved into the oldest part of the cemetery, stopping in the shadow of a crumbling mausoleum some twenty-five yards distant from the new grave site.

Bolton waved away the undertaker with the umbrella.

Had any of the mourners looked back, they would have glimpsed his figure, head again bowed, lingering for a last moment with his sister.

But Annie could see his face. It was for a singular, heart-stopping instant transformed. His lips curved up in satisfaction.

Annie knew, as clearly as if he'd shouted, that James Bolton was exulting. A murderer twice over, safe, secure, successful. A rich and powerful man.

"James."

His face reformed into sad repose as he turned toward Miss Dora.

The old lady took her time, each step obviously a painful task.

Annie slipped free of her raincoat, unfurled a navy umbrella—Sammie Calhoun had quite willingly given her mistress's umbrella to Miss Dora—and undid the scarf covering the curly white wig.

Miss Dora, her wizened face contorted in a worried frown, peered up at James Bolton.

"James, I've had the oddest"—the raspy voice wavered—"communication. The ouija board. Last night. Never been a believer in that sort—"

"James . . ." Annie held a high, light, musical tone, then let her voice waver and drop like the sigh of a winter wind. In her own ears, it didn't sound enough like the recorded interview the local radio station had found of Constance Bolton speaking out in a League of Women Voters forum on abortion. She tried again, a little louder. "James . . ."

It must have been better than she'd thought.

James Bolton's head whipped around, seeking out the sound. His face was suddenly gray, too, the color of old putty.

Annie glided from behind the cover the mausoleum, one hand outstretched. "James . . ." Then she backed away, just as a dimly seen figure might drift forth, then disappear. Once out of Bolton's sight, she darted in a crouch from stone to stone until she gained the street. Quickly pulling on the scarf and raincoat, she hurried to Miss Dora's.

"Heh. Heh. Heh." Miss Dora's satisfied cackle would chill the Devil. She poured a cup of steaming tea.

Annie sneezed. The heat against her fingers helped a little, but she didn't feel that her bones would ever warm from the graveyard cold.

Miss Dora glowered. "No time to flag. Young people today too puny."

"I'm fine," Annie retorted crisply and knew she was catching a cold. But she couldn't afford to sneeze tonight. She and Miss Dora weren't finished with James Bolton.

"Scared him to death," Miss Dora gloated. "He looked like bleached bones. Her raisin-dark eyes glittered. "Mouth open, whites of his eyes big as a platter. And when I pretended I hadn't seen or heard a thing, thought he was going to faint. That's when I told him about the ouija message: Pillow. Find pillow." She cackled again.

Annie took a big gulp of tea and voiced her concern. "Miss Dora, how can we be sure he didn't destroy the pillow?"

Miss Dora's disdainful look infuriated Annie.

"Classical education taught people how to think!" the old lady muttered. "Crystal clear, Young Miss. He dared not leave it behind. He had to take it with him. Then what? He couldn't keep in his house. Old Beulah Willen's his housekeeper. Not a single spot safe from her eyes. So, not hidden in his house. No incinerators permitted in the city. Besides it's too bulky to burn well. Joe Bill Tompkins drives James. So, not in his car. I talked here and there. He's not been out to any of the plantations since Constance died. So where is it? Somewhere not too far, Young Miss." Another malicious cackle. "James thinks he's so smart. We'll see, won't we?"

The rain had eased to a drizzle. Annie was warm enough. A black wool cap, thermal underwear, a rainproof jacket over a wool sweater, rainproof pants, sturdy black Reeboks. The nylon hose over her face made it hard to breathe, but it sure kept her toasty. From her vantage point she could see both the front and rear doors to James Bolton's house. She had taken up her station at nine-thirty. Miss Dora was to make her phone call at nine-thirty five and play the recording Annie had made and remade until Annie's whispered "James . . . I'm . . . coming . . . for . . . the . . . pillow" sounded sufficiently like Constance Bolton to satisfy Miss Dora.

The back door opened at nine-forty. James Bolton, too, was dressed for night in dark clothing. He paused on the top step and looked fearfully around, then hurried to the garage.

Annie smiled grimly.

He reappeared in only a moment, carrying a spade.

Annie followed him across the Bolton property and through a dank and dripping woods. She stepped softly along the path, keeping his shaded flashlight in view, stopping when he stopped, moving when he moved.

Whoo-oo-ooo-ooo.

Annie's heart somersaulted and she gasped for breath.

Bolton cowered by a live oak.

Annie wasn't sure which one of them the owl had frightened the most.

Iron hinges squealed, and Bolton stepped through the opened gate to the old graveyard, leaving the gate ajar. He moved more cautiously now, and the beam from his flashlight poked jerkily into shadowy pockets.

Did he fear that his dead sister awaited him?

Annie tiptoed, scarcely daring to breathe. One hand slipped into her jacket pocket and closed around the sausage-thick canister of mace, relic of the days when she lived in New York. The other hand touched the Leica which hung from a strap around her neck.

Bolton stopped twice to listen.

Annie crouched behind gravestones and waited.

When he reached the oldest section of the cemetery, he moved more boldly, confident now that he was unobserved. He walked directly to a winged angel atop a marble pedestal, stepped five paces to his right, and used the shovel to sweep away a mound of leaves.

Annie was willing to bet the earth beneath those leaves had been recently loosened.

He shoveled quickly but placed the heaps of moist sandy dirt in a neat pile to one side.

Annie crept closer and closer, the Leica in hand.

She was not more than ten feet away and ready when he reached down and lifted up a soggy newspaper-wrapped oblong.

The flash illuminated the graveyard with its brief brilliant light, capturing forever and always the stricken face of James Bolton.

He made a noise deep in his throat. Wielding the shovel, he lunged blindly toward the source of light. Annie danced sideways to evade him. Now the canister of mace came out, and as he flailed the shovel and it crashed against a gravestone, Annie pressed the trigger and mace spewed in a noisome mist.

Annie held her breath, darted close enough to grab up the sodden oblong where he had dropped it, paused just long enough—she couldn't resist it—to moan, "Jaaammees," then she ran faster than she'd ever managed in a 10 K, leaping graves like a fox over water hazards.

The headlines in next morning's *Clarion* told it all: JAMES BARTON CHARGED IN MURDER OF SISTER.

Miss Dora rattled the newspaper with satisfaction then poured Annie another cup of coffee. The old lady's raisin-dark eyes glittered. "We showed him, didn't we? Saved Constance's good name."

For once—and it was such an odd feeling—Annie felt total rapport with the ill-tempered, opinionated, impossible creature awaiting her answer.

Annie grinned. "Miss Dora, we sure as hell did!"

Annie bought her own copy of the newspaper before she took the ferry back to the island. She wanted to have it to show to Max. Especially since his telegram had arrived last night: "Retrieval accomplished. No fireworks. Boring, actually. Only action caused by fleas Laurel picked up in jail. Plus tourista tummy (me). Home soon. But not soon enough. Love, Max."

Swap Meet

by Beverly Taylor Herald

The identical twin sister of Barbara Taylor McCafferty and the co-author of the Nan and Bert Tatum series, Beverly calls Slaughters, Kentucky, home. Though the twins may look alike, you'll find their stories vary in most aspects except both are compelling fiction.

You can never tell what a crazy person is going to do. I suppose that pretty much goes without saying.

And it wasn't as if all of her friends didn't know Carla was going crazy, either. We all did know. At least, we all knew that if Carla had not exactly arrived at crazy, she'd certainly taken the on ramp there, beginning that Saturday night at the weekend swap meet.

Of course, as I remember it, Carla wasn't the only one who'd gone a little nuts that night.

My own heart had dropped to my knees when I saw the sheriff and his deputy push through the front double glass doors of the abandoned hardware store that housed the swap meet. That queasy feeling that I had when I saw the two of them come in wasn't because having the police at the swap meet was all that unusual. They always stopped by—although not on official business, of course. Just about everyone in the county stops in at the swap meet sometime during the weekend. Our swap meet is what other parts of the country call a flea market or a rummage sale. Folks come by to trade knives or buy some trifle or just shoot the breeze. There just isn't much else to do in a little town like Bittersweet, Tennessee.

I noticed Sheriff Lucius and Deputy Bernard when they walked in because they were both wearing The Look. Lucius's bland face looked like whatever he was thinking about was pulling his face down with the weight of it. And Bernard's jaw muscles were working; and he wasn't looking anybody straight in the eye. The last time I'd seen The Look on their faces was five years ago, when they strolled up my front sidewalk to tell me about my husband, Ben. When Ben's big rig had flipped over on Interstate 60 and then caught fire. Before that day, the word "widow" had just meant a spider to me.

I realized that I was actually holding my breath as the deputies in their neat tan uniforms turned right and headed my way. Of course, the first thing that my mind leaped to was my two kids, away at college. A car accident? The two men marched right past me, though, and kept on walking, past the first three booths in the aisle—my "Bette's Bakerie" is flanked on either side by "Morene's Markdowns" and "Eunice's Antiques." They headed straight for "Carla's Crafts."

We four girls—I reckon I should say women—Morene, Eunice, Carla and I—had all hung around together in high school about a million years back. Back in high school, we'd all had our claims to fame. Carla was the "pretty one", Morene the "sexy one", and Eunice the "plain one." I reckon I was the "brainy one." After high school, we'd all done the usual—married whoever was handy, and some of us had even had the usual allotment of kids. Twenty years later, all those kids were pretty nigh grown up, and the four of us had time on our hands.

So we'd taken these swap meet booths—nothing fancy—just a couple or three card tables set up with various things to sell. Certainly, nothing to draw cops to our booths.

I threw a worried look over at Morene and Eunice, as we watched Carla glance up at the two policemen who'd stopped in front of her. She was hot-gluing a drooping bow on one of her hand-painted plywood cats.

"Why, Lucius, Bernard—what are you two boys looking so long-faced about?" she asked, stooping to fluff the tissue bow.

"Yeah, Lucius, what's wrong?" Morene piped up. Morene, being Morene, had taken one gander at the two men and stomped over there after them, her long dark hair trailing behind her and her high heels clipping on the linoleum. (Morene would wear high heels to bowl.)

On the other side of me, Eunice straightened her eyeglasses and walked down there, too. I preferred to listen from where I was.

"Carla," Lucius said, "you best be sitting yourself down."

Carla stopped fluffing then and took a long look at the men. "What on earth is going on, Bernard? Lucius?" Carla asked, her clear blue eyes bouncing back and forth between the policemen. Bernard was studying his shiny black shoes. Not a good sign.

"It's . . . um. . . really bad news, Carla, "Lucius said. Then his words came out in a sudden rush. "I'm awful sorry to have to tell you this, Carla, but Robert's passed on to his eternal reward."

A gasp broke the stillness, before I realized it had come from me. Oh my God. On either side of Carla, Morene and Eunice put their hands to their mouths, their eyes wide.

But Carla herself wasn't having any. She just frowned, looking confused. She stared at Lucius so long that I guess he thought he should be more clear.

"Carla, your husband is dead," Lucius said flatly.

"Don't be silly," Carla said. "That can't be so." Her blonde curls bounced as she shook her head. "You've made a mistake, Lucius. Robert's gone over to the library. He was just in here a couple of hours ago. Ask them," she said, gesturing toward Morene, Eunice, and me with one sweep of her arm. "Why, Robert told me right then I'd better plan on getting home before him. As if I cared. He was going off to do some silly old research at the Bittersweet Public Library. Looking up some old stupid things about some old stupid stuff." Robert was the history teacher out at the community college, and Carla did not share his enthusiasm for higher learning.

I noticed that when Carla mentioned the word *library*, Deputy Bernard blinked a couple of times and looked away.

"Carla, it *is* your husband," Deputy Lucius said, patient-like, but with a little more force this time. "I identified him myself. The maid who found Robert's body called us. She read his name on his driver's license."

That must've done it, because Carla dropped like an anvil then, sitting down hard on one of her hand-painted pillows. Knowing how fastidious Robert was, Carla must've figured he'd had to have been dead to let anybody go through his trousers to get his license.

I felt as if I could hardly feel my feet, as I walked down the aisle toward Carla. Tears welled in my eyes.

"There, there, honey." Eunice put an arm around Carla's shoulders, while Morene's eyes began to stream mascara. "I'm right here for you," whispered Morene hoarsely, pushing Eunice's arm aside and taking Carla's hand in hers. Eunice removed her eyeglasses with her other hand and pressed two fingers to her eyes, as if she could hold back her tears. From behind, I rubbed Carla's back, not even bothering to wipe away the tears running down my own face.

Carla stared dry-eyed straight ahead at absolutely nothing.

"It was probably a stroke, the county coroner says," Lucius added. "Real sudden. You can take comfort that Robert didn't suffer."

"I'll say he didn't," Bernard added. I turned to look at him. He seemed to be smirking some.

Carla didn't seem to notice. "Well, well," she said and then stared at nothing some more. "Well, then," she said again. She turned around and looked back at me. "I reckon I'm a widow, then. Just like you, Bette."

Tact never had been a virtue of Carla's. Then she gave herself a little shake, looking up at the deputy. "Well, I guess I need to go see to him," Carla said, standing up. Then she frowned again. "What was that you said, a *maid* found Robert? What's a maid doing at the library?"

Lucius looked a bit pained right then. "Um . . . Carla, Robert wasn't found at no library."

Both men exchanged looks and cleared their throats in unison. I wondered if this particular news might be even more difficult to deliver than the first.

"Well, where is Robert then?" asked Carla, sounding as if she thought they might've misplaced him.

Lucius took a deep breath and issued another rapid news flash. "Robert's body was found, lying on a bed in a motel outside of town."

There was a shocked silence while that news sunk in.

"He was fully clothed," Lucius added. Evidently, he thought that Robert being found with all his clothes on might be a comfort to Carla.

Even so, Morene's and Eunice's mouths had formed little *O*s. Carla, though, just did what she did best—she frowned and looked confused.

"Well, that can't be," Carla said, her eyebrows knitting together. "Goodness, Lucius. You gave me such a scare. That can't be my Robert. Robert doesn't go to motels. He has a perfectly nice home."

Morene, Eunice, and I exchanged looks. I could tell they were thinking what I was, and could easily figure out what Robert might be doing in a motel. Carla, unfortunately, was a little slow on the uptake.

Lucius was a little firmer this time. "Carla, it *IS* Robert. I told you that. I'm sorry to have to tell you this, but he had only one motel key on his person. The other key is missing. No evidence anyone else was in the room. Yet. He was obviously waiting for someone."

Morene was the first one to react. She jumped in to give Carla an easy out. "Wasn't Robert expecting you, Carla? That was it, wasn't it? Didn't Robert give you his motel room key when he came by earlier?" She nodded encouragingly, begging Carla with her eyes to say *yes*.

The rest of us caught on real quick. "Sure, Carla, that's it," I said, patting Carla's shoulder like I was encouraging a puppy to speak. "Tell Lucius about your romantic getaway."

"You two were planning on doing a little second-honeymooning, weren't you, Carla, honey?" Eunice asked, her plain face a bright pink behind her glasses.

All of us all but winked at Carla.

Carla stared. "Are you all nuts? Me second-honeymooning with Robert? That's just stupid. That'd be like you, Morene," Carla turned to look at her, "second-honeymooning with Mike."

Carla often made up for her lack of tact by being very insensitive. Still, it wasn't exactly a secret that Morene's marriage to Mike had been on shaky ground for quite some time—mostly because Morene referred to Mike all the time as "the slug I married."

"Or it would be like Beau," Carla turned to Eunice, "taking you away for a romantic getaway. Can you imagine?"

Eunice colored slightly and said nothing. Rumors of her husband Beau's infidelity had been making the rounds for years.

"Romantic getaway," Carla repeated. "Why, that's just plain silly." She looked at each of us, bewildered. Then her blue eyes slowly narrowed as she finally made the connection. She turned to the two deputies. "Which motel was Robert at?"

Lucius cleared his throat. "The Morning Glory."

"The Morning Glory!" Carla exclaimed. "Why, everyone knows that folks go there for only one thing. Why, I hear-tell they run those nasty X-rated movies, and—"

"You got that right, the TV was playing when we come in the room, and there was old Robert—" piped up Bernard. His voice trailed off when Lucius turned to glare at him.

I glanced at Morene and Eunice, and knew they were thinking the same thing. Picturing scholarly Robert sitting up in bed, alertly watching a dirty movie, probably for the first time in his life. And then, quietly having a little fatal stroke.

Carla was on her feet now, her fists clenched. "Well, now I know for sure that it isn't Robert. He . . . he wouldn't do that to me. He wouldn't dare!"

I could tell from the looks on Morene's and Eunice's faces that they weren't that sure. Watching Carla, I have to admit I was surprised by her reaction. I wondered why she was so all-fired upset. She seemed more upset at her husband's going to a motel than at his up and dying. After all, hadn't Carla whispered to us, giggling, about her own one-night stands with some hunk or other who was passing through town?

I couldn't believe Carla would even mind. For the last several years, she hadn't even seemed to like Robert very much. "Boring, boring, boring," she'd sing whenever her husband's name came up—and Carla would never be the one who mentioned him. She and Morene would both go on and on about what sorry husbands they had, while Eunice complained about being neglected by hers. I'd always felt cheated somehow—Ben and I had adored each other; and, wouldn't you know it, I was the one who didn't have my man around anymore.

"Oh, no, this just can't be true," Carla said, her eyes going from Morene to Eunice, as if looking for confirmation. Her gaze came to me. I thought she could read it in my face. Because bad things did happen—right out of the blue, too. Oh, yeah, they sure did. I absolutely ached for her right then, and for me, too.

Carla turned back to Sheriff Lucius and stomped her foot. "I still say your dead guy isn't Robert."

But, of course, he was.

Four days later, by the time Robert's funeral rolled around, Carla had pretty much decided Robert really was dead, and she'd switched to an entirely different concern.

At the Bittersweet United Methodist Church, with the air sickeningly sweet with about a million flowers, I sat with Carla in the front pew, Robert's closed casket a few feet in front of us. I was sitting with her because she really didn't have any family to speak of. Carla and Robert had been the one couple among us who'd had no children—she had said more than once that she wasn't going to get stretch marks all over her body just to satisfy Robert's ego in producing an heir. Looking at his closed casket, I couldn't help it—my eyes kept filling with tears. Robert had been such a very nice man. I'd never heard him say an unkind word to anybody.

Behind us, Morene sat, already sniffing, while her husband, Mike, sat next to her, already snoring. When they'd married, high school basketball star Mike had been six-five and about 185. Now an insurance salesman, he could only be weighed by livestock scales, according to Morene. Poor Mike did seem to fall asleep anywhere he had to sit for more than five minutes. But he was a good provider and Morene had never had to work outside the home—at least, that's what she kept saying. Still, it was no wonder that Morene spent so much time away on buying trips for her swap meet booth. She always seemed to be going out of town. In fact, she'd just returned from one of her trips, a couple of days before.

On the other side of Carla, Eunice sat with her own husband, Beau, the high school football coach. Handsome Coach Beau had barely made it back in time for the funeral, returning to town from one of his own recruiting trips. Even here—at a funeral, of all things—Coach Beau sported a short sleeve T-shirt that emphasized his bulging biceps. At least, his T-shirt was black.

Every now and then, Morene would pat Carla's shoulder, and Eunice, right on cue, would pat the other shoulder, dabbing a Kleenex beneath her glasses.

Dry-eyed, Carla frowned and looked confused as Brother Miller began his remarks. "Friends and loved ones of this fine man," he began, "we're here to say good-bye. Cut down in the prime of his life, Robert was—"

"—playing around on me!" Carla muttered to no one in particular, a shrill, breathy sound that had to have been heard through the entire church. "Can you imagine? Robert was playing around on me!"

Brother Miller glanced at Carla uneasily and continued on. "A good provider, a community leader, and a family man of the highest ideals—"

"Oh, bull doo-doo!" Carla hissed.

Brother Miller gaped at her and then seemed to lose his place in his notes. "Cut down in the prime of his life, Robert was . . . I mean, this fine man will be missed by so many—"

"Especially by HER," Carla snarled. "Whoever that little hussy was." She turned around to face Morene in the pew behind her. "How could Robert do this to me?" she asked. "Especially when he was so . . . so . . ."

"Boring?" Morene offered, but Carla had gotten to her real point.

"It had to have been HER," Carla said. "That hussy did it. SHE made him do this to me. So who is she?" Carla whispered through clenched teeth. "Who was the woman Robert was waiting for in that horrible, horrible motel?"

"Oh, Carla," Eunice whispered, stifling a sob as she patted a tissue to her lips. "You mustn't torture yourself." Her cheeks were a bright pink.

"Eunice is right, Carla," I whispered, "What does it matter now? Robert is dead and gone. This kind of thinking can just kill you." I instantly regretted my choice of words.

"Kill!" Carla hissed. "KILL! We'll see about *kill* if I find out who that home-wrecker is! I'll show her!" She leaped to her feet, pointing a finger at the minister like he was the guilty party. His eulogy had dwindled off, pretty much due to a lack of interest, as the entire church strained to listen to Carla's ranting.

"Just you wait, Reverend," Carla announced. "I found Robert's handgun in his underwear drawer. And I'll show that thieving hussy—I'll show that whore, you just wait. You'll be having yourself another funeral, Brother Miller, when I find out who she is. And don't you think I won't!"

Brother Miller's eyes bugged. Apparently, death threats didn't happen too often at his funeral services. Or the use of the word *whore*.

"Carla's just distraught," I announced, yanking at her arm, trying to pull her back down. "She doesn't know what she's saying."

"I do so know what I'm saying!" Carla jerked away from me and turned around toward the entire congregation, lifting her arms as if she were about to lead a choir. "Doesn't anyone here know who that bitch is?"

Since everyone in Bittersweet had heard what happened, there was no question about whom Carla meant. There was a flurry of murmured *no*s and shaking heads, and then everybody in the pews around us looked at her own lap. I snagged Carla's arm, trying to drag her down again. Eunice grabbed for the other arm.

"You mean no one saw them together?" Carla demanded, flouncing away from us. She marched up to the pulpit in front of Robert's coffin. "You expect me to believe that? In THIS town? What do you take me for?" She leaned toward Brother Miller, putting her hands flat on the coffin lid. "Okay, Reverend, who is she? Give me a name." Carla got only an embarrassed head shake in reply. Brother Miller's eyes were huge in his crimson face.

She looked at the organist and then at the choir. "Somebody tell me who this bitch is!" Carla yelled. She kept on yelling the question over and over, turning toward the sections of pews around her. It was when she started down the aisle to question the ushers that we three girls rushed after her. Lifting her by the elbows, we carried her out.

"WHO IN HELL IS SHE?" Carla bellowed to the congregation as we sailed her through the front doors.

Weeks later, Carla was still asking that same question. She was missing one swap meet after another, too. Rumor had it that she was spending her spare time phoning every household in the county to see if anyone had ever seen Robert with another woman. According to Eunice, who'd heard it from Morene, who'd heard it from Carla herself, Carla was working her way through the white pages and was already on the *H*s.

"It's just plain crazy," Eunice said, sitting at a table in her booth. It had been six weeks since Robert's funeral, but we were still talking about little else. "Nuts. Bonkers. Cuckoo." Eunice's eyeglasses caught the light as she made out a price tag for one of her figurines. "She's gone off the deep end. She needs professional help. One thing for sure, though, we can't force Carla to go to a doctor for some help unless she wants to."

"A doctor?" Morene asked, sewing a button on one of her discounted dresses. "Oh, Eunice, you're so dumb. Carla doesn't need a doctor; she needs a shrink."

Eunice colored slightly. "That's what I meant," she said, very low.

"That's not what you said," Morene said.

It seemed a good time to interrupt. "I can't believe Carla's carrying on so," I said, "about who the other woman is." I tucked fresh brownies into a clear cellophane package. "Carla always acted as if she didn't care two cents about Robert. And she was always having affairs herself."

"Doesn't everybody?" asked Morene, snipping a thread.

Eunice blushed again. "Carla did act like she didn't much care about Robert when he was alive."

Morene shrugged, tossing her dark hair over one shoulder. "A lot you know, Eunice. Of course, Carla didn't want Robert. But she sure as hell didn't want anyone else to take him from her, either." Her tone was matter-of-fact. "Not until she was ready to give him up." She glanced over at me, her eyes searching. "Do you think that Carla's crazy enough to kill this other woman if she found out who she is?"

"Oh, surely not," Eunice said. "Carla's just, you know, acting out. It's only because she's so hurt."

Morene threw a look of contempt at Eunice. "Eunice, I wasn't asking you. I was asking Bette. What do you think, Bette?"

I shook my head. "I don't know. That possibility does worry me some—she's certainly been talking nutty enough lately. If only we could get Carla's mind off Robert and his affair—"

"With all those reminders of Robert throughout her house?" Eunice said. "Goodness, she's got an absolute shrine to him over there. I don't know how Carla can ever process her grief with all that stuff still lying around."

"Process? You make it sound like bologna," Morene muttered.

"I know what Eunice means," I said, "You do some really stupid things when you lose somebody, but you do get through it. You go on. I know I felt a whole lot better when I finally gave Ben's things away to charity."

"That's it," Eunice said. "We've got to get Carla to finally let it go. And we can start by getting her to go through her closets and finally get rid of Robert's things."

"You know, that's a very good idea," Morene said slowly.

Surprised, I turned to look at her. Morene had never said Eunice had a good idea since grade school.

"Then it's settled," Eunice said. "I'll go talk to her."

"No!" Morene said quickly. "I mean, let me do it. I can leave the swap meet early today and see what I can do," she added.

I stared. It was certainly out of character for Morene to offer to do something like this. But it was also true that Morene was probably the best one to go. I wasn't sure I could go through a dead man's clothes again; and Eunice, with her submissive ways, might not be forceful enough to convince Carla to do it.

As it turned out, Morene must've been a woman of powerful persuasion, because on Sunday afternoon when I walked into the swap meet, Carla was back in her booth, fluffing bows and rearranging plywood chickens and pigs. Sure, she was bustling around, like maybe she had a lot of pent-up energy; but, unbelievably, she was there.

I couldn't help staring. Goodness, was that actual humming Carla was doing?

I walked over to Morene's booth, where she was hanging up some dresses on a rack. "What on earth did you say to Carla?" I asked.

Morene shrugged. "I just didn't take no for an answer. We went through Robert's closet and books and stuff together, and we sorted them. Then we packaged them all up and took them to the Salvation Army dumpster. Mission accomplished."

I grinned. I really had to hand it to her. As I walked back to my own booth, though, I happened to glance over at Eunice's area. White lace cloths still covered her locked cases, and the shelves holding her figurines and antique doodads were swathed in tablecloths.

I felt the first chill of unease. Eunice was never late.

About then, I spotted Deputy Lucius and Bernard coming through the front double doors. Just like the last time, they turned right and headed our way. But, this time, the look they both wore held something I couldn't read. Maybe something with a touch of anger in it.

The two men passed Morene and me and stopped directly in front of Carla's booth once again. Morene and I followed them over there, right to where Carla was lining up a family of plywood ducks—a mother with a kerchief and three of her painted ducklings. Looking up, Carla smiled at the two men.

"I think you know why we're here, Carla," Lucius said. "Do you have the gun you used over at Eunice's house this morning? "

"What," I said, my hand going to my mouth.

Morene stared at Carla, an odd expression playing around Morene's mouth. "Carla?" she said slowly. "What did you do? What in God's name did you do?"

Carla's eyes shown with a strange light. She pulled a small gun out of her apron pocket. As she did, a small piece of paper fluttered to the ground. Morene and I gasped at the sight of the gun. The two policemen stiffened, but they needn't have worried.

"Here it is, right here, Lucius," Carla said with a smile. Then she simply handed the gun to him and smiled again. "You know, it was only fair, Lucius," Carla went on. "I said I'd do it and I did. Eunice never should have done that to me."

"Eunice?" I blurted. "What did Eunice do?" I stooped to pick up the paper that had fallen out of Carla's pocket. It was a typed note, and I glanced at it. It began with the words, "My dearest Eunice, I adore you . . ."

The note pretty much went on in that vein for a few more paragraphs and misspellings. The note was unsigned.

I looked up to see that Carla had been watching me read it, her eyes intense.

"You see, Bette?" Carla said, the light in her eyes making them seem as brittle as glass. "Eunice is HER—the woman who took my Robert from me. She never should've done that to me. I told everybody I'd use that gun when I found out who that home-wrecker was."

I couldn't believe my ears. "EUNICE?" I asked. "*Eunice?* Are you crazy?" Though anyone could see that Carla was.

Carla gave a sly little smile. "Crazy like a fox. That's proof right there in your hand. Robert must've been writing it to her. It fell out of one of Robert's books—yesterday, when Morene and I were gathering up all of his things."

Beside me, I could feel Morene shrink back a little. I turned to glare at her. I could almost picture how it had happened. What Morene had done. Morene palming the piece of paper and, while sorting Robert's books, letting it flutter to the floor. Then, being oh-so-shocked as Carla read the note.

I turned to look at her. "Morene, what were you thinking?" I asked. "Couldn't you get Beau to divorce Eunice? Or did Beau want to stay married to Eunice so he could continue playing around with more women than just you?"

Lucius had already taken Carla by the arm, to lead her away; but he looked back at me at that one. Morene glanced at the sheriff and then glared back at me. "Bette, I don't know what you're talking about."

"Come on, Morene," I said. "You've been seeing Eunice's husband for years. Did you really think that no one would notice that Coach Beau's little recruiting trips and your little buying trips happen at the same time?"

"Bette, you don't know what you're talking about," Morene repeated, but her voice was shaking now.

I took a deep breath. "I'm talking about using Carla to murder Eunice so you could have Coach Beau. Just like with a gun. I'm talking about doing the same thing as loading Carla and pointing her right at Eunice."

Carla frowned, looking confused. Her vacant blue eyes went from me to Morene and back again. "What was that about loading me?" she asked.

I ignored her, as Morene spoke directly to the sheriff. "Lucius, Bette is making all this up."

But I couldn't stop now. "Come on, Morene. You used Carla to get rid of Eunice for you!" I said. "Do you really think that anyone will believe educated Robert wrote that note—look at all the misspelled words! And you better not have used your own typewriter." I turned to the sheriff. "Tell her, Lucius. I watch those crime shows on HBO. Tell Morene that you've got ways to detect if a particular typewriter was used to type a note."

Lucius opened his mouth to speak but Morene jumped in first. Her eyes shot sparks in my direction. "Okay, so what? What if I *did* write that note? It was just to help Carla along a little. Eunice was the woman seeing Robert. That's all I've got to say."

I put my hands on my hips. "Eunice? EUNICE?"

Morene put her hands on her hips. "So how do you know Eunice wasn't meeting Robert after the swap meet—huh? Just tell me that." Morene stuck her chin out, daring me to speak.

I stared at her. Had she guessed the truth? I thought of the motel key at the bottom of my purse.

I needed to throw that thing away. I wasn't even sure now why I'd kept it. Maybe because it was the only thing Robert had ever given me. He'd been such a sweet man, so lonely, so sad. Just like I had been. All these years. How could I have ever known that Carla would care so much if he were unfaithful? Our affair had never even gotten started, but what a mess it had made of so many lives.

But I couldn't let myself think of that now. If I did, I'd go crazy myself.

I stared levelly back at Morene. "Maybe I *don't* know the woman wasn't Eunice," I said. "But you can't know for sure it *was* Eunice, either."

"But it *has* to be Eunice," Carla insisted, her eyes wandering around as if maybe she was looking for it to be written somewhere. "It has to be." She turned to the sheriff. "I said I'd show her, Lucius. I wanted her to know just how I felt. Having my husband taken from me like that."

Morene wasn't even listening. She was looking first at me and then over at Barnard, who dropped his eyes to his shoes. Morene finally addressed Lucius, her hands out as if she were pleading her case. "Look, Lucius, I didn't do anything wrong," Morene said, her voice cracking with tension. "Okay, so maybe Carla had made a few threats. I couldn't know for sure that Carla would actually shoot anyone."

"You could just hope that she would," I said.

"Bette, stay out of this." Morene turned to Lucius again. "There was no way on earth I could know for sure that Carla would actually shoot Eunice."

The deputy's head went up at that. "You're wrong there," Bernard said. "You and Bette both are."

Morene was already shaking her head. “I did not do anything illegal.”

The sheriff interrupted her. “He’s not talking about that, Morene. He’s trying to tell you what happened.” He cleared his throat and took Carla by the arm to lead her away. “Carla didn’t shoot Eunice. She shot Eunice’s husband. She’s killed Coach Beau.”

I couldn’t help it. I gasped.

I did better than Morene, though. She let out an anguished scream that turned heads aisles away.

Marti's Secrets

by Grant Devereaux

Devereaux is the co-author of WordPerfect For Legal Professionals *from CFMS Press and contributor to several anthologies including one on relationships from Random House in 1998. Originally from Spartanburg, South Carolina, he now lives in Nashville.*

I love the crisp smell of autumn, especially after a rain. Smoke rises from chimneys, filling the air with the comforting scent of burning pine and oak. People gather around those fires, turning their backs on the damp chill winds outside, away from strangers, inward to the comfort of their families. They leave the loneliness of the rain-drenched streets at twilight to people like me.

Those streets are the only place I can find peace. Peace before the winter comes, before the cold blanket of snow smothers the life from everything. I should be at home, in bed, sleeping, but I can't. Neither can Marti. Living with a murderer in the family is a troublesome thing.

I need to get back home, back to Marti. When she was really little, she used to be so afraid to be alone, in the dark. Now she seems afraid all the time. That's why I need to get back. I don't want her to get scared, to second guess, not now. We're a team. In good times and bad we have to stick together.

It's been three years since it happened. In some ways, though, it seems longer. It was the first snow I could remember that was more than a few inches. A treacherous eight inches of snow followed a night of blinding sleet and rain, leaving the roads slippery with gray slush and ice. Only the foolish or the brave ventured out in their cars that day.

Mary Beth asked me to walk to the store. That's what we called her, Marti and I. *Mary Beth.* Marti said she didn't deserve to be called *mother.*

Britt's Grocery was just five blocks from our house, and Mary Beth knew it would be open. Old man Britt was always open, except on Sundays. The law saw to it that he stayed closed on the Sabbath or everyone knew he'd have been open then too.

I didn't mind going. I actually liked the chanced to get out of the house. I usually just went out the back gate and down the alley, across Plum Street, and over to Main. I could get there and back in about ten minutes.

For a dollar I could buy enough candy for Marti and me to keep us happy for a week. Mary Beth didn't eat candy. Didn't allow us to have any, either. Not any she knew about anyway. We figured what Mary Beth didn't know wouldn't hurt her . . . or us.

That day, of all days, a pair of frolicking chipmunks caught my attention just outside our back gate. I followed them back into our yard just in time to see Mary Beth push Winston down the back stairs. Just the day before, she warned him, told him, that she had washed his last diaper. I guess she meant it.

Just as she pushed him, she glanced up and saw me. With a look of absolute certainty, she let me know she had no fear of me. Then she smiled and turned her satisfied gaze to poor little Winston, lying lifeless in the snow. She knew I would keep her secret, and I did. I went on to the store. What I didn't know then was that Marti had seen it all, too, from her bedroom window upstairs.

Did I tell you Mary Beth pushed her twin sister into a bonfire? That's what I always heard anyway. They say her father built a huge bonfire one Halloween. He went inside the house to get some marshmallows, and that's when they say she pushed her. Mary Beth was only about eight years old at the time, but people say she stood and silently watched as her twin sister burned alive. By the time her father got back and pulled his little girl from the fire, she looked like a roasted pig. The sight of his charred baby drove him mad.

Mary Beth never shed a tear. Jealousy. After that, everyone knew about Mary Beth.

Then there was Mary Beth's mother. Marti called her Granny Lynn. Granny Lynn came to live with us after a stroke but she didn't live long. Died of asphyxiation. Mary Beth told everyone Granny Lynn got tangled up in her bed covers. Everybody knew Mary Beth used a pillow to suffocate her, but no one did anything. Some people even said it was good Granny Lynn was out of her misery, like Mary Beth had done a good thing.

The kids in our neighborhood never came over to our house. Their parents wouldn't let them. No one ever came to our house. Mary Beth had a way about her that kept even grown ups at a distance. Yet she lived her life in relative peace with Marti, Winston, and me, teaching English literature at the local high school.

When the ambulance came, no one asked why a two-year-old was outside in the snow with only his pajamas on. No one seemed curious about anything. They just came and wrapped up his tiny blue body and said how sorry they were for Mary Beth and for Marti and me.

Later there were questions; the police became suspicious. Winston had bruises and cuts. They even thought maybe I had done it. I wanted to tell them that Mary Beth had pushed him down the stairs, that I had seen it all, but I didn't. They wouldn't have believed me. Mary Beth would have said I had done it and they would have listened to her. Everyone always listened to Mary Beth.

After Winston's "accident," Mary Beth's moratorium on sweets was mysteriously lifted. She began routinely baking treats for Marti and me on a regular basis. Her elaborate pink colored confections always smelled suspiciously of mothballs.

I never ate them. I pretended to, but I didn't. I warned Marti—told her I thought Mary Beth was trying to kill us. That's when I found out that Marti had seen Mary Beth push Winston, too.

So I guess you could say that's how I got my idea. From Mary Beth and her mothball-flavored treats. Just put something in the food, but I had to be clever at it. It had to be something that didn't smell funny. Something she wouldn't suspect. Something no one could trace.

I began to read up on poisons, reading every story I could find about unsuspecting campers eating poison berries or mushrooms. The idea became an obsession. I needed something simple, something even a kid could find, and something that wouldn't leave trace. That was the hard part.

It took me almost two years, but I found the answer in a newspaper article on poisonous landscape plants. Azaleas—even poinsettias—could make you sick, but there was one thing that could kill you dead. Kill you for certain. Oleander leaves. People had died from burning its branches in a campfire. Just died from the fumes. Children who had innocently chewed on a leaf had died too.

But the best part was that as few as three leaves cooked in a pot of food could kill everyone who ate from the pot. They die of a heart attack. No trace. There was only one problem. We were in

North Carolina, and oleanders didn't grown there. I knew where they did grow though, in Florida, and we went to Florida every summer! So I waited.

It was so easy. In Florida, oleanders are as plentiful as they are poisonous. Covered with pink or white blossoms, they line almost every highway. Shopping centers and homes use them for landscaping. All this poison, all this death, right in your front yard. I suddenly wondered how many people in Florida who had died innocently of heart attacks had really been murdered.

This is the best part. Mary Beth caught me breaking a branch, covered with white blossoms off an oleander bush outside our hotel room, late at night.

"What are you doing!" she demanded.

I looked at her sheepishly and extended my arm, offering the branch to her. "For you."

She tried not to smile, tried to betray her delight at the offering. Finally she took the branch, smelled deeply of the flowers, and then said, "Back to bed. Now!" I recognized that tone of her voice, knew what she meant. I hurried back to my bed. She pretended to chase me. For a moment I felt a pang of guilt, but only for a moment. All I had to do to dispel it was to remember Winston.

Mary Beth put the branch in a vase and kept it by her bed for days. I kept hoping against hope that somehow the fragrance would be enough to kill her. Just before we left, she tossed the branch into the wastebasket. I retrieved it, stuffing seven or eight leaves inside a clean sock and putting them in my duffel bag.

I knew if Mary Beth found the sock, she would just think I was nuts. She would never guess that she was now the hunted. Still I was afraid. I would lie awake at night, wondering if I was crazy. If I was not just like her. The thought made me restless. Truth is, it still does.

It was October before I used them. Mary Beth was making a big pot of spaghetti sauce, the kind you simmer on the stove all day long. Her specialty. She made it fresh, mushrooms, tomatoes, garlic, and bay leaves. I looked in the pot on the stove, and there they were, floating in the thick, bubbling sauce. They didn't look exactly like the oleander leaves, but both were long, slender, and dark green. Covered in sauce, they couldn't look much different.

I told Marti what I was going to do, showed her the leaves, and asked her if I should. A look of panic crossed her face. *No*, she said. *We can't!* She covered her ears and begged me not to tell her.

I pulled her hands from her ears and softly whispered his name. *Winston.*

I reminded her how cute he was, how he used to laugh when she would blow air on his tummy. She smiled at the memory and then began to cry. I reminded of her of his plunge to his icy death, of him lying alone in the cold white snow, dead just before Christmas. Sweet, chubby, little rosy-cheeked Winston. Barely two years old when Mary Beth pushed him down the stairs to his icy death.

Then I told her I knew I would be next, and then she would really be alone. Alone with Mary Beth. And one night, alone, in the dark, Mary Beth would come for her. Smother her like she had Granny Lynn, take a pillow and just push it her face and smother her.

"Stop it!" she cried out.

I put my face over her mouth, afraid Mary Beth had heard her. That was the first time I saw Marti look at me with fear. I wish it had been the last. Finally she agreed to my horrible plan. She just didn't want to know any more about it. She went to her room and locked her door.

When Mary Beth was down in the basement doing the laundry, I fished the bay leaves out of the pot of hot steaming spaghetti sauce and replaced them with my oleander leaves. I watched as the churning bubbling sauce, the color of blood, slowly took them in. It was wicked how much they looked like bay leaves, wicked how easy it was all going to be!

As soon as I was through, I went upstairs and told Marti the deed had been done. We only had to wait now.

Marti was having second thoughts. She knew Mary Beth was evil. She knew she had killed Winston. Marti even acknowledged that she had even tried to kill us. But this was murder, and I could see Marti didn't have the stomach for it.

"We have to tell her. We have to stop her!" she pleaded. She ran for the door and I grabbed her by the arm. I pulled on her hard, hard enough to hurt her.

"No!" I said. Don't you see? It's either her or us. Don't you see that? And if you tell her now, if you tell her, Marti, she'll make me eat the spaghetti. She'll make me eat it. And she'll make you watch me. She'll make you watch me die, Marti. Tonight." I dramatically reached for my throat and pretended to gasp for air. "She'll do it. You know she will."

"No," she began to cry. "No!"

"We can't go back now, Marti. It's too late. We're in this together. Through the good and the bad, together. Don't desert me now, Marti. Not now. "

"I won't tell," she whimpered, her breast heaving, her words short and chopped as she sobbed, "I promise."

"You can't tell, Marti. Not Mary Beth. Not anyone, not ever. Do you understand? It's Mary Beth or me. There's no other choice. You tell and she'll either kill me or tell the police. Either way, I'm gone."

"I know, I know. I won't tell, anyone, ever. I promise." Her face grew cold. Her red eyes stared at me with silent anger. I was almost sorry now I had done it. Sorrier still for telling Marti.

"Maybe you should go to a friend's house," I suggested. How about Connie Harrell's, or Maybe Nita Cannon's?" Marti's face brightened a little. "That's it. I'll walk you to Nita Cannon's house. You can call from there later, to ask for permission to spend the night."

"She won't let me," Marti answered defiantly.

I didn't answer. I just looked at her until the realization hit her. She wouldn't need Mary Beth's permission. Not tonight. Not ever again. I could see her struggle with the mixed emotions that brought.

I took Marti outside and walked her down the street. We took an unfamiliar route, walking down streets where no one really knew us. We walked until she stopped crying. I worried—worried that people might see her crying. If they did, they may figure it all out. That would ruin everything!

After Marti calmed down, and her eyes were not so swollen, we made our way back up the street to Nita Cannon's house. Nita and Connie Harrell were jumping rope in the front yard. Marti joined right in, laughing and playing, just like it was any other day. I dropped her off, and then took my time going home.

Mary Beth liked to taste her spaghetti sauce as she cooked it. She would use a big wooden spoon, and taste and season, taste and season, all day long. I guess I never realized how much she tasted it. Maybe that day she was trying to get rid of that strange bitter taste. Anyway, by the time I got home, she was already dead on the floor, the wooden spoon still in her hand.

I sat on the kitchen chair and just looked at her. I had heard parents say their children look like angels when they are sleeping. Not Mary Beth. She looked like the devil.

I wanted to just wait. Wait until morning. Just to be sure she was really dead. Then I realized witnesses probably saw me come in, and if I didn't report her death, they would be suspicious. I could call the police, but they may notice I was not upset. I had to be upset.

I imagined getting caught. I imagined going to jail. I thought of Marti all alone, and I began to cry. Tears poured down my face as I thought of what I had done, and what could happen to me, to Marti, if I were caught.

Then a calm swept over me. Yes. *Cry! Cry!* I told myself. The more tears, the more convincing it will be, and I let the tears come. All the tears, all the terrible tears I had held inside for Winston, for Marti, and for myself.

When my face was red and swollen from the tears, I went next door to Mrs. Godfrey's house. I was convincingly hysterical, sputtering half phrases. Choking on tears of panic and fear. She sat me down, tried to make me drink some tea, but I pushed it away.

"She's dead!" I blurted out. "I just got home. She was lying there on the kitchen floor."

"Marti?" Mrs. Godfrey asked. That's when I knew for sure. She knew about Mary Beth.

"No. Mary Beth," I answered.

"Who did it? How?" she asked, incredulous at the revelation.

"I don't know. She was just lying there cold—no pulse"

"Did you call the doctor, an ambulance?"

I looked up at her; a feeling panic engulfed me. "No," I answered. "Oh, God, I should have, shouldn't I? I didn't think . . ."

"Don't you worry. Of course you didn't. You're in shock. I'll take care of it. Where is Marti?"

"She's down the street. The Cannons' house," I answered.

"Let me make some phone calls. You stay right here. You'll be all right, won't you?"

"Yes, I guess so. No. I don't know."

"Just take it easy. There's nothing you can do to change anything, now. What's done is done."

I wondered what she meant by that. *What's done is done.* Did she suspect something? Who was she calling? The police? I tried to stay calm. I couldn't panic. Not now.

I tried to remember Winston. I began to wonder why I hadn't told people then that Mary Beth had done it. Why had I kept her dirty secrets? And then I thought of Marti, and her keeping my secrets.

Had I become just like Mary Beth? Had the evil in her now taken possession of me?

No! It wasn't my fault! It was all Mary Beth. She was the bad one. She was the evil one. She had forced my hand. It had to end up this way.

Mrs. Godfrey came back into the kitchen and together we went back to my house. Mrs. Godfrey gasped when she saw her. It's never easy looking at death, I guess. She knelt beside Mary Beth and felt for a pulse. I knelt beside her too, crying. Crying from fear, crying for joy.

I had one more moment of panic when flashing lights and sirens arrived, but they were just there to take Mary Beth away. No one acted the slightest bit suspicious.

So I guess the murder went off without a hitch. The death certificate recorded the cause of death as a heart attack. Mary Beth was only thirty-four years old.

The funeral was lovely. Nice flowers, nice eulogy by the Baptist preacher from the church we almost never attended. He did a good job, though he called her Mary instead of Mary Beth. It was all very respectable. I think even Mary Beth would have been pleased.

Lots of people came, which surprised Marti and me. We never thought of Mary Beth as having friends. I finally figured out they were mostly her fellow teachers from the high school. Of course some of Marti's friends and their parents came, as did some my friends and their families. There was no family there though, other than Marti and me. There was no family left. Mrs. Godfrey assumed the role of mother hen, protecting us from the good intentions of a rush of relative strangers. She held a wake after the services at her house. Everyone was very nice, but they seemed to talk more to each other than to us.

I wandered through the crowd, accepting a few well meaning hugs, pats on the back, and words of encouragement from people I hardly knew. I finally found Marti sitting alone at the bottom of the stairs. She was humming something to herself, holding fast to her Cabbage Patch doll and gently rocking back and forth.

"Marti, you all right?" I asked.

My voice startled her. She looked up at me. No answer, just a cold empty stare. Marti hadn't said a word since Mary Beth died. Not to me. Not to anyone. She returned her attentions to her doll and her humming.

I couldn't help but notice that Marti now looked differently at me. Like I was Mary Beth.

Mrs. Godfrey put her hand on my shoulder. "She'll be all right in time. You both will be. I know it seems hard to believe, but one day the pain will get bearable and you will get on with your lives. Time heals all wounds."

I hugged Mrs. Godfrey, "Thank you. I hope so. Right now it's just so hard. For both of us."

"I understand," Mrs. Godfrey said, and then she left us alone with our grief.

Marti went on singing to her doll, pretending I wasn't there. I knelt down beside, tilted her face up with my hand and asked, "Still love Daddy?"

Living with a murderer in the family is a troublesome thing.

An Unmentionable Crime

by Toni L. P. Kelner

Toni Kelner considers herself an expatriate, having grown up in North Carolina and later moving to Boston. Her novels and short stories are set mostly in North Carolina as well, except when portraying how the North looks to a good Southern woman. Her Laura Fleming series is set in a small fictitious mill town in her home state.

If Sue had been anywhere else, talking to anybody else, she'd have said, "Now don't get your panties in a bunch," but she knew Ida would fire her on the spot if she dared say such a thing to Annabelle Lamar while working at Petticoat Junction. Especially when it was her salmon pink panties that Miz Lamar was mad about.

Miz Lamar's nostrils were flaring, her eyes were flashing, and she was doing all the other things folks do when they're too highfalutin to cuss.

"Were there or were there not panties sent with my ensemble?" she asked.

Sue shrugged and looked pointedly at Ida. She was the manager—let her take the heat.

"Well . . ." Sue could see that Ida wanted to blame the supplier, but Miz Phelps, Tori Dupont, and Tori's daughter Marie had been watching when she opened the box, and they'd seen her hang up the panties along with the bra, camisole, and garter belt. Lee Fredericks had come in later, but he'd seen the complete set, too. So, naturally, Ida got out of it by passing the buck to the only other person around.

"Sue," she said sternly, "I told you to keep an eye on things while I was helping Miz Phelps. What happened to Miz Lamar's undergarments?"

Ida had said no such thing, but Sue wasn't willing to lose her job over saying so. "I don't know, Ida. I was helping Tori and Marie, like you said to."

"She helped me, too," Lee said, which was nice of him.

Unfortunately, Miz Lamar wasn't so nice. "Are you saying that anybody off the street could have taken my panties?"

"Of course not," Ida said. "Nobody's been in here except—" She stopped, but it was too late. The only people who could have taken those drawers were right there in the store. In other words, Ida herself, Miz Phelps, Tori, Marie, and Lee. And Sue. It didn't take a whole lot of smarts for Sue to figure out which one Ida would rather blame.

"Call the police," Miz Lamar said. "I prepaid for this ensemble, and I insist on having it complete."

"I'm sure we have another pair of panties in stock that will go with the set," Ida said.

"Don't be ridiculous," Miz Lamar snapped. "The color, the trim—they're unique."

Sue had to admit that Miz Lamar had a point. There really wasn't anything in the store that would work, and no place else in town carried anything like it. There might be something close in the mall in Hickory, but Sue was willing to bet that it wouldn't be an exact match.

Ida swallowed hard but managed to get out, "Then I'll refund your money."

"Unacceptable! I ordered the set to wear to the cotillion tonight, and I will accept nothing less. Call the police."

The other customers were getting irate, and Sue didn't blame them. Miz Lamar had as good as accused one of them of stealing her panties. What did she think the police were going to do? Strip search everybody? Miz Phelps looked indignant, Tori was holding onto her daughter protectively, and Marie was mortified. As for Lee, he was sweating bullets. Sue didn't have any idea that he had stolen anything, but he did have a secret, and it might come out if the police got involved.

"Sue," Ida said in a strangled voice, half begging her to come up with something, half warning her that her job was on the line if she didn't.

Getting the police involved was a sure way of losing some of their best customers; even if one of them really was a thief, it would be awfully bad for business. And if Petticoat Junction closed, Sue could kiss a new minivan goodbye.

The day had started out bad and gotten worse. First off, Amber was teething and wouldn't stop whining. And Crystal snagged Sue's panty hose while she was chasing Jason, which meant that she'd had to dig up another pair. Then Tiffany announced that she wasn't speaking to her because Sue wouldn't buy her a bra. If all that weren't enough, Ida had been on her back from the minute she got to work.

"Sue, have you seen the mailman?" Ida said.

"Not yet," Sue answered for the umpteenth time.

"Fiddlesticks!" Ida said. That was the closest thing to cussing Ida would allow herself at work. She wouldn't let Sue cuss either, but Sue had decided she'd rather say nothing as to say *fiddlesticks*.

Sue turned back to her customer, and said flatly, "You go ahead and buy that bra if you want, Miz Phelps, but I'm telling you, it ain't up to the job."

Mary Jacobs Phelps, who was anything but flat, glared at her. "I like a feminine bra."

"Suit yourself, but if you get that bra, your boo—" Sue stopped herself just in time. Words like *boobs*, *hooters*, and *butt* were also forbidden at Petticoat Junction. "Your breasts are going to hang halfway to your knees. At your age, they don't stand up on their own."

"I'll have you know that my breasts are as firm as they were the day I got married."

Sue was willing to believe her, but before she could say so, she saw Ida in the mirror, hovering behind them. Ida raised her eyebrows at Sue in a clear message. So Sue said, "Is that right? Well, that's nice, that's real nice."

Miz Phelps looked suspicious but went back to admiring herself in the mirror.

Sue was tempted to let her go ahead and buy that pitiful excuse for a bra, even though she knew it would be stretched out of shape in no time.

The only thing was, if she did, Miz Phelps would come back and squawk that they'd sold her inferior merchandise, and Ida would blame Sue for it. So she was going to have to be tactful, even though tact wasn't her strong suit.

Sue smiled the way she'd seen her husband's cousin Vasti smile when she was sucking up to somebody. "You know, Miz Phelps, since you are so firm and all, I should show you the Le Bustier 3000. It emphasizes the bust line a lot more than that bra, and it would be a shame not to show off a figure like yours." Actually, Miz Phelps had a figure like a tugboat.

Ida was still hovering, so Sue decided to lay it on even thicker. "We don't stock many of the model I'm thinking of, because most women aren't big—aren't well enough endowed to carry it off. You wait here and I'll get you one out of the storeroom."

While Miz Phelps simpered, Sue went in back and got the Le Bustier Model 3000, which they kept out of sight because it was so huge nobody would admit to needing it. She pulled off the size tag and started to replace it with a tag with the size Miz Phelps thought she took. Then she had an inspiration and replaced it with a tag for one size smaller than that.

Sure enough, Miz Phelps checked the tag as soon as Sue handed it to her. She looked doubtful, but was all smiles when she opened the slatted door to the dressing room and said, "It fits!" in a tone of amazement. "Of course, it's not as pretty as the other one—"

"Maybe it's not as low cut," Sue said quickly, "but it seems to me that men want women to leave a little something to the imagination." She smiled the Vasti smile again and held her breath while Miz Phelps thought it over.

"I believe you're right," she finally said. "I'll take six of these."

"Yes, ma'am," Sue said, mentally adding up the commission and how much closer it would get her to a minivan.

Miz Phelps went back into the dressing room to get changed, and Ida nodded approvingly at Sue. Then she had to go and ruin it by saying, "Don't forget to wrap them."

"Yes, ma'am." Sue had forgotten once last week, and Ida was never going to let her live it down. She went out back and pulled out five more Model 3000s, making sure to change all of the tags, and then wrapped the bras in the pale pink tissue paper Petticoat Junction stocked.

Wrapping things in paper the customers were going to toss away the second they got home made no sense to Sue, and once again, she wished the store's owner were still running the store. She and Bobbie Jo had gotten along real well, but Bobbie Jo had retired and hired Ida as manager, and suddenly the place had to be high-falutin.

First Ida had moved the store to Rocky Shoals, because she said there was a better class of customer there. Sue didn't mind that because it was closer to her house, but she did mind having to wear dresses and panty hose to work, and she didn't much care for the other changes Ida had made, either.

Now everything in the store was pink, from the carpet to the curtains to the doors on the dressing rooms. Even the cash register was pink. And now they sold *undergarments* instead of *underwear*, *panties* instead of *drawers*, and *stockings* instead of *panty hose*. If her station wagon weren't on its last legs, Sue never would have put up with it, and if Bobbie Jo hadn't insisted, Ida never would have kept her. Ida was itching for an excuse to get rid of her because Sue wasn't prissy enough to suit her, but Sue wanted that minivan something fierce. So if Ida wanted her to waste time wrapping bras in tissue paper, Sue would wrap bras in tissue paper.

Sue had to admit that the store was making more money than when Bobbie Jo was in charge, so maybe Ida knew what she was doing. Who'd have thought women could be so particular about their bras and so embarrassed about what size they wore? Sue herself had no interest in wearing gauzy nothings.

After four breast-fed children, all she wanted was support and comfort, and her own bras made the Le Bustier 3000s look as flimsy as the pink tissue paper they were wrapped in.

Sue was ringing up Miz Phelps's bras when the front door opened, and Ida went to greet the new customers. Sue recognized Tori Dupont, who had been in her graduating class, and Tori's daughter Marie, who was a friend of Sue's daughter Tiffany.

"Can I help you ladies?" Ida asked, smiling as warm a smile as she could manufacture.

"I hope so," Tori said while Marie looked in every direction other than at Ida. "My daughter here is ready for her first bra."

Sue would have cussed if she could have. According to Tiffany, Marie was the only girl in her class who didn't wear a bra. Other than Tiffany, that is. Tiffany was as flat as a flounder, but every other day she was whining that she needed a bra and that girls who were flatter than she was wore one. First off, Sue didn't think it was possible to be flatter than Tiffany, and second, if those other girls' mothers wanted to waste money on bras their daughters didn't need, that was their business. The problem was, Tiffany didn't see it that way, and when she saw Marie wearing a bra come Monday morning, she was going to be impossible to live with.

Miz Phelps had paid for her bras and was heading for the door when the mailman came in. Sue couldn't help grinning. As pink as the store was, it was nothing compared to the color that fellow turned every time he had to deliver something. He could get away with sliding letters under the door, but this time he had a package.

"Special delivery," he said in a choked voice.

Sue reached to take it from him, but Ida said, "I'll take care of this, Sue. You help Miz Dupont. And Miss Dupont." She smiled at the girl, but Marie was still trying to find something to look at that wouldn't embarrass her.

Sue took Tori and Marie over to the part of the store that had the sign NEW BEGINNINGS hanging overhead, but Tori and Marie were more interested in seeing what was in that box. People around Rocky Shoals didn't get many special delivery packages. Mrs. Phelps was waiting around, too. The mailman, on the other hand, left as soon as he got Ida's signature.

"Thank goodness!" Ida said as she ripped the box open, not even bothering to use a letter opener to protect her manicure. She tossed wads of lavender tissue paper out onto the floor before reverently pulling out and unfolding a complete set of salmon pink lingerie: matching bra, panties, camisole, and garter belt. Marie finally stopped looking at her sneakers, and even Sue was impressed.

"That's just what I need for the cotillion," Miz Phelps said, even though it was plain that she'd need two or three sets like that to cover her. "How much is it?"

"I'm sorry, Miz Phelps," Ida said. "This ensemble is already sold. Miz Lamar special ordered it. According to the catalog, these are exactly like what Princess Diana wore on her wedding day. Only hers were white, of course."

The customers oohed and aahed while Ida pulled out one of the satin padded hangers they used for negligees, and delicately arranged the set.

Then she hung it on the hook between the two dressing rooms, the place of honor reserved for the store's best. "I was afraid that it wouldn't arrive in time for the cotillion tonight, and Miz Lamar would have been so disappointed."

Disappointed? Sue knew darned well that Miz Lamar would have been mad as a wet hen. No wonder Ida had been a pain all day. Miz Lamar had probably been worrying her to death.

"Sue," Ida said, "clean up this mess while I call Miz Lamar."

Sue tried to smile instead of gritting her teeth as she gathered the box and packing material and took it to the storeroom. When she came back out front, the store's customers were clustered around the royal undergarments.

"Does it come in other colors?" Miz Phelps was asking.

"I believe so," Ida said, "but I have to warn you that it's quite expensive."

Sue whistled softly. It must be high for Ida to admit that to a customer. Ida called a thirty-dollar bra "one of life's necessities," and a forty-dollar bra "a little indulgence."

Ida said, "Come on back to my office to look at the catalog." Sue raised her estimate even more. Ida kept her office fancier than the store itself, and she only did business there if she thought she was going to make a big sale.

Sue wasn't pleased. Miz Phelps was her customer, but if Ida made the sale, she wouldn't have to pay Sue a commission. At least she had Tori to wait on. A few bras for Marie should help with the minivan. Sue said, "Marie, put your arms down so I can get a look at you."

Marie wouldn't meet Sue's eyes, but she did move her arms away from her chest, such as it was. She didn't have much more than Tiffany. Sue pulled out three different triple As, bras so small they had spandex panels instead of cups. "Give these a try, and see which one feels the best. Now remember—you're going to be wearing it all day long. Make sure it's comfortable."

Just then the door opened again, and Lee Fredericks, one of Sue's regular customers, came in. Marie's eyes got wide as saucers because of a man seeing her with bras in her hand, and she fled into the dressing room and slammed the door behind her.

Tori smiled. "I still remember how embarrassed I was when I got my first bra."

Sue didn't see what the big deal was, but she nodded anyway. "If you'll excuse me a minute, I'll go see what Mr. Fredericks needs."

"Hey, Sue," Lee said.

"Hey there, Lee. What can I do you for?"

"I just dropped by to see if you had anything new. For my wife."

"How did she like that last batch of panties?"

"Loved them," he said.

"Well, we've got some new ones in that same line, only the lace is softer. Pretty colors, too."

"Let's see them."

"Did the size tens fit all right?"

"Perfectly," he said, with a gleam in his eye.

Just like with bras, Ida didn't keep the larger sizes on display, so Sue went out back to get the panties in red, black, dark blue, and pine green. Just for the heck of it, she pulled out some tiger- and leopard-skin prints, too.

She laid them out on a table in front of Lee, and while he looked at them, she went back to the dressing room. "How are you doing in there, Marie?"

"Okay."

"Let me take a look."

Marie opened the door only a crack. She wasn't taking any chances that Lee would be able to see the little bit she had.

Sue peered in. "Turn around."

Marie obeyed.

Sue pulled at the midriff band. "This one's too big. Let me get you a smaller size."

"Smaller than this?" Marie said in anguished tones.

"Not the cup size," Sue explained. "I'm talking about the band. It's got to fit right to support you the way it should."

Sue closed the door so Marie could try on the next one.

Tori whispered, "Did I hear you getting that man size ten panties?"

Sue nodded.

"His wife must be huge! I didn't wear panties that big when I was pregnant with Marie."

Sue shrugged. Lee lived in Charlotte, so she didn't have any idea of what his wife looked like. Besides, the woman never got any of those panties he picked out anyway. Sue had figured out ages ago that he wore them himself, and he probably had a pair on under his khakis right now. Why else would he buy panties in Rocky Shoals, when there were plenty of bigger places in Charlotte? Size ten was big for a woman, but it wasn't big at all for a man.

"Marie," Sue said, "I'm handing you the other size over the door."

Marie's hand reached up to take them.

Tori said, "You know, while I'm here, I may as well get a couple of new bras, too."

Sue looked over at Lee to make sure he was all right, and saw him admiring the salmon pink lingerie set. She was pretty sure that garter belts were too much for him, but she sure would have liked the commission from selling it to him. Anyway, since he was occupied, she helped Tori look for what she wanted. Except they didn't have what she wanted. That model had been discontinued.

"But I've been wearing the same exact bra since high school," Tori said.

"You did develop all at once, didn't you?" Sue said. Tori had left school at the end of freshmen year flat as a pancake but had had all the boys chasing after her when she came back in September. "Le Bustier makes one that's nearly the same. Try one on and see what you think."

"Are you sure I can't get the old one?"

Sue sighed. Not only were women particular about bras, but some were loyal until death. "You might be able to call around and find somebody who's got one left, but you may as well go ahead and get used to something else." She pulled one from a rack. "Try this one and tell me if you don't like it just as well."

"I don't need to try it on."

"You heard what I told Marie. An uncomfortable bra can ruin your whole day."

Sue handed it to her, and Tori disappeared into the dressing room.

While she was gone, Sue spoke to Lee, then went into the back room to get him more of the animal-print panties.

Sue was trying to make sure everybody had everything he or she needed when Annabelle Lamar swept in, nose as high in the air as ever. Ignoring the fact that Sue was busy with other customers, she said, "I'm here to pick up my order."

Ida must have heard her, because she pushed Miz Phelps out of her office so she could usher Miz Lamar in. Then she rushed back out to get the salmon pink lingerie and say, "Sue, I told you to get that trash out of the floor."

With so many customers in the store, Sue couldn't even cuss under her breath as she grabbed a wad of white tissue she'd missed and shoved it into her pocket. It wasn't as though she didn't have plenty to do. Lee was waiting to pay for his panties, Miz Phelps wanted her to write up the catalog order, Tori had decided to get the new bra but wanted Sue to find her two more, and Marie couldn't make up her mind which bra felt the best.

Sue was trying to get them all squared away when Miz Lamar realized that her panties were missing.

Now Sue was trying her darnedest to figure out what had happened. She hated to admit it, but Miz Lamar was right: somebody in the store had to have those panties.

Miz Lamar said, "Ida, if you won't call the police, I'll do it myself."

Not that she actually reached for the phone, of course. She was too used to people doing whatever she wanted. So that gave Sue enough time to think the situation over.

The way Sue figured it, if Ida had wanted to take the panties, she wouldn't have made a point of opening the box in front of everybody.

Besides which, she'd own up to it now to keep Miz Lamar from calling the police. As for Miz Lamar, Sue wouldn't put it past her because the woman enjoyed making a fuss, but she didn't think she'd had a chance.

That left the other customers. The lingerie had been hanging in plain sight, and since Sue and Ida had been going back and forth to the storeroom and office, there'd been plenty of time for somebody to grab them.

Sue didn't think even Miz Phelps could convince herself that she could stuff herself into those panties—Miz Lamar had to be fifty pounds lighter than Miz Phelps. And Miz Phelps had enough money to buy herself a set of her own if she wanted it. Of course, she and Miz Lamar were both involved in what passed for high society in Rocky Shoals, and Sue knew that fancy cotillions meant fancy feuds. Could Miz Phelps have taken the panties just to get Miz Lamar's goat?

Then there was Lee Fredericks. But wearing women's panties was one thing; stealing them was another. Not to mention the fact that he couldn't wear them any more than Miz Phelps could. Besides, Lee had the most to lose by being caught—a story like that could easily reach all the way to Charlotte, especially if he was found wearing the baby blue panties he'd bought last time. Sue really didn't want it to be him anyway. Commissions from his shopping trips had already paid for the spare tire on the minivan, and she was hoping for a stereo.

That left Marie and Tori. As embarrassed as Marie was about bras, would she have risked being caught stealing panties? Especially panties that were way too big for her. Tori could have worn them, but if she was the kind to always buy the same bra, Sue didn't think she was likely to have a sudden urge to wear fancy panties.

So nobody needed or wanted the panties, and Sue couldn't see somebody stealing them just to torment Miz Lamar. Of course, it was Ida who was in trouble, and Ida made people mad every day, but Sue could think of a whole lot better ways of getting back at her than stealing panties. As for Sue herself, even if she'd annoyed one of the customers that much, there were worse things they could do to her, too.

Sue stuck her hands in her pockets, a habit Ida said wasn't businesslike or ladylike. That's when she figured it out. "Hold on a minute. Maybe those panties are still in the box. I better go check." Ida started to protest, but Sue talked over her. "Just so it doesn't look like I'm pulling something, I'm going to take somebody in the back with me to look. Tori, how about you?"

Tori looked reluctant, so Sue added, "Marie will be all right for a minute."

Tori nodded and followed her into the storeroom.

Once they were out of earshot, Sue took a good look at Tori and deliberately poked her friend on the right side of her chest. It made a noise, like crinkling paper. Then Sue poked the left side. There was no noise, but she knew doggoned well that she wasn't poking the woman's boob either.

"Tori, how long have you been stuffing your bra?"

Tori's face turned bright red, but she knew she'd been caught. "Ever since high school."

"Why would you do such a fool thing?"

"Because I was the last one in our class to need a bra. Don't you remember?"

"What about Lou Ann?"

"I saw her the summer after freshman year, and she'd started wearing one, so I got one of my own and—And I stuffed it."

"Geez, Tori."

"You don't know it felt, Sue. You got your bosom in junior high school. Nobody ever laughed at you."

"Nobody ever laughed at me because I wouldn't let them," Sue pointed out.

"I guess you're right," Tori said, "but I was pretty insecure back then."

If she was still stuffing her bra, Sue figured that she must still be mighty insecure. "You do have a bosom now, don't you?"

"Of course I do, but it's not as big as I'd made myself out to be. I knew people would notice if I changed sizes, so as I got bigger, I used less and less stuffing. I thought sure I'd catch up some day, but I never did."

Did Tori really think people paid that much attention the size of her boobs? What did she do about her husband? Sue shook her head, just not understanding. Then she reached into her pocket and pulled out the wad of tissue paper that Ida had told her to pick up. "Is this yours?"

"Is that what happened to it? It rolled out of the dressing room while I was trying on the new bra, and I couldn't find it. I had to find something to put in my bra—otherwise it would have showed!"

She was right. The shirt she was wearing would have made it pretty obvious. It was too tight for her to hide anything. Other than Miz Lamar's panties, that is.

Tori went on. "I looked out of the dressing room, but the only thing within reach was Miz Lamar's lingerie. I was meaning to come out of the dressing room and find something else to use and then put the panties back. I didn't mean to cause any trouble."

"There's not going to be any trouble." Sue held out her hand. "Give 'em here."

Tori reached into her bra and pulled out the crumpled panties. Sue gave her the stuffing back, then took the panties and shoved them into a corner of the shipping box. "Just agree with whatever I say, all right?"

They went back into the store, with Sue carrying the box.

"Are they in there?" Ida asked, the strain showing in her voice.

"I'm not sure." Sue made a big show of pulling out tissue paper, then acted real surprised when she found the panties. "Well, here they are. They must have been here all along."

Miz Lamar looked suspicious, but Sue and Tori looked innocent, so there was nothing she could say other than to demand a discount for their being so wrinkled. Ida took care of it while Sue got the other customers squared away.

Miz Phelps still looked indignant, and Sue was willing to bet there were going to be fireworks at the cotillion. Marie and Tori just acted glad to be getting out of there, but Tori did turn back and mouth, "Thank you," to Sue. Lee had one eyebrow raised as if he thought Sue had pulled something, but he was too nice to say so. He did loudly mention that Sue ought to get a bonus for saving them all a lot of trouble. When Miz Lamar agreed, Ida gritted her teeth and said they were right.

By the time they were all gone, there was only an hour or so until closing time, and Sue spent most of that hour looking at the New Beginnings bras. Come closing time, she wrapped up five of the smallest, daintiest bras Petticoat Junction sold. She figured that with her employee discount, she was still making a profit from the bonus Ida had promised her. Maybe Tiffany didn't have anything to fill the bras with, but Sue would rather she wear them empty now as to go on a panty raid twelve years down the road.

Waiting for Snow

by Elaine Fowler Palencia

Elaine Fowler Palencia is the author of Small Caucasian Women, *a book of short stories set in the mythical (and mystical) Blue Valley in the real state of Kentucky. Her new book,* Brier Country, *from the University of Missouri Press, is set in the same area. She counts herself as a devoted mystery fan and Southerner.*

Except for the Christmas lights swinging in the wind, nothing had moved on the street for the last fifteen minutes before the man appeared down at the end of the block. Slowly he worked his way toward me, slipping from doorway to doorway in the rainy night. He wore a wide-brimmed hat and a long coat, and he kept looking behind him.

I was sitting in the front window of the bus station, watching the rain and recollecting other Christmas Eves—most, like this one, spent in eastern Kentucky. A car had gone by about 8:30, and I didn't look for another one before closing time. There's a Wal-Mart outside of town that gets the last-minute shopping now, plus a couple of years ago the city fathers paved over the railroad right-of-way to make a bypass of downtown, all five blocks of it. There wouldn't be many folks riding the bus, either. I could have locked up and let people wait outside, but I had too many memories of lonely streets not to stay open till the Bluebird went through at 10:30.

Rhonda, she understood I had to do it. "You're a nurturer, Tiny, that's why I married you," she said. She gets stuff like that off TV talk shows, but whatever. I'm just glad she said *yes* all those years ago.

When he got opposite the station, the man darted across the street, opened the door, and slid a glance around.

"Hidy. Come on in," I said.

He looked bad. His face was that gray-white shade you get when you're going to pass out. Lurching down the line of booths along the wall, he flung himself into the last one.

When I got myself back, there he was, hunched over on his elbows, staring at the table top. Without looking up he muttered,

"Gimme something to eat."

I said, "How about some homemade pie? I got lemon meringue, butterscotch, chocolate, and apple. My wife makes them."

"Anything."

"Coffee?"

"Yeah."

Time I got a piece of the butterscotch and a cup of coffee to him, he'd laid the hat aside. He hadn't shaved or washed in a while, but with his looks he could have been a country music star.

"You all by yourself tonight?" he asked, unbuttoning his coat.

That's when I saw he was carrying.

For some reason I'll never understand, seeing the gun made me sit down across from him. It was a pure instinctual thing, almost like I wanted to keep myself between him and somebody else, like I was trying to protect someone. At any rate, I don't keep a gun at the station, only a baseball bat, and it was across the room under the counter. Heavy as I am and the way I move with this prosthesis, I'd never make it over there.

"Yeah," I said, keeping it loose, "it's just us chickens tonight. Ordinarily my wife'd be keeping me company, but it being Christmas Eve and all, she's got stuff to do at home. If you're wanting a bus there's one more at 10:30, for Huntington." I thanked the Lord that Rhonda decided to stay home and finish a dress she was making for Kimberly.

After he wolfed down the pie, he lit a cigarette, drew in a lungful of smoke, and let it out with his eyes closed, like it was medicating his soul.

"You from around here?" he asked.

"Carter County originally. Been here going on nineteen years, though."

He nodded.

It occurred to me that he didn't have a plan. I'd been robbed before; drugs have changed eastern Kentucky in a lot of ways. And with TV and all, even your teenage dopehead has some kind of a half-assed strategy.

But this old boy seemed to be thinking of something else. Not that this relieved my mind exactly. The man was some kind of trouble. The only question was what kind and to who.

"What happened to the couple used to run this place? Way back," he said.

"My in-laws, the Conns. You know 'em?"

He gave me an up-and-down look. "Your in-laws, you say."

I said, "They retired and moved back to Big Woods six years ago. Me and Rhonda took over then. Of course, Rhonda always did make the pies here, even when she was working at Aquastream."

He closed his eyes again, ducked his head, and pressed his thumbs into his temples, massaging in little circles. He looked plumb worn out.

"You got any kids?" he asked.

I didn't like bringing in my family. "I reckon I'd better wash out the coffee pot," I said, making a move to leave.

"I asked you a question," he said, steely and low.

I thought, *Okay, whatever sails his boat.* "Kimberly's our one and only. She just turned twenty."

His head snapped up. "Twenty."

"Yep."

I never saw a man try so hard to look casual.

"When's her birthday?" he asked.

"In September."

"Got a picture of her?"

I nodded.

"Lemme see it."

He had unusually close-set ears. An idea started crawling up the back of my neck. All at once it seemed like I'd been waiting my whole life for this man to show up.

I got out my billfold and fumbled it open to the family portrait we got done at Olan Mills for Easter. Somebody's breath was whistling in his nostrils and I actually turned my head to see who might be in the next booth before I realized it was me.

He took the wallet from me and slid his thumb slowly back and forth across Rhonda's and Kimberly's faces. His knee started jiggling under the table, rocking the booth. "How long you been married?"

"Fifteen years last October."

"So she isn't your daughter."

"Kimmy was five when we got married. We've been in our house fourteen," I said, my tongue like cotton.

He studied the picture. Softly he said, "She don't favor you."

I swallowed hard. "I met her mama when she was three, but I'm the only daddy she's ever known. She's my pride and joy."

The phone rang.

He looked me in the eye and shook his head, giving me a big negatory. "We'll just sit here. It'll quit."

I said, "Look, Buddy, it's Christmas Eve. I don't want any trouble."

"Neither do I," he said as he lit another cigarette and sat back, one arm along the back of the booth. But the knee was still dancing and now he started drumming his fingers. He was trying to decide something.

When the phone finally quit, he frowned. "That was somebody that expected you to be here."

I was thinking that if it had been Rhonda, she'd be down in a New York minute to see what had happened to me. Which gave me something else to worry about.

"Who do you think it was?" he asked, chewing his lip.

"Probably somebody wanting to know if the bus is on time." A big drop of sweat slid down my spine. I thought about our toy poodle Fifi, about the way she'd nibble Rhonda's corn pads off while we were sleeping and Rhonda'd wake up giggling. I wondered if I'd ever hear Rhonda laugh again and feel Fifi's cold little nose in my ear.

He narrowed his eyes and squinted at the front windows. "Your daughter live here in town?"

"No."

"She smart?"

"She's real smart. Takes after her mama." I didn't want to tell him any more, but it's like I couldn't stop myself. "Right now she's working for 3M. She went to Berea two years and then she wanted to go out to St. Louis and specialize in physical therapy, but we didn't have the money to send her."

Just then I heard a car pull up to the blind side of the building.

He slipped his hand inside his coat.

A young couple came in. The girl was way along, maybe eight months. She was so skinny she looked like a pregnant broom handle. The boy, same spindly type, was carrying a little flowered suitcase. They sat down on the first two counter stools, put their heads together, and went to whispering. We weren't part of their world at all.

"When's that next bus?" he asked.

I told him that the Bluebird was due in ten minutes. Then, it's like my tongue was loose at both ends and hinged in the middle. I informed him that it's part of the last private bus line from here to Wheeling. I called up memories of riding on it as a boy going to see family in Fort Gay and of how Daddy would always buy a packet of Chiclets for us kids. Next I philosophized about the age of trains dying and now the age of buses was dying, making places like Blue Valley a secret known only to the people who live here, for we don't figure on the national map of travel connections anymore. I was into the pluses and minuses of the local lumber industry when he snapped at me.

"Is that the bus?"

The rain had quit. In the distance I heard the growl of a big engine, coming this way. He must have been pretty rattled to mistake that sound for a bus. Me, I'd know the horses Earl's got under the hood of his patrol car anywhere. "No," I said, "it's the police."

I got myself upright and walked to the front doors and leaned out.

Nobody shot me in the back. Earl was barreling up Main Street, blowing through stoplights with his siren off. To my left, the Bluebird was struggling up Bishop Avenue from the bypass, wallowing in the wind like a whale.

Everything went into slow motion. With a big oily sigh, the bus pulled in slaunchwise to the front door. The young couple stood up and went into a movie smooch. An old lady got off the bus with a shopping bag full of presents. She waved at a pickup truck that pulled in from the other direction and stopped nose-to-nose with the bus. Earl screeched up on the other side of the bus, jumped out of the patrol car, hurdled the bumper of the pickup, swiveled around the old lady, pulled open the door, and shoved past the couple.

"How's come you didn't answer the phone?" he yelled at me.

"There was this man—" I said, not in my real voice.

"Where is he?"

The back booth was empty.

Earl rushed to check the rest rooms. The young couple went on outside to the bus and in a second I heard the boy yell, "My car!" just as an old red Camaro peeled around the bus and took off up the street. Earl heard it too and sprinted for his vehicle. The fellow must have gone out through the kitchen. Earl wasn't halfway to his wheels when a black late-model Ford streaked past. The two buggy-whip antennas on the back told me it was an unmarked cop car.

After the bus left, I went outside and looked up the street. What I noticed right away was what wasn't there: There were at least two cop cars chasing the Camaro, but I didn't hear any sirens.

The rain had started again. I locked the front door and went to wash up the plate and cup the man used. That's when I saw my wallet on the table. With everything happening, I'd forgot to get it back from him.

The picture of Rhonda and Kimberly was gone. In its place lay folded ten pictures of Grover Cleveland, the first thousand-dollar bills I'd ever seen.

Late the next afternoon, after we'd opened our gifts and eaten Christmas dinner out at Papaw and Mamaw's, Rhonda and Kimberly took Danny, her new boyfriend, over to Aunt Cosby's to show him off. I was trying to stay awake to watch the game on TV. I hadn't slept all night and tried to call Earl twice, but nobody answered. He's divorced and lives alone since his twins went off to the deaf school.

Just as I was dozing off, a knock came at the door. Earl walked in and tossed his hat on top of the Lexington paper on the coffee table. From the wrinkles and smudges, he was still in yesterday's uniform.

I raised a hand. "What do you know for sure?"

He sat down in the other recliner kindly gingerly, like his back was bothering him again, picked his hat back up, and turned it around and around by the brim. Earl and me, we've run together since we were four years old. We don't have to talk about something to be talking about it.

Just him being there meant we were already discussing an item buried in the state news section of the paper: HIGH-SPEED CHRISTMAS EVE CHASE RECOVERS STOLEN CAR.

For a while we watched the game without talking.

Then during a beer commercial Earl said, "I've been thinking about retiring."

"Seriously?"

He fiddled with his hat band. "I've had a good run, met lots of people."

This is true. Down in Frankfort one time, he peed in the urinal right next to John Wayne.

"I'll get a good pension," he said.

"Was it right what the paper said?"

"About what?"

"That you didn't catch the driver of the car."

Earl sighed. "Not exactly. I was trying to get to him first and take him into protective custody."

"Then the other car, the black Ford—?"

Earl reached in his shirt pocket, took out the photo of Rhonda and Kimberly, and handed it to me. There was a smear of rusty red across one corner. I wondered who had shot first.

We looked at each other real straight.

"This was something big," I said.

"You don't want to know how big. It wouldn't be healthy for you to know." He sat back, gripping the armrests of his chair, eyes on the TV.

"Law enforcement."

The Lions scored on a bootleg.

Probably I'd seen the stranger at his worst. But I hadn't gotten the feeling he was mean or evil, only scared and desperate. I wondered if he'd had time to draw his gun. After a while I said, "Do you think he came back for Rhonda?"

"Rhonda? No. He had too much else on his mind last night. We think he was headed for Curranville." Out of the corner of my eye, I saw him turn and look at me. "You know who he was?"

"Not for sure," I said, fingering the picture, "but I have an idea." Kimberly has his coloring and the same close-set ears.

"Are you going to tell Rhonda you saw him?" asked Earl.

The first week we met, I had asked Rhonda to marry me. She told me she was waiting for someone and that she'd never love anybody like she loved him. She told me that someday he would come back and get her and she'd live like a queen, once he got some things straightened out. It took me almost three years to convince her to marry me instead of waiting. He was the *big* dream, the trip to California and Vegas. I'm the *small* dream, the one that fixes your washer and makes your house payments. We've had a good life together and we don't talk anymore about what she said at the beginning. Most of the time I manage to believe she stopped waiting for him. But sometimes I think that maybe what's keeping her with me is the waiting for him. If he wasn't out there any longer for her to wait for, would she wake up and want something else?

"No," I told Earl. "I'm not saying a word to her."

We walked out to his car.

Earl looked up at the gray sky. With his head slanted back, I noticed the white starting at his temples.

"More rain in the forecast. Remember how it used to snow on Christmas when we was kids?" he said.

"You never get snow in the Knobs on Christmas," I said. "But sure, I remember it."

He thought for a minute, then grinned. "Yeah, I guess it's just something we can't do without thinking we grew up with. Like once upon a time, everything was perfect. Hoss, you take care."

On New Year's Eve, I told Kimberly I had the money for her to go to St. Louis. When Rhonda asked how I came by it, I just said I worked a deal. Rhonda's not good with money, so she just accepted it and hugged my neck. After everybody went to bed, early in the morning of the New Year, I wrote out an undated note saying that the money for college came from Rhonda's birth daddy, who was no longer living. I sealed it in an envelope marked "In the Event of My Death, Tiny Whitaker," and put it in the Gideon Bible I keep in my chest of drawers. I didn't like taking credit for another man's generosity, but I didn't see any other way for the time being. Also, I figured if something happens where it would do more harm than good for them not to know, I'll tell them.

Come summer, we packed up the truck and got Kimberly moved to St. Louis. Danny, the boyfriend, stayed behind to work in Cynthiana, and pretty soon they were history. To this day Kimberly's still in school out there, doing well and loving it. Somehow I doubt she'll ever live close to us again, now that she's seen the world, and I know in my heart of hearts that if it'd been my money, I wouldn't have had the nerve to send her out there. Sometimes early of a morning when I'm opening the station and nobody else is around, I find myself thinking real hard toward that stranger, almost like I'm praying. I try real hard to get through to him, try to let him know that it took both of us to do it right. I gave her roots, he gave her wings.

Damn if it didn't snow the next Christmas.

One Man's Treasure

by Andrew Kantor

Andrew Kantor started writing short fiction in elementary school (although it has improved considerably in the last twenty-five years). He's been a "real" writer since the early 1980s in New York, when he headed Stuyvesant High School's science-fiction magazine. Since then, he's been earning a living as an editor of Internet and computer magazines, including stints at PC Magazine *and* Internet World *(where he made an appearance on "60 Minutes" showing Lesley Stahl how to forge e-mail). Kantor now lives in Cincinnati; this is his first published fiction since writing about "Orion's Crystal" in the April 1997 issue of* Games.

My friend had this treasure map, see, and we were going to help him dig for gold.

It wasn't actually a map. It was instructions to follow. And technically he didn't even have that. What Alex really had was a sheet full of numbers and an inclination that it was a coded map to a treasure. That's what you get when you have a crazy relative.

Friday

Kara and I were headed down I-75 toward Louisville. An empty highway, in part because we were—as far as I could tell—in the middle of nowhere, and in part because it was six in the morning on a Saturday.

"Virtuous people are up and about," my uncle used to say, waking us up at—well, at around this time on the weekend. Then and now, I'd rather be malevolent and asleep. The virtuous have bags under their eyes.

A couple of months ago, my friend Alex and his wife, Casey (Cassandra, but no one I ever knew called her that), had moved into his family's farmhouse, about twenty minutes outside the city. (If you could call Louisville a city. Being from New York—the City, with a capital *C* thank you—I think of anyplace smaller than Chicago as a large town with airs.)

But here we were, tooling toward farm country because Alex

and Casey might be rich. Besides, we hadn't seen them in half a year, and this was as good an excuse as any to take a week off. Better, if there really was treasure to be had.

"Rest area, five miles ahead," Kara said, glancing up from the map she had cradled since we left the hotel in Cincinnati that morning.

"A comment or a hint?" I asked.

"Just a comment. I usually don't hint if I need a rest stop."

"Good point."

"This is a big one, though," she added. "It's got a circle around it."

"A *fancy* rest stop," I replied. "Maybe even a Burger King."

"The circle doesn't lie."

When we traveled, Kara was navigator—sometimes her sense of timing (or direction, or both) was good enough that she'd steer us through local roads without looking up from the map. On highways, where the only way to go was forward, she'd amuse herself by saying things like, "Rest stop, six miles," a minute before the REST STOP: 5 MI. sign appeared.

She kept the map in her lap and Casey's instructions in the car-door pocket; Kara said she's trust a fellow woman's directions better. We passed the circled-so-it's-fancy rest stop and kept going—eventually exiting the highway, down a state road, turning on smaller and smaller roads until we came to Alex and Casey's.

The house was a half mile down, a well-kept, recently painted Victorian with Alex's Acura in the driveway, a porch swing ("How cliché," chuckled Kara), and our friends coming out the front door.

One thing Victorian houses have above every other kind is that they look like houses. Homes nowadays—what the real estate agent calls "contemporary"—look like boxes with windows and maybe a garage. Victorians, like Alex's, have style. There were things sticking out all over—cupolas and balconies and rooms and chimneys. It clearly wasn't a cookie-cutter kind of place; few homes from the 1800s are. Houses like Alex's have a personality.

His looked to be in great shape, too. A lot of old homes seemed to be owned by old people—the people who have lived there forever and don't see the slow deterioration of the shingles or the sagging of the porch. But his was clearly well-kept, and I recalled that Alex mentioned something about caretakers. Maybe they were the ones who kept the place shipshape.

Before he was officially our friend, we knew Alex as the younger brother of a college friend—my news editor when I worked on the *Student Press*. So I had a couple of years on Alex, although home ownership would soon age him, I knew.

Kara and I joked that when we were in our eighties, Alex would *still* be the kid brother. He was in his early thirties now, thin to the point of lankiness, with brown hair that, like his brother's, always seemed in need of a haircut.

Like Alex, Casey was also in her early thirties, her hair still short and dark like it had been when Kara and I first met them. She was a head shorter than Alex's five-ten, and just as energetic—"perky" we called it back then.

Evidently she had snapped into hostess mode and was wearing khakis and a dark blue top, both looking washed and pressed. Alex, evidently trying for the native look—or, more likely, what he thought other people would expect the native look to be—was in a red flannel shirt, blue jeans (not worn enough yet, I bet he thought), work boots, and baseball cap. I didn't have the heart to tell him that any caps worn by the natives wouldn't be the 100-percent wool, Major League Baseball-approved variety. If you want to blend, try the "given away by John Deere" style. But Alex was always the guy who wanted to be on the cutting edge, whatever that was.

Still, he made me feel a bit less scruffy in my worn jeans and "Newton State" sweatshirt, although I reminded myself that I had the drive as an excuse. Kara always looked good, long drive or not. She's one of those people whose pants are always creased and whose sweater always matches her top. At least from a husband's point of view.

We got out of the car. Greetings were exchanged. Hugs were had. The drive was described. Directions were praised. The neighborhood was admired. You know how this goes.

"This is a great house," Kara said as we walked in the front door. "How old?"

"Built in 1852," Alex said. "We've got this plaque. Big brass thing, I think from the Historical Society. We have to put it—or we're *supposed* to put it—on the front of the house. One of those 'historical homes' things. Just haven't gotten around to it." Alex always sounded like he had ten things he wanted to say and only time for nine. You could almost feel the words bouncing around in his head before some of them shot out.

The requisite nickel tour took a good hour. That's the beauty of older houses, especially Victorians: There always seems to be another room, or an almost-forgotten corner with something interesting in it. They're made for people to live in a long time, so stuff accumulates. Just like the outsides of today's houses are boring, the insides usually are, too—mass-produced blocks that require the people who live there to give them every drop of personality. An old Victorian, though, comes with at least a small, prepackaged soul built in.

Alex's house had been in his family a long time, so it was infused with . . . well, with something. It was a home, not a house. We saw rooms that were bedrooms, and bedrooms that were offices, or a library, or a sewing room. Family heirlooms (that is, stuff that no one else wanted, but no one else wanted to throw out, either) were everywhere. One room at the back of the house had three old telescopes. One had drawers full of maps of the state, county, and town. One was decorated (if you could call it that) with carefully labeled insects from the area, some of which I hoped had become extinct since 1852. And it kept going up—three floors of living space, plus an attic with a roof high enough to stand under.

But the place didn't feel old, just well-used. It wasn't worn out, wasn't dusty or musty or creaking . . . much.

"This place is 150 years old?" I asked. It was in great condition—freshly painted, polished wood floors, a beautiful rug in the living room, all the windows clean and unbroken. "Where do you find the time?"

"Not the time," said Casey, "the money. And not ours."

"My great-grandfather built it," Alex explained. "Built the house, left money in his will. For a caretaker. So even when someone wasn't living here, there was somebody taking care of it—keeping it up."

"Must have been a lot of money," I said. "A hundred and fifty years? That's a lot of polishing and dusting."

"Before vacuums and Pledge, even," Kara said.

Alex nodded, smirking. "Great-granddad was rich. On the wealthy side."

"Rolling in it," added Casey.

"Rolling, jumping, dancing," said Alex. "At least until he died."

He waved his arm, follow-me style. "Come. I'll tell you the tale of Great-granddad Webster. And his money."

"And his treasure map," said Kara.

"Yes. Quite possibly," said Alex.

We headed down to and through the kitchen, into the family room behind it. "Watch your step," Casey said, pointing down. The family room was a good inch and a half lower than the kitchen—enough to trip, but not enough to be a true step. "Old houses," she said with a shrug.

The family room was warm and cozy. Again, a well-polished wood floor, darker than the living room, but also rug covered—this one was a braided oval with lots of browns and greens. A wood stove sat in one corner, and Alex and Casey had arranged the sofas and chairs (none matching, but that's the way it was supposed to be) around it, with a large, well-worn coffee table (oak or cherry, I guessed) in front. On the wall opposite the stove were two bookshelves filled with a mix of old and new. Some old-fashioned kitchenware sat on top; now it was art.

We arranged ourselves, Kara and me on the sofa, Casey and Alex each in a chair. Alex leaned back in what I assumed was his best Alistair Cooke pose. "Let me tell you a story," he said, "before I show you anything."

"Tell and show," quipped Kara.

Alex nodded. "My great-grandfather was born over in—that is, down in—Tennessee and moved to Kentucky when he was little. He made a pile of money by making supplies for the Army—I mean the U.S. Army. And I think some state militias. But then he started giving them—well, selling them—to the Confederate Army. When the war started."

"A patriot through and through," I said.

"A patriot for *someone*," Kara agreed.

"He was a big believer in the South. In the Confederacy," Alex said. "The kind of guy who hated anyone named Abraham. You know, Lincoln. On sight. Slavery, Dixie, Robert E. Lee—the whole nine yards. That was great-grandpa."

"Or so we thought," Casey interjected.

"Or so we thought," Alex agreed. "Wait a sec. Back to that in a minute. Clarence—great-grandpa—was rich. Really rich, for the time. But he was also a bit of a loon."

"Not that those ever go together," I said.

"Granted. In his case, they did. He was the crazy guy in the attic. The guy the family would keep there, anyway. If he didn't own the house, that is. He used to sit around with maps—maps of his property—making strange marks, writing things on the edge that no one understood. He was into astronomy and beekeeping and guns and all sorts of stuff."

"And codes," Casey said.

"And codes," Alex said. "We found notes. Little ones on scraps of paper, some whole pages. All of it in weird codes. Bunches of letters on a page. Symbols, sometimes. Sometimes numbers, or a mix."

"So you had a crazy, rich great-grandfather," I said. "Always nice."

"He used to give lots of money to the Confederacy. Other things, too," Alex went on. "But then the war dragged on. And Clarence's son—my grandfather, Jeffrey—left. He left the farm and moved to Cincinnati."

"Up north," said Casey.

"Technically," said Alex. "And that's what counted. Counted for Clarence, anyway. Grandpa Jeffrey abandoned the cause. He was a traitor—you get the idea. From his letters, it looked like Clarence spent the rest of his life spending money and grumbling about Jeffrey."

"Sounds normal," I said. "For back then."

"For now, even," Kara agreed. "So then what?"

"Well, that went on for a while—a good ten or fifteen years. But in his later letters it looked like he had begun to forgive my grandfather. The war was over, things weren't bad for him. He made some comments in his letters about who would get what when he died."

"And he stopped bad-mouthing Jeffrey?" I said.

"Pretty much. But when Clarence finally did die, and everyone gets together back at the farm, guess who's hardly in the will."

"Grandpa," Kara and I said together.

"Bingo," said Alex. "So much for time healing all wounds. But his other kids didn't either. Didn't get any money, I mean. He left money—Clarence left money for the care of the house, and gave some to his two daughters, but not a lot."

"Not the family fortune," said Casey. "Not all the money he probably had."

"So where," asked Kara, "is the fortune?"

"Maybe he lost it," I suggested. "Supporting the losing side of a war isn't always the best investment."

"That's what we thought," said Alex. "That he lost it all. Or that he gave it away. Maybe to some The-South-Will-Rise-Again cause. Maybe the Klan. But he didn't."

"And you know this how?" I asked.

"There were a lot of hints," Casey said. "Kind of a gestalt about it—you got the feeling that he still had his money, somewhere."

"But not for any of his offspring," I said.

"Right," Alex agreed. "Well, almost. I think. I didn't tell you what he *did* leave my grandfather." He paused for effect. "One small iron box and the contents within."

Another pause. Then Kara: "And they were?"

Alex grinned. "Paper. A single piece. Written in—"

"Code," I said. "Of course."

"Score one for Andrew. It's a sheet of code—it's been sitting for over a hundred years. In that box. Or somewhere. People saw it—they must have. But no one bothered to try to decode it."

The obvious question: "Why not?" asked Kara.

"I wondered. I wondered the same thing," Alex said. "Maybe no one . . . maybe everyone figured it was a waste. Of time, money, whatever. Maybe it was a will. Maybe not, and maybe they figured that if Clarence left anything it was just junk. Worthless, and no one figured to work it—no one had the mind-set to bother. So it sat in my dad's attic forever. Until I inherited it. Then I got this house and started thinking about that."

"And how did you get this place, anyway?" I asked. "Being on the wrong side of the Mason-Dixon line and all."

"I actually inherited it from my Aunt Sophie, who got it from her father. Sophie didn't have kids, and she and I were always close. I guess she figured the war was over, and she could give it to someone who lived up yonder."

Kara was chomping at the bit. "So do you have any clue what's on this paper? Is it directions to the treasure? What's the deal?"

"The answers," said Alex, "are 'No,' 'Probably,' and 'We have to find out.' Sophie left me a whole pile of Clarence's letters. She was the family genealogy buff, at least for a while. And I started to go through them—the letters, I mean. To cut to the chase, it looks like Clarence didn't hate my grandpa after all."

He reached over and slid open the drawer of the coffee table, pulling out a manila envelope that he opened. He handed Kara what looked like an old letter. "Read the last paragraph."

Kara scanned it, then read aloud. "'Don't worry. When I finally leave this earth I'll make sure to take care of all of you, including Jeffrey—'"

"Jeffrey was my grandfather," Alex reminded us.

"'—but it may be a while before he figures it out. God preserve the South.'"

"There are other things," he said. "Things like that. Comments in letters. Like about Jeffrey deserving more. Mixed in with other stuff—commentary about things changing after the war, about things being different. Always some comment about God preserving the Confederacy. Something like that. But you could *feel* that he was thinking of things differently."

"I think I'm getting it," I said. "Clarence is rich. He doesn't hate your grandfather, but he only leaves him this coded message. And he doesn't leave much money to anyone."

"I like to think," Alex said, "that he figured if my grandfather was smart—smart enough to figure out where his inheritance is—he deserved it. We think he left a good chunk to him. My grandfather. Maybe all of it."

"So where is this stash?" Kara asked.

"We think the instructions are in this message," Casey said.

"He had to be difficult about it," said Alex. "And that's the problem."

"And that's why we're here," said Kara.

Alex nodded with a smile. "In part. We wanted you to visit, though. We wanted you here. A code-deciphering treasure hunt—potential treasure hunt—sounded like fun. Or not. We could just sip lemonade and sit on the porch for a week."

"I like the money idea better," I said. "And we would split this how?"

"Sixty-forty," said Alex.

"Fifty-fifty," said Casey, at the same time. She glared at her husband.

"Fifty-fifty," Alex agreed, "but—" Another glare. "Fifty-fifty," he repeated. "But I can't promise anything. I mean, there may not be any."

"Blood, toil, tears, and sweat will be fine," I said. "And half of whatever we find sounds fair. Let's see this path to riches."

Resigned to his fate, Alex grinned at the chance to show off whatever it was he had. He reached back into his envelope to pull out a sheaf of papers. At first I thought this was a long letter, but they were copies—he gave one to each of us.

427718718271 31116217 4213195217345 421279031116 42795 31127 116902420895217208 42110537131662 421721731

2724 31116217 421105208217 274 31116217 4213195217345 101662 31116217 1017183416212 134718249031 3195217217 6622790718718 410524208 34 718349592217 95279024208 421312724217

421313424208 1052492 2724 31116217 421312724217 11621734208 2724217 116902420895217208 42110537131662 410510217 20821792952172 17421 101662 31116217 162753634421421 42795 3111695217217 116902420895217208 2171059211631 410510217 421721731 111621795217 6622790 1105718718 410524208 3424 105952724 1013495 10524 31116217 9295279024208

495275 31116217 1013495 11621734208 4105431662 208217929521721 7421 3424208 9227 2724217 116902420895217208 421721731 3127 34 16718217349510 52492

162724242171631 31116217 2082731421

20810592 20810592 20810592

11163431 6622790 410524208 105421 662279095421

9227208 36952174212179510217 31116217 421279031116

"I'm guessing that *1* isn't *A*, I said after a moment.

"Nope," Alex agreed. "It looks like a mess. I mean, we can figure that *34* is *A* or *I*, but that's about it. Unless *3* is *I* and *4* is *T* or something."

"Are you sure this mess means anything at all?" I asked. "Could it be a hoax?" Sometimes I've seen code that looks like code. But this was just a sheet of numbers. No punctuation, no apostrophes, no nothing. At least there were spaces and line breaks.

"What I figure," Alex said, "is that it might be nonsense. Garbage. Maybe Clarence went through a little trouble to screw around—to create a lot of trouble for my grandfather. But then I figure, what's the point? My granddad wasn't obsessive—he wasn't the sort of guy who would run around—who would spend the rest of his life trying to decode this. You figure—at least *I* figure—that if he was going try to drive my grandfather up a wall, he'd do something a bit better. More inventive."

"Sometimes simple is best," Kara said.

"Ask a fashion model," I agreed. I held up the paper. "You want us to spend the next few days trying to decode this?" I said.

"I have faith."

"That we can decode this?"

"That at least one of us can."

So we sat around the family room, staring at the sheet of numbers. There didn't seem to be any pattern or anything recognizable. I noticed that Alex and Casey didn't stare at the sheet nearly as much as we did. "Believe me, I've stared at it forever," Alex said. "I want some fresh sets of eyes."

Those fresh sets of eyes were becoming less and less fresh after an hour of staring and scribbling. We broke for dinner; Alex grilled us some well-done (but medium-rare) sirloins and we talked to them about future plans for the house.

"I'd like to add a greenhouse someday," Alex said. "Behind the family room, or maybe even upstairs."

"My understanding of greenhouses is that they require a lot of windows. Like a glass roof," I said. "Upstairs has the traditional opaque kind."

"Ah, but you notice the third floor, it doesn't cover the com— the entire—the whole second floor," Alex explained. "We can take the baby's room and convert it by taking out the ceiling. That is, the roof. We cut the joists on the top, then extend the—"

"Stop," I said. "You're wading into homeowner-speak."

Alex look confused. "But don't—I mean, you own your house."

"But I've never used the word 'joist' in conversation," I pointed out. That's the difference."

Kara, able (as usual) to focus like The Boy Who Couldn't Stop Washing, said, "Baby's room? Is there something we should know?"

"Baby's *room*, not baby," Casey told her. You saw it—the one with the yellow paint and the cute wooden crib. It's only pine," she lamented. "But that yellow paint shouldn't be too hard to cover. Actually, it's more of an ochre."

"Oh, yeah," I said. "Make that into a greenhouse. Hmm. I guess

I can see it."

"Crib," said Kara suddenly. She was staring, but not at any of us. Not at anything in the room, either. Her eyes started to glaze with that one-moment-while-I-try-to-remember-something look.

"Crib," Alex agreed.

"Small wooden box that holds baby," I added. "Has blankie."

"Crib," Kara said again, starting to smile. "Sonofabitch."

I stared at her blankly, like someone who just heard what was supposed to be a complete sentence, but wasn't. "A crib," I repeated. "We need a verb."

"Come on, you know—a crib. Not a baby crib, a . . . a crib crib." She gave me a half glare. "You're smart, but not that smart. You must have used cribs in college. Crib sheets."

"Ah," I said, finally understanding. "I was just more honest about it. We called them 'cheat sheets.' Your point is?"

Kara was now back on Earth, and I could see the pieces of whatever puzzle she was working on falling into place. I just had to wait her out so it could go from her brain to her mouth to us.

She spoke slowly, making sure to get the idea right. "If you want to break a code, you might be able to use a crib. If you know what some of the words are, you can use that to decipher the rest of the message."

"Like hitting the HINT button," Casey said. "Sneaky."

"Smart," I added. "You think there's a crib to be had?"

"Can I see some of your great-grandfather's other letters—the ones Sophie had?" Kara asked.

Alex shrugged. "Sure." He disappeared up the stairs.

"What kind of crib do you think you'll find?" Casey asked.

"Alex said something about the letters all saying something about God preserving the Confederacy," Kara said. "Or maybe it's just a 'Dear Sophie' or 'To Whom it May Concern.'" But if there's anything consistent about his writing, that might be the way to crack it."

"This just . . . came to you?" I asked. "Like lightning?"

"The voice in my head," she replied. "The one that keeps telling me to undercook your chicken." She winked. "Actually, it's from doing word puzzles."

"And when do you have time for those?" I asked. "During your copious free time?"

"At work. Online. At lunch. There are lots of sites with puzzles, and you can work 'em with your mouse while you eat with your other hand." She grinned. "I've got it down to a science. Anyway, there's one where you have to decipher a scrambled quote. If you can guess some of the words, you can solve it pretty easily. So if the quote's from, say, a philosopher, you can guess that a big word might be 'philosophy.'"

"A crib," said Casey.

"Right."

Alex returned, letters in hand. "Careful. They're old."

We spread them on the floor and coffee table, each of us with a few in front. Then we started reading them. "Concentrate on the first few words or the last few," Kara suggested. "Look for a turn of phrase—the bigger the words the better."

It took us less than five minutes, and Kara had her crib. Alex and I didn't find much, because he had the oldest letters—the pre-Civil War ones—and I had the later ones, long after the war. But Kara and Casey had the middle ground, during and just after the war. That's when, as Alex had said, he ended every letter the same way: "God Preserve the South."

Kara picked up her copy of the coded message. "See the last line? It's pretty short. Let's assume that it stands for 'God Preserve the South.'"

"It's still a bunch of gibberish," Alex said.

"But look—the number *217* is in there, four times," she said. "Three *E*s in *preserve* and one in *the*. Four. I bet *217* is *E*."

"We're on our way," said Casey.

As anyone who's driven with kids knows, being on your way and being there are two entirely different things. But we had at least a feeling that we were headed in the right direction. We had *E*s, *S*s, *R*s, *T*s, and a few other letters. Of course, figuring out which combination of numbers corresponded to a particular letter wasn't easy. Was *427718718271* broken up as *427-718-718-271* or *42-77-187-182-71*? Or something else?

Turns out Clarence didn't use a simple cipher like *217* was *E*, *218* was *F*, and so on. No, he had to mix 'em up, sometimes using a two-digit number, sometimes using a three-digit number, and for all we knew, sometimes using a one-digit number. I say "for all we knew," because after about two hours of playing with the thing, my eyes glazed over and I was ready for something else. Kara, on the other hand, is a pit bull when it comes to puzzles, and she barely looked up as one by one Alex, Casey, and I headed for the kitchen for a snack, then into the living room to talk.

Every now and then I'd check on Kara and was rewarded with a "Hmm?" and an occasional "Could you bring me some more paper?"

Conversation, time, and paper came and went, and it was well past one in the morning when we were all too tired to be polite anymore. Alex and Casey went to bed, and I stopped in to see how Kara was doing before turning in.

"Good luck," I said. "I'm off to sleep. See you . . . er . . . later."

"Luck is not a factor," Kara replied, not looking up. "If you were going to give someone some kind of directions, how would you start them?"

"With 'Start' or 'Begin' I guess."

"That's what I figured, and I think figured right. That gives me *T*, and that's the second most common letter in English." Now she looked up. "I'm getting there. I can do this."

"I have no doubt," I replied. "I can do sleep. I'm going to do that now."

"Hmm? Oh, okay. See you later." Back she went to the paper, and up I went to bed.

Bed, yes. Sleep no. Well, not much. It seemed like thirty seconds after I shut out the light (leaving a Casey-provided night-light on) I was woken by a frantic blonde shaking me.

"IdiditIdiditIdidit!" Kara was shouting. Well, *saying*, but in the dark in the middle of the night it certainly felt like shouting. And she was definitely shaking. Me, that is.

"You did it," I managed, trying to make sure it sounded like a statement instead of a question, lest she feel the need to explain it.

"I did! I got the whole thing, from start to finish." She furrowed her brow. "Well, from 'Start' to 'South,' actually. But I got it. I'm getting Alex and Casey. Let's go treasure hunting."

I grabbed her arm before she could ruin two good friendships. "First of all," I said, now wide awake, "it's"—I looked at the clock—"three-twelve in the morning. My guess is that Alex and Casey have other things on their minds."

"At three in the morning?"

"I meant sleep. And second, even if I let my sanity take a break and woke them, are you sure you've got it right?"

"Ha!" said Kara. "Damn straight—don't doubt me, sleepy boy. I mean, it makes complete sense, and all the letters work out, and the chances of there being some other combination of letters and words that fits those numbers is zero. Z-E-R-O."

"Lemme see."

She handed me a sheet of paper where she had written out the whole message in neat block letters:

> START BY FACING OUT FROM THE BACK DOOR OF THE HOUSE
>
> WALK STRAIGHT TWO HUNDRED EIGHTY FIVE FEET INTO THE WOODS TO THE BLACK OAK TREE
>
> HEAD WHERE THE LOWEST LIMB IS POINTING FOR ONE HUNDRED SIXTY FIVE FEET TO AN ARROW ON THE GROUND
>
> FOLLOW THE ARROW ABOUT EIGHTY FEET TILL YOU HIT THE STREAM
>
> FOLLOW THE STREAM SOUTH FOR TWO HUNDRED SIXTY FEET
>
> ON THE SIDE OF THE STREAM BY THE BLACK WALNUT TREE YOU'LL FIND A LARGE ROUND STONE
>
> STANDING ON THE STONE HEAD ONE HUNDRED SIXTY FIVE DEGREES BY THE COMPASS FOR THREE HUNDRED EIGHTY FIVE FEET WHERE YOU WILL FIND AN IRON BAR IN THE GROUND
>
> FROM THE BAR HEAD FIFTY DEGREES AND GO ONE HUNDRED FEET TO A CLEARING
>
> CONNECT THE DOTS
>
> DIG DIG DIG
>
> WHAT YOU FIND IS YOURS
>
> GOD PRESERVE THE SOUTH

"You got all this from that crib?" I asked.

Kara nodded. "From that, from guessing that 'start' might be the first word, and from staring at the thing till my eyes turned red." They were back to being green now.

"This is amazing," I said. "You amaze me. Incredible." And I meant it.

"We have to find it," Kara said.

"Well, yeah. But not at 3:00 a.m. How about, say, eight? I'll set the alarm."

"Make it seven-thirty." She crawled into bed, still grinning, and only the weight of the blanket keeping her from bouncing onto the floor. "Geez, how am I supposed to sleep?"

I reached over and unplugged the night-light. "Put your head down. Close your eyes. Think happy thoughts."

A moment passed. "I'm not going to be able to sleep," Kara pronounced in the dark.

I was pretty awake myself, and now in possession of all my faculties. "Well, I have one idea."

Saturday

Tempting as it is, I won't bore you with the details of waking, waking Alex and Casey, showering, dressing, and having breakfast. And you can imagine their reaction to Kara's work.

"I've got some kick-ass compasses in my camping equipment," Alex said—or, more accurately, exuded. "And I think I know where my range finder is." He jumped from his seat.

"Range finder?" I said.

"Compasses?" Kara said. "Plural?"

Alex stopped in mid-bolt-for-the-other-room and looked back and forth between us. "Compasses plural because what if we got separated."

"In your yard?"

"Out hiking," he retorted. "Actually, one's for working with maps—it's designed to be used flat—and one's for being outside in the field where you have to sight on something in the . . . you know, far away."

"Uh-huh," I offered. "And this range finder?"

"Geez, you never hearda one? You use it to measure the distance across a room," he explained. "It's good for calculating, you know, the dimensions."

"Like a tape measure," I said.

Alex hmphed. "Yeah, yeah, but it's a lot more accurate. It uses a laser. We can send someone out in the right direction holding up, I dunno, like a big, white piece of wood. We point the range finder at that, and we can measure the distance exactly."

"Then whoever's holding the wood moves closer or farther until you say 'Stop,'" I finished.

"Yeah, yeah. Exactly."

Kara pondered this a moment. "Assuming your great-grandfather didn't have one of these—"

"A good assumption," I agreed.

"—then what's the point of being laser-accurate if he wasn't?"

Alex and I exchanged glances. "Um," he said. "Well, y'know . . ."

"Um," I concurred. "Sweetie, it's not about using the *best* technology. It's about using the *most* technology."

"Oh." She turned to Casey for support, but Alex's wife was in the kitchen, probably baking trail food or preparing sandwiches. Kara nodded and smiled slightly—the kind of smile, I suspected, she would give an escaped mental patient. No sudden moves here. With Alex, that was often the best policy.

We agreed to return to our respective rooms and get ready to start hunting, meeting around the kitchen table a few minutes later. Kara and I were in jeans and sneakers, but Alex had on something designed for a trek into the mountains of Tanzania. Khakis with enough pockets to hold a Craftsman 200-piece tool set, and big enough to hold any small children that wouldn't fit in the crib in the ochre room. He also wore what I thought was a photographer's vest but now knew to be a treasure-hunter's. More pockets, some already with things in them—extra compasses, I assumed. And here I was, wondering if a walking stick would be too much.

"I don't need to ask if you're ready," I said.

"You betcha," Alex replied, patting his pockets. I didn't ask. Casey joined us a minute later, without the pockets but with four Ziploc bags with what appeared to be granola bars. Condensation was forming inside the bag, indicating they were still warm—indicating these were homemade granola bars. I wasn't surprised, for some reason.

"Granola bars," Casey confirmed. I have Kool-Aid, too." She indicated her backpack. "Grape."

"Er—" I started, but Kara shot me a look. "Great," I said instead. "Although we're probably only going a few hundred yards."

Casey shrugged. "I know, but it's fun to have an excuse to bake."

Pausing a moment, then nodding at each other, the four of us headed out the back door from the family room into the yard, Kara clutching her newly deciphered cipher. As we stood on the back porch, she read: "Start by facing out from the back door of the house. Walk straight 285 feet into the woods to the black oak tree."

Alex reached into a pocket and produced a small black box that had a display on it, then reached into another pocket and pulled out a small piece of white cardboard that he proceeded to make into a *large* piece of cardboard by unfolding it. I could see that he had taped it together to make it foldable. He handed it to me and pointed into the woods. "Go out there and hold this up. I'll sight on it." He held up what must have been his laser range finder. "Kara and Casey can make sure you're going straight." He pointed. "That way."

I took the cardboard and (quietly counting) paced out ninety-five steps, which I figured to be about ninety-five yards. Close enough for the moment. The woods weren't dense yet, so I was able to keep a straight line. That changed soon, though: Not too far in front of me the trees started to get thicker. If the instructions called for a 350-foot walk, I'd have been in trouble. I looked toward the house. The others stood by the back door, with Alex pointing his black box at me, Star Trek style.

I saw Casey cup her hands to her mouth. "Come! Closer!" she shouted. I took a couple of steps in while Alex looked at the range finder. "A! Little! More!" she yelled. Two more steps. "One! Step! Back!"

I did that, then shouted, "This is close enough! Get! Over! Here!" I waved my arms, figuring that anywhere from 275 to 295 feet would be close enough for treasure-hunting work. I saw them discussing something—I assumed Kara was reminding Alex that his great-grandfather didn't have a laser range finder—and then start walking toward me. I started looking for that black oak tree.

Even though I had passed a couple of dark-looking trees, I didn't see anything that looked like a black oak where I was. Or even nearby. And if I continued walking away from the house for another dozen feet or so, I'd bump into a large rock.

"We did something wrong," I said as Alex, Casey, and Kara arrived. "There's no black oak here." I pointed behind me. "There's a rock, though. Are you sure we walked straight from the back of the house?"

They all nodded. "You bet," said Kara. "And you're standing right at 285 feet."

"Two hundred eighty-six," grumbled Alex.

"This is a highland oak," said Casey, patting one tree. "Highland live oak, actually."

"Not a black oak," Kara said.

"Nope. I think we passed a couple of black oaks back there, though. I didn't look carefully."

"Not fair," Alex said. "I figured if we were gonna be stuck, it'd be later. Not right away. First instruction. Sheesh."

Kara repeated the instruction: "Start by facing out from the back door of the house. Walk straight 285 feet into the woods to the black oak tree." We all looked around again. No black oak had appeared, Ivanhoe style.

"That was the back door, right?" I said. They all looked at me. "Right?"

"Can I use sarcasm in my answer?" Kara said.

"Well maybe it's the back door now, but was it the front door back then?" I countered. "Who knows where the road was in 1865?"

"Same place," said Alex.

"So there's no side door now that could have been the back door then?"

"Nope."

"And I supposed it's pointless to ask if the range finder is accurate."

"Pointless," agreed Casey, before Alex could say a word.

"Maybe someone took down the tree," said Kara. "Is there a stump around?"

We all looked, but the trees around us seemed intact. Kara, I noticed, was staring at the house, her brow crinkled. I knew a thought was coming, and waited it out. I didn't wait long.

"What if the door moved?" she said.

"Moved?" said Alex. He shook his head. "Didn't move. Not a lot of room on that wall for it to move."

"I was thinking," she went on, "that maybe the back of the house now wasn't the back of the house then."

There was a pause as we processed and absorbed that, then Casey started nodding. "The family room floor," she said.

Kara was grinning. "Exactly."

"Exactly?" I said. "Exactly what?"

"Exactly not aligned with the kitchen floor," she replied. "I bet the family room was added later. That's why we had to step down."

"Different kinds of floor, too," said Casey. "The kitchen and living room has two-inch maple boards on the floor. The family room is two-and-a-quarter-inch pine. And it's polyurethaned. The rest of the house is varnished."

"I thought varnish and polyurethane were the same thing," I said.

"Polyurethane is a kind of varnish, but varnish isn't polyurethane," Casey explained.

"Different floors, different times," Kara said to me.

"Different floors, different doors," I said. "The door to the family room was the back door. How wide is the family room?"

"Twenty feet," said Alex. So the family room added twenty feet to the house, and we had to subtract twenty feet from where we looked for the black oak. As the glow from this new light bulb washed over him, Alex pulled out his range finder.

But I was already pacing off twenty feet toward the house, without a laser. "About here," I said when I had removed the width of the family room from the calculations. And right next to me was a tree with dark gray bark, leaning slightly into the path I had just walked. It looked like it had a bad case of whatever passes for acne in the tree world—the bark was pretty gnarled and scaly—and a quick look at a leaf told me it was an oak.

Casey confirmed it a moment later. "Looks like a black oak. Probably a California black oak. *Quercus velutina* or *kelloggii.*" We all stared at her. "So I took Latin!"

"So this is the right place," I said, getting away from Casey's high-school days. "From the door of the kitchen, 285 feet."

"Give or take," grumbled Alex.

Kara looked at her instructions. "Now we 'Head where the lowest limb is pointing for 165 feet to an arrow on the ground,'" she recited. We all looked up at the tree. The lowest limb wasn't low—it was a good thirty feet in the air—and pointed at an angle to the right. "That way," said Kara and started walking.

"Not so fast," I said. "Look closely." They all did.

"Ah," said Alex.

"Ah," repeated Casey, then Kara. About ten feet below Kara's lowest branch was a close-cut stump of a branch, painted with that stuff to keep cut limbs from infecting the rest of the tree. It was a dark gray like the tree, so you could miss it easily, especially if you had treasure on the brain.

"Now what," said Casey. "We can't tell if it was pointing straight or at an angle or what."

"Not easy," said Alex. "Not gonna be easy at all. This whole thing."

"What, you don't want to work for your treasure?" Kara said. "Let's just try a best guess." She pointed in the direction the tree limb might well have pointed. "What was it, 165 feet? Alex, get your range finder out."

The woods were getting more dense here, so it wasn't a straight shot. We had trees to get around, so the 165 feet took about ten shorter trips so we could work our way around trees and through the underbrush. Eventually, though, Alex announced that we were in the spot.

We all looked at the ground, expecting, I expect, to see a glowing-green arrow in the dirt. No such luck; it was just dirt, with a few stones and leaves thrown in for good measure.

"And then," I said, "depression set in."

"You wanted what, a burning bush?" Kara asked.

"A flaming arrow would have been nice," I said.

"I vote," said Alex, "that we clear things. That we clear some of this brush away. Look on the ground. Maybe we'll see something."

We cleared, discovering all manner of things that crawled, stung, pricked, or—I had a feeling we would realize later—itched. Casey ran back to the house at one point, returning with several kinds of gloves and pruning shears, which were gratefully accepted.

It was, in fact, Casey who had the aha moment. "Aha," she said. "Lookee here. Obsidian."

"Is that important?" asked Kara.

I walked over to where she was standing. "It is when it's in the shape of an arrow," I reported. And it was: eight pieces of shiny, black obsidian arranged in the shape of an arrow, under a wild rose bush that Casey had pruned back. "I bet Clarence did that on purpose," I said. "Planted that rose bush over the arrow."

"Wouldn't surprise me," said Alex. "Or poison ivy."

The arrow pointed us farther away from the house, deeper into the woods.

"Next we 'Follow the arrow about eighty feet till you hit the stream,'" Kara instructed. Alex had the range finder out, and—feeling bad about pacing off the twenty feet without his help a few minutes ago—I decided to play along. I got out the white card and started walking.

We moved in stages again, fifteen or twenty feet at a time, with Casey and Kara making sure we were still headed in the right direction. When we reached eighty feet, we collected again. The woods still weren't very thick, but more importantly, there wasn't any water—stream, brook, river, or otherwise.

"We should have done this a long time ago," I said.

"Like a hundred years ago," Kara agreed. "Before things changed."

I nodded. "The good ol' days."

"Yeah? Think about those good ol' days next time you're at the dentist."

But Alex summed things up well. "Now what?" The ground didn't look any different where we were standing, or even a few feet in either direction. There wasn't any hint of a stream. There were paths through the trees that said stream *could* go, but nothing in the here and now. After a hundred years, trees grow and streams, apparently, disappear.

"All right," I said, after the four of us stood around feeling and looking dumbfounded. "Let's assume we went in the right direction and for the right distance."

"We did," Alex said.

"That's the point," I replied. "So let's assume we're standing in a streambed, or what was once a streambed."

"Okay," Kara said.

I went on. "The next instruction is . . ."

Kara glanced down at the paper. "Follow the stream south for 260 feet."

Alex was shaking his head. "But the stream probably wasn't straight. We can't just go south. We can't just guess. That'll throw it off."

"Agreed," I agreed. "But we know that from this spot"—I pointed at my feet—"we have to at least start heading south. So we have a crib here, basically."

Kara was nodding. "Got it. We know that the stream must at least start going south. Figure at least ten, maybe twenty feet before it really begins to turn a lot."

"Right. Alex, get out one of your compasses. Tell me which way is south."

He reached into a pocket, pulled out a compass, and after a moment said, "That way. Pretty much."

I pointed 'that way' and said to Kara, "Walk over there, like ten feet or so." She did, stepping around or over the brush. "Okay. We can assume the stream flowed from where I am to where Kara is. So let's see if we can find something that says, 'Once there was a stream here.'"

Kara and Casey started looking up and around, maybe trying to decide if there were different trees growing where the streambed had been. Alex and I were looking down and around, hoping to see, I don't know, fish skeletons or something.

Alex found the something. "I think I've got it," he said. "Catch." What I caught was a small rock.

"So?" I said. "There are rocks everywhere." I tossed it to Kara.

She tossed it back. "But not smooth ones," she said. "Smooth rocks mean water."

"That was my point," said Alex. "Follow the rocks. The smooth rocks."

"Aha."

Easier said than done. Casey made another trip to the house, this time for trowels to help us dig down a couple of inches, where most of Alex's smooth rocks were buried. After about an hour of digging and following the remains of the streambed, we broke for lunch.

Casey, I wasn't surprised to see, had already prepared a monster cold-cuts plate (probably slicing the stuff herself, if not actually slaughtering the salami). We dug in, keeping the conversation to something other than the fact that we had to follow 260 feet of stream essentially a few feet at a time.

Eventually the desire to find the treasure overcame our lunchtime inertia and we headed back to the woods. And that's where we spent the next four hours: digging, scraping, and following the course of a stream that hadn't seen water since who knew when.

We worked in five- or six-foot jumps, uncovering smooth rocks. When we found enough to be sure we were still in the streambed, we moved farther. If we lost the trail, we would dig to either side until we found more of the right kind of rock. Occasionally, in a bout of frustration, Kara or Alex would take a guess about the course and dig twenty or thirty feet downstream. More often than not, they lost the trail; the stream wound around quite a bit. But the few times they struck gold—or, rather, struck *smooth*—it saved us a bunch of time.

On we went. When it started to get dark, we decided to check our progress. Alex got out his range finder and we did the ten-foot hop trick from where we started, moving along the uncovered streambed, around curves, avoiding trees, stepping over underbrush. We got to our last digging point, and Alex started counting on his fingers. Then he said, "Oops."

"Oops what."

"Where you're standing," he said. "Right there. It's 286 feet."

"You're kidding," said Kara. "We went twenty-six feet farther than we had to?"

Alex shrugged. "No one was keeping track."

"Wasn't that your job?"

"My job was figuring out how far we got."

"That's the same thing!"

"I'd say that's enough," Casey cut in. "Let's mark the 260-foot spot and head home. I have to start cooking."

We paced back twenty-six feet, and—just to be sure—Alex, the range finder, and I paced off the distance to the starting point. When we were comfortable with the spot, he pulled a small can of orange spray paint from a pocket and sprayed a dot in the former streambed. "Until tomorrow." We headed back.

Sunday

It's amazing what a good dinner and a good breakfast can do for your spirits. And a hot shower helps, too. By nine Sunday morning, we were ready to roll again. By a quarter after, we were standing over Alex's orange dot.

"Here we are," said Kara. We all agreed. "All right, then. 'On the side of the stream, by the black walnut tree, you'll find a large round stone.' That's what we need to find next."

"The black walnut tree," I said. "He's got a thing for black trees."

"They both live a long time," Casey said. "Black oaks and black walnuts. Also easy to find, I guess."

"Just look for walnuts," Kara suggested.

But Casey shook her head. "Not this time of year. Late summer, fall. It's too early for walnuts."

"But there should be some on the ground from last year, right?" I asked.

"You underestimate the power of squirrels," Kara said. "But we might find some shells."

"What does a black walnut tree look like?" I asked, as we started to scour the ground—this time for walnut shells. My back was beginning to have second thoughts about treasure hunting.

"It looks like this," Casey said a moment later. She was standing about five feet from Alex's dot, her hand resting on a tree. I looked up. It looked like a tree. I looked down. Scattered around the tree were what looked like golf-ball-sized rocks, that turned out to be walnuts, or parts of them. Black walnuts, I assumed.

"That was easy," I said.

"So's this," Kara said, pointing to a large, round stone a foot from the tree.

"Small favors," Casey agreed. "You think this is the right one?"

Just in case, we searched around the tree some more, but—

although we found plenty of rocks, stones, and pebbles, none was as obviously large and round as Kara's.

"This is it," Alex pronounced. "Gotta be. What's next—the next instruction?"

Kara removed the paper from her pocket. "Standing on the stone, head 165 degrees by the compass for 385 feet where you will find an iron bar in the ground."

Alex was already pulling out his compass. This one was significantly more complicated looking than the one he used yesterday to determine "south." I assumed he preferred a "kick-ass" model for figuring exact direction. He flipped open a cover on the thing, using the metal flap as a sight. Then, standing on the stone, he rotated his body, all the while sighting along the compass lid.

"Andrew," he said, not taking his eye off the compass, "Go out. That way. Till I tell you to stop. Then I'll tell you to move left or right."

"Right." I headed out in what was roughly 165 degrees, already pulling out my white card for use with the laser range finder I knew would soon be making its appearance. When I was a good distance away but still visible to Alex, I held up the white card to make it easier for him to see me through the trees.

"A few steps left!" he shouted. I moved to my left. "Other left!" I moved to Alex's left. "Keep going!" A few more steps. "Hold it! That's it! Don't move!" I saw him disappear a moment as he bent down, then he reappeared with the range finder, which he pointed at me. "Ninety-two feet!" he shouted. "Remember that!" Then he, Kara, and Casey made their way over to me.

We repeated the process: I walked away at roughly 185 degrees, Alex moved me left or right, then he figured the distance. After five such legs, he announced we were at 385 feet from the black oak and the stone. No iron bar was jutting out, so we began to search, making our way out from the 385-foot point (which Alex sprayed with another dot—blue this time).

We continued to search. And continued. After what seemed like an hour, no luck, and my back was getting stiff.

"There's got to be an easier way," Kara grumbled off to my left.

"There must be a technological way," I agreed, moving what I hoped wasn't poison-anything out of the way.

"Oh!" shouted Alex.

We stood and turned. "Got it?" I asked, glad this was over.

"No," he said, as we all met by the blue dot. "But you're right.

There's technology. I mean, there's a technological solution. Wait here." And he scampered—no joke—back *towards* the house.

"He worries me sometimes," Kara said. Casey only nodded.

Alex returned a few minutes later with a . . . a *thing*. It looked like two oval loops of steel joined by a five-foot rod with a box in the middle. The box had a bunch of switches and dials on it, as well as a handle of some sort.

"Planning to contact the mother ship?" Kara asked.

"Funny," said Alex. "This is the Tokahama TM9000 Metal Detector."

"*That's* a metal detector?" I said. "I thought those had a round disk, like a frisbee."

"And a beach," added Kara.

"Those are the cheesy models," Alex replied. "This is a professional one."

"There are professional . . . er . . . metal-detector users?" I asked.

"Detectorers," Kara suggested. "Metal detectives."

"All I know," Alex replied, somewhat indignantly, "is that this thing will chirp if you even think about metal near it. An iron bar in the ground will set off bells." He started flipping switches.

"If my watch stops, you owe me," I said, backing away from Alex and the TM9000.

He moved one of the two ovals a couple of inches above the ground by the blue dot and began moving it back and forth slowly, in widening circles, working in between trees and pushing aside undergrowth. The three of us watched with a mix of awe and fascination. Mostly fascination.

Every now and then the detector would bleep, chirp, or beep, and one of us—usually me—would dig around the spot. Unfortunately, all that got us was a few bottle caps and six cents. (Although that included a buffalo nickel, which I thought might be worth something.)

After a while, we let Alex alone, digging only once when the TM9000 gave a slightly longer beep. It turned out to be a chunk of rusty metal, but after a brief discussion we decided it wasn't an "iron bar" and Alex continued.

As exciting as it was, after an hour of watching Alex sweep the ground, we began to get restless. Also, it was getting past noon. "My inclination," I finally said, "is to break for lunch. There's really no rush."

"You never studied compound interest," said Kara.

"We've got all week," Casey said. "Banks are closed today anyway."

I could see Alex look up and nod in reluctant agreement. "I'd never decline one of your lunches, anyway."

"Cranky people are no fun to treasure-hunt with," Kara finished. "I can put this off for an hour. The anticipation will keep me company."

"Done," I said. "Lunch it is."

Like all Casey's meals, lunch was terrific: chicken and pasta salads with fresh rolls—homemade ones. I still had no clue when she had the time, but I wasn't about to ask. Deals with the devil are the dealmaker's problem.

"I don't get it," said Alex, as we sat around the table. Casey was back in the kitchen, presumably cleaning lunch and preparing dinner at the same time; she refused assistance. Se we tried to figure out what we had done wrong. "We know we're in the right place," Alex continued. "We found the black walnut tree. And we found the round stone. And I *know* we went the right way and the right distance."

"Maybe the iron bar moved," Kara said. "Weren't there earthquakes?"

"I think that was before his time," I replied. "Early 1800s, if I remember. But I don't think that would move an iron bar. Bury it, at worst."

"The TM9000 would find it, then," said Alex. "Unless it's way, way deep. And even then."

"Let's work this through step by step," I said. "First, we're assuming the black walnut we found is *the* black walnut. Then we're assuming the round stone is *the* round stone. Then we're assuming we headed in the right direction for the right distance. Right?"

"Right, right, and right," agreed Kara. "Is there any reason to think that the tree was wrong? Was there another black walnut around?"

Casey walked in from the kitchen. "I didn't see one, no. And I looked. I can use the walnuts for cooking and dye-making." There was a pause as we absorbed that.

Then Kara: "All right, then. So that has to be the right stone."

"And even if it's not, the right one has to be close," Alex said. "It wouldn't make that much of a difference. If we started out a bit off, I mean. We'd still be there—in the right place. Or at least the right area."

"I want to ask this next question without getting anyone into a huff," I said. "But Alex, are you *sure* you used that compass right?"

Alex nodded. "Yep."

"I mean, just an observation, but it looked new."

"It is. Well, not used. I mean it's new, but not used yet," he said. "But I know how to use it. Line the needle with the *N*. Turn till you're facing 165 degrees—you sight with this wire here. I lined you up with the wire."

"There's no point asking if the compass is accurate, is there?"

Alex looked insulted. "The Director 15-A compass is accurate within one-tenth of a degree," he said. "As long as the North Pole hasn't moved, that was 165 degrees."

"Hmm," said Kara.

"And the distance was right, too," I said.

"Yep," Alex agreed. "And even if we were off a bit—which we weren't—but even if we were, I searched all over."

"Hmm," said Kara.

"I'm guessing here," I said to Kara, "that something's on your mind."

"Yessss," she replied. "I think the North Pole *does* move."

"Reindeer accidents?"

"Funny. Just a natural process." She held out her hand to Alex. "Lemme see that compass." He dug around and handed it over; Kara popped open the cover and stared at the dial. She started to grin. "See there?" She was pointing to the face. "That dial—it's for correcting for magnetic north."

"What do you mean, 'correcting for magnetic north'?" Alex asked. "Isn't north, north?"

"Not quite," Kara said. "Some norths are more north than other norths. You have to correct for magnetic north depending on where in the country you are." She looked at me. "Don't you remember that orienteering class we took?"

"Vaguely," I replied. "I remember being distracted by you."

"Hmph. Anyway, there should be a guide that came with the compass to tell you what the correction is for Louisville. I bet it's a few degrees off."

"And that would move the search area by at least a few feet," I said.

Alex bolted upstairs and returned a few minutes later with the instruction book. "Bingo," he said. "Right here. Magnetic declination. We have to correct for it."

"What's it say for here?" asked Kara.

"It's a small map, but this area looks like about three degrees. We have to correct three degrees West." He looked up. "I never knew that. This is great!"

Kara was smiling. "College wasn't a waste of time. Let's go."

"Once more into the breach," I said as we got up. Alex grabbed Casey, and soon enough the four of us were standing back at the black walnut tree and the associated round stone. Alex and I repeated the compass/walking/range finder process, this time ending up several yards from where we had been searching.

Alex turned on the TM9000, we all backed away, and the search continued. I expected it to last ten minutes, tops.

Two hours later, we were back in the house, grumbling. We had crawled, dug, and scanned. No iron bar. Alex must have recalibrated the TM9000 a dozen times, but the best he ever got was a couple of Civil War bullets six inches underground.

We went through the same process as last time, reviewing each step and trying to figure out where there could be a mistake. Nothing jumped out at us. The angles were right, the distance was right (Alex assured us of both), but the iron bar wasn't.

After arguing, sketching, considering, and rethinking the whole thing, we decided to get out of the house for a bit, heading for one of the local malls where we spent a good couple of hours browsing, shopping, and forgetting about treasure. We grabbed dinner at a local Mexican place and headed home. By mutual agreement we put the hunt aside till the next day, instead playing Scrabble and watching the History Channel. We finally turned in near eleven.

A little after midnight, as I teetered on the edge of sleep, Kara jolted me awake. "Oh, duh!" she said from the dark.

"Mmph?" was all I could manage.

"I know where the iron bar is," she announced.

"You do?"

I heard her shuffle around, probably propping herself up on the pillows. "I'm pretty sure. Follow this. We assume Clarence put that iron bar at 165 degrees from the stone. Meaning, 165 degrees true."

"I'm following you so far, but I have doubts about the future," I said. "You mean 'true,' not . . . er . . . 'compass,' right?"

"It's called 'magnetic,'" she said. "We looked at 165 degrees magnetic, but that's not the same as true 165 degrees. That's because the magnetic pole moves, but the true north pole doesn't. Otherwise Santa would have to move every few years."

"Of course. So we were off by three degrees. But we corrected that the second time around," I pointed out. "Then we were looking at 165 degrees true."

"I know. But what if Clarence didn't? Didn't correct the magnetic and the true."

I thought about this. "Then the bar would be in the first place we looked, right? It has to be one or the other, right?"

"No, it doesn't." She turned on the bedside light. "You're assuming that Clarence either corrected for magnetic north by three degrees, or didn't correct at all. But what if magnetic north wasn't off by three degrees back then? What if it was off by more or less?"

I gave her the incredulous look that four years of marriage had perfected. "Are you kidding? Are you saying that not only is magnetic north not the same as true north, but that it changes every year? How do people keep their compasses straight? How does Santa get home every year?"

"It doesn't change much, I bet, but after a hundred years it may be different enough. Clarence's compass may have put him at an entirely different 165 degrees."

"How the heck are we supposed to find out where magnetic north was in 1890-something?" I asked.

"Alex's office. He's got a whole Internet in there," she grinned. "If anyone can find it, you can."

"Do you do all your best thinking at night?"

"Among other things."

After the frustration of the day, Alex and Casey weren't as upset as normal people would have been when we woke them to explain Kara's idea. We went to Alex's office—equipped with enough electronics to keep the Japanese economy stable for years—and he connected to the Net. "You have the conn," he said, getting out of the chair.

"Go get some coffee or something," I told them. "This might take a bit."

They took my suggestion, leaving me alone with all I needed: A Web browser and a search engine. I started typing in keywords like "compass," "declination," "magnetic north," and "correction."

Slowly but surely I found my way to the information I needed. And wouldn't you know it: It was from the government.

"Any luck?" Kara asked, making me jump from my seat.

"Yep," I said, taking the coffee mug she offered. "Courtesy of the National Geophysical Data Center." I pointed to the screen. We can look up changes to magnetic north going back to 1900."

"That's close enough," Alex said.

I nodded as I filled out the form with latitude and longitude (I looked those up) and selected January 1, 1900. In a moment, it spit back the answer. We all leaned in. Kara made the official announcement.

"Two degrees, eleven minutes east," she said.

"And we were looking at three degrees west," Casey said. "We were almost six degrees off the first time."

"But only two degrees off the second," Alex said. "We should have found it."

"After 385 feet, that two degrees probably means fifteen or twenty feet, and that's assuming Clarence was really careful," Kara said. "We might have been thirty feet away."

"I'll break out the flashlights," Alex said.

"You'll do no such thing," Casey shot back. "It's almost two. This can wait till morning."

Monday

We didn't need any encouragement to get out of bed on Monday. By 7:30 we were all dressed and breakfasted, and Alex had checked the nuclear reactor on the TM9000. We headed out.

Once again, Alex and I started at the black walnut tree and headed out, this time at 165 degrees the way we hoped Clarence had calculated it. I marked the 385-foot mark, and Alex came over with the metal detector.

It turned out that Clarence wasn't quite as good with a compass as we would have hoped. Luckily, technology was on our side. Ten feet from where we started, the TM9000 gave a long beep. We cut back the brush and found a thick, rusty, metal rod sticking about an inch out of the ground. Casey tried digging it up, but it was clearly buried deep. It didn't matter. It was the right rod. We were almost there and, as Kara pointed out, banks were open today.

"Next," she read, "From the bar, head fifty degrees and go one hundred feet to a clearing."

Compass out. Range finder out. Andrew walking away, white reflector card in hand. Alex calling directions. Casey and Kara watching with amusement. This time, we corrected for Clarence from the get-go. When I reached what Alex determined was the 100-foot mark, he called out "Stop!" and the four of us gathered there. Alex marked the ground with a green dot.

Unfortunately, we weren't standing in a clearing. We were still, as far as I could see, in the middle of the woods.

"Spread out from here," Kara suggested. "In case Clarence was off. Look for a clearing." We did, but the woods were pretty dense and never opened up into any space wider than a half-dozen feet across.

"Maybe Clarence was a really small guy," I suggested back at the green dot. "Maybe he had a different idea about what a clearing was." This wasn't greeted with enthusiasm.

"We need to find the clearing and the dots to connect," Kara said. "That's the next part: Connect the dots. And I don't think it means Alex's paint spots."

"That would be too easy," I agreed. "So how do we find a 150-year-old clearing?"

"Oh, that's easy," said Casey. "Size *does* matter."

"Huh?"

"Big trees and little trees," she explained. "Old ones and young ones." There was a long silence. "Okay," she continued. "If there was a clearing here 150 years ago, there were trees around it, right? So the trees that popped up in the clearing are new. They're younger."

"And smaller," I said.

"Right. Look around you," Casey said.

"We missed the forest for the trees," quipped Kara.

Once we knew what to look for, it was obvious. All around Alex's green dot, the trees were significantly smaller than the ones a few yards away. Some were bigger than others, but you could even tell by the condition of the bark: Newer trees had smoother surfaces.

Alex, green spray paint in hand, started marking the approximate edge of the clearing. In a few minutes, we had a rough circle around us, about twenty-five or thirty yards across.

"All right," Alex said, "The dots. Anyone want to take a guess what he meant?"

"The sun and the moon?" Casey suggested. "Maybe at a certain time of year."

"Tree stumps?" I offered. "But they'd be rotted away by now."

"Fruit trees," said Kara. "Maybe that's what he means by dots." We all looked up and walked around but didn't see anything bearing gifts. "Casey, are any of these apple trees that haven't sprouted or fruited or whatever?"

Casey shook her head as she walked around. "I don't see any. They should have at least flowered by now."

We stood by the dot—Alex's, not Clarence's—in thought, trying to figure out what "connect the dots" might mean. Nothing came to mind.

Then Alex said, "Oh, forget this." He picked up the TM9000 and flicked it on. "There is no problem so large it cannot be solved by enough technology."

"But you don't know where to look," I said.

"The way I see it—the way I figure it—is that it has to be here. Inside the circle. This clearing. Or else why bother sending us here? So it's just a matter of finding the right place. And digging." He started from the center and started waving the loop over the ground.

Kara nodded. "Makes sense. Without a metal detector this would be tough. You'd dig for months. But we can look underground with that thing. We don't need to connect the dots." Neither Casey nor I disagreed. We all stepped back to give Alex—and the TM9000—room to work.

It was clearly tough going. When this was a clearing, it would have been simple, but with all the trees and brush, he had to make his way between trunks, branches, and leaves.

Every now and then the TM9000 beeped. "Anything?" I asked each time.

"Nothing major," said Alex, continuing to sweep the detector's loop over the ground. Forty-five minutes had passed.

"I'm having doubts about this," I said.

Then the TM9000 screamed.

It took Casey less than five minutes to run back to the house and return with two shovels and two trowels. This was good, because Alex looked ready to dig with his hands. Instead, he and I started in with the shovels.

"That thing tell you how deep it is?" I asked.

He looked surprised. "Well, yeah." He dropped his shovel and turned the TM9000 back on, waving it over the spot again, this time with the volume turned down. He consulted whatever readout the thing had and adjusted a few settings before announcing, "Fifty-four inches."

We dug. At exactly fifty-four inches—due credit to the Tokahama Corporation—I hit something solid. A moment later, so did Alex.

It took us over an hour to clear away the rusty metal box, Alex and me with the shovels, and Kara and Casey with the trowels for the close-in work. It wasn't huge: I figured it to be about twenty-four by eighteen inches and a foot deep. We cleared a hole several feet around it—and a few inches underneath on either side—so we could reach in and get a grip. It was heavy, but not too heavy. With a "One, two, THREE," Alex and I lifted it out and put it on the ground next to the hole we had dug.

It was a big metal box, dirty and rusty, with some hinges on one side and a mud-clogged lock on the other. "Your choice," I said to Alex. "Open it here or drag it back to the house?"

"Here," all three of them said at once. To confirm the decision, Alex took one swing at the lock with a trowel and smashed it open. He pulled out the pieces of the lock and lifted the cover.

Whatever was inside the box was wrapped in a waxy cloth. "Waxed cotton," Casey explained. "Waterproofing." We carefully unfolded it, revealing a sheet of yellowed paper on top of more waxed cotton.

Wiping his hands on his jeans, Alex carefully lifted the paper out. A moment later, he snorted. I leaned over to read it.

> Traitors like you ruined my country, so you can inherit the spoils. I hope you and your Yankee brothers choke on it.

I repeated it aloud. Casey reached over and unfolded the top of the second layer of cloth. Underneath the second layer of waxed cotton was, neatly stacked, what appeared to be piles and piles of money. "I don't believe it," Alex said, leaning away from the box.

It was Confederate money. Stacks and stacks of worthless Confederate cash. Clarence had the last laugh.

While Alex shook his head in disbelief, Kara and I carefully looked through. "It's worse than that," I said. "It's mostly fives and tens. There's probably only a few thousand dollars here, tops."

Kara didn't say a word.

"I guess he didn't forgive your granddad after all," said Casey.

"Crap," said Alex.

We carried the box, the shovels, and the metal detector back to the house, stowing the gear and putting the box on the floor in the family room on top of some old newspapers to protect the rug. Casey started taking out the stacks of bills and counting them, while Alex and I sat there in disbelief, sipping beers. Kara disappeared upstairs.

"About twelve thousand," Casey announced a few minutes later. "Give or take a few hundred. It's mostly fives, with a few stacks of tens."

"And absolutely worthless," Alex grumbled. "Except to a museum."

"That's not quite true," said Kara, coming back into the room. "Before you decide to burn the money or give it away, have either of you thought about how much Confederate cash is worth?"

"Not a lot," I said. "They lost the war. It's like rubles."

"Er," she said. "Not quite. You oughta go online and check out what this stuff is worth."

"You think it's worth something?" said Alex, perking up.

"I know it is. I checked."

"How much?" we asked in unison.

"I don't know, exactly—it depends which bills those are, when they were printed, and all," she said.

"Give. Us. The. Ballpark. Figure," I said.

She smiled. "Those bills are in good shape. Each one is worth at least twenty to fifty bucks. And that's assuming there aren't any really special ones—some might be worth over a grand."

The wheels of math were churning in my head. "Twelve grand in fives would mean about 2,400 bills."

"Some are tens," Casey pointed out.

"So let's say 2,200 bills. Fives and tens are worth the same?" I asked Kara.

"Roughly. I mean, it depends on the individual bill, but most are worth at least twenty or twenty-five bucks. Even the fifties and hundreds, if you had those."

"Twenty-two hundred bills at twenty bucks a pop," I said.

"Forty-four thousand bucks," said Alex. "Minimum."

Kara was looking at the money. "Better. These are all from 1861. I think that makes them worth more. I think it's time to get a safe-deposit box and look up some collectors."

We looked at one another and started to smile. I raised my glass, and Alex clinked it.

"God preserve the South," I said.

The next month

Not being sure which bills were worth what, we split the piles evenly, agreeing to let everyone know if any were particularly valuable. Alex and Casey went to a collector down there, and Kara and I found one at home. In the end, the find was worth about $58,000.

Alex and Casey decided to keep most of their Confederate money as an investment, getting some advice from a local collector on preserving it, which they passed on to us; we planned on keeping all ours . . . for the moment. They did sell some—enough to pay for the greenhouse they had been talking about.

On a Saturday, we were sitting around the kitchen table having yet another Maybe-we-should-buy-such-and-such discussion when the phone rang. It was my friend Tom, who just bought a house up in Danbury, Connecticut, with his wife, Kelly. "What's up?" I asked.

"Wanna come out here for a visit?" he asked.

"Maybe. Why-for?"

"There's something you and Kara might be into."

"What's that?"

"Well," he said, "You'll never guess what we found at the bottom of the well."